What the Green Rushes Whisper

What the
Green Rushes
Whisper

Vonnie Banville Evans

WEXFORD

Code Green Publishing

ISBN 978-1-907215-12-4

Version 1.0

Cover design by Barry Evans
Illustrations by Vonnie Banville Evans

Published by
Code Green Publishing
Coventry, England
www.codegreenpublishing.com

In memory of James F. Evans
who encouraged this book and
who was its first reader...
amor vincit omnia.

Dedicated to my beloved grandchildren:
Aoise & Shara, Mila & Priya and Dermot.

Author's Note:
While the story uses a backdrop of historical events and real people,
it is, nevertheless, a work of fiction and must be read as such.

'For the land will be for honest men to live in
The innocent will have it for their home'
(Pr.2:21)

Prologue
NOVEMBER 1946

I hear the drone of voices through the wall. It's a nuisance, an unwelcome intrusion into my reverie, like the distant buzzing of bees on a summer day.

Lizzie tells me I am becoming a recluse, a hermit, sitting here in the semi-darkness instead of joining them in the kitchen. I suspect she thinks my mind is going. Certainly it becomes more and more of an effort to lay the dreams aside.

I chose my exile a long time ago when my work was finished, when I was no longer needed.

I heard Lizzie in the hallway last week making a great drama of the fact that I am sitting in the dark waiting to die. I laughed out loud and quite frightened myself.

My son comes and sits with me now and then. He brings the little girl. They are comfortable with my silence.

I think I have worn out my life, certainly my body is useless, I cannot even walk. It hardly seems to matter. I have everything I need inside my head. I close my eyes and rise up, young again, to meet the past. I took John's book down today and copied the piece he loved to read for me. I am sure I heard the echo of all their voices as I read. It was a strange experience. I almost feel I must stand up to make them welcome.

> *For see, winter is past,*
> *The rains are over and gone*
> *The flowers appear on the earth*
> *The season of glad songs has come,*
> *The cooing of the turtle dove is heard in our land .*
>
> (Song of songs. 2:12)

Part 1

Chapter 1
JANUARY, 1890

Julia stepped out into the lane and shook the shawl down from her head. She lifted her arms and, catching her long hair, threw it up from under her clothes and tossed it into the wind. Lifting her thin little face, she closed her eyes and smiled into the freezing cold January day. She pulled the shawl around her narrow shoulders and anyone looking at her would have thought she was shaking with cold but the girl's slight frame was convulsed with pleasure.

This was her birthday, she was fifteen today and old enough to take up her new job at the big house. Her Dada was going away for the whole week with the horses and her Mama was well enough to get up and sit at the fire.

Kitty had given her second best shawl to her and Miss Helen had promised to let her have a pair of boots, if she was there tonight to help her get ready for the tennis dance in Kilrane. She would stay all night, Mama said she could, and she would risk sleeping under the stairs in the boot press. It was worth it for a pair of Helen's shoes. She never wore them out and they were only a bit too big - they only hurt her toes for a few weeks, then she got used to them.

Bloody Lonegan would be too drunk to bother her tonight. When the master was away he spent his time in the stables drinking anything he could steal from the house. Nobody knew how he managed to sober up when the time came, but he was always standing in the yard to help the master down off his horse when he arrived home.

Crafty old devil, Julia thought to herself, like me Dada, he can sober up when he has to.

She glanced quickly over her shoulder to make sure she could not be seen from the house. No need to worry Mama, who was always on to her about keeping her head covered and keeping warm in case she caught a chill.

1

'They won't keep you on as scullery maid if they think you are ailing alannah,' she said. 'You are lucky to be taken on up there now that I can't work. They are good hearted enough in their own way and if you work hard, and keep a still tongue in your head, you might be able to work your way up the stairs in time. Miss Helen is fond of you, you know, and I heard her telling the mistress you are a wonder at the hair dressing.'

Julia stopped in her tracks when she remembered the look on her mother's face. Poor Mama, she was failing fast, fading away before their eyes. Kitty tried her best to look after her. Being the eldest she had always managed to stand up to their Dada. As long as Julia could remember, Kitty had faced him, even at his worst, when he was footless with the drink, she would try to stand between him and their mother. Even now when he could see her dying on her feet, he gave her no peace.

Poor gentle Mama, who would not be with them much longer.

Julia's happiness faded and her chest tightened at the memory of his last attack the night before.

They all knew what to expect when he arrived in at supper time, kicking the door shut behind him and swearing at the dog who was not swift enough to make his escape.

He was in an ugly humour, not sober and not drunk enough for his own liking - how often Julia had heard him roaring, as if in agony, that it would be better to hang a man than to leave him half drunk.

Last night he had been just that, half drunk and ugly, looking to make sure they all shared his misery.

Mick Whelan was a big man, tall and heavy, with wide shoulders and mighty arms, strong as an ox from physical labour. His hair was sparse now and grew close to his head, grey and matted, his eyes small and close set. Julia hated him! When she was younger she pretended he was not her Dada. She liked to believe she was a fairy child, like the ones in Mama's stories. She used to wonder why her Mama had married him at all. Mama who could read and write, and whose voice was so soft and gentle.

Kitty told her the story of their marriage when she found her in the outhouse, crying, one night after he had wrecked their few possessions in a drunken frenzy and beaten his wife senseless, calling her a useless cow and a travellers' whore. 'Was our mother a tinker?' Julia asked her sister as she blew her nose in her skirt-tail and wiped her eyes with her sleeve.

'Your mother came from good stock,' Kitty answered angrily,'don't ever forget that - good stock. Her father had land up past Ross, but he lost it trying to keep people alive during the famine. He caught the fever himself and left his wife and daughter destitute. They had to take to the road and the only answer for our mother was a 'made match'. God help her, she never set eyes on that auld devil inside until she met him at the alter. Sixteen she was, and beautiful, with a head of long red hair down past her waist. She could read and write. And that fellow knew he was getting a bargain. God forgive her mother for allowing it - but the poor woman was on her last legs and she wanted to see her daughter settled before she went to her Maker. Settled! I wonder can she see her now, and did she see her all the years since - bringing six of us into the world and trying to fend for us and keep that bastard from killing her until we were reared. Well poor Pat is gone to heaven and Jack and Jim look as if they won't follow in Dada's footsteps - he won't encourage them to take to the drink anyhow, there's never enough for himself. Sadie is too delicate to work, so it's up to you and me to see to her and we will. Hush now, don't start your bawling again' she said, putting her arms around the little girl.

But tonight Mick Whelan was in no humour to be appeased and Kitty knew, as she put his supper down in front of him, that they were in for a bad time. She put the mug of buttermilk down beside his plate and lifting the heavy black pot of potatoes off the open fire, she tipped some of them out onto the middle of the scrubbed table. He sat where he had thrown himself onto the chair with his head sunk into his chest - his two sons, the twins, Jack and Jim, who had followed him into the cottage stood awkwardly behind him until he roared at them to stop skulking around and sit down.

3

They took their places at the table opposite, afraid to raise their heads. The boys who favoured their mother, had her reddish hair and slight build - they were afraid of their father, with a cringing terror that moved about them like an aura, they had none of Kitty's courage in his presence and looked to her for protection.

Sadie, who was a year older than Julia, never left the fireside - she was dawny, their mother said, born delicate before her time and her father ignored her, leaving her alone even when his humour or drunken state was at it's worst.

Their mother, Nan Whelan, sat on the three legged stool on the hearth, her long hair flowing around her shoulders, her worn face beautiful in the soft light from the fire.

The doctor had been to visit her earlier in the evening and he spoke kindly, telling her to rest and take the medicine he left for her. But when Kitty followed him outside the door he turned a grave face to her and shook his head.

'Give her two drops of that bottle when the pain is bad and keep her warm and comfortable. There is nothing more I can do, I'm afraid she won't last the winter.'

'Does she know how sick she is?' he asked.

'I think she does' Kitty answered, 'But we don't talk about it. She tells us she will be strong enough to turn over the plot soon - but that is only for Julia to hear.'

Doctor Cosgrove nodded.

'Do your best my girl, and call me if you need me. Good day to you now,' he said gruffly, as he mounted his horse.

Poor woman, he was thinking to himself as he rode away from the cottage - she will be better off dead. That girl will manage the rest of them and be better able for her monster of a father than the wife ever was.

Kitty resumed her stance behind her mother and started back to brushing her hair gently. Nan Whelan closed her eyes and sighed softly, hoping against hope that Mick would eat his supper and go back to Leigh Court to get the horses ready for their morning departure. Thank

4

God, she thought, he will be away for the best part of a week at the shoot in Begerin. But as if reading her mind her husband sprang up and kicked back the chair, throwing the plate of bacon against the ground.

'Rotten fat meat!' he shouted. 'Is that what a man gets to eat in this kip on a Sunday night after working his guts out all the week. You two lazy whelps - get out and get the cart ready. I have to go to town, and you, you lazy bitch, get up and do something for your keep.' He made a lunge at his wife and before Kitty could stop him, he had kicked the stool from under her and she fell with a moan onto the stone hearth.

Kitty flung herself at her father, her face contorted with fury she clawed at his cheeks with her nails. He caught her and flung her away from him with an oath.

'You mad rip,' he roared, but he stopped as he saw the look in her eyes. She put a protective arm over her mother's sobbing frame. He stood undecided for an instant and then turned with an ugly laugh.

'Oh well, I won't have to put up with you much longer, you're rotten with disease the doctor tells me. You will be six feet under before spring.'

The door banged after him, shaking the little thatched cottage. Kitty lifted her mother's frail body from the floor and carrying her into the room, laid her gently on the iron bedstead.

The cold and the memory of that night made Julia shiver now and she pulled the shawl back over her head and moved into the shelter of the ditch. The muck under her bare feet was beginning to harden with frost - it would be a cruel night. The sky was darkening already and the clouds that had been plumped up, like Miss Helen's pink eiderdown, had lost all their colour and were just piled like the dirty white laundry, on the upper landing, waiting to be gathered.

She had been enjoying that sky. She loved to lose herself in the landscape the clouds made on a day like this. Earlier on, the huge massed pink clouds could have been turreted castles in a strange sky-world of princes and fair maidens, or maybe the hills and mountains of Hy-Brazil, the Isle of the Blest.

5

Miss Helen had read that poem for her last week when she went to clean up the schoolroom.

The girls' governess, Miss Armstrong, never let Julia near any of the books. She caught her looking at the pictures one evening; Julia dropped the book like hot coals when the woman's strident tones rang out.

'You dirty little creature, how dare you touch my books.'

'Sorry Miss,' Julia mumbled as she backed away hurriedly.

'Never put your dirty hands on my property again or I will have you dismissed,' she hissed, bending to retrieve the fallen book.

Helen, who had followed her into the room, spoke now in a bored voice. She felt nothing for the servants really, but she intensely disliked the bony governess.

'Come now, Miss Armstrong, Julia meant no harm, she likes books.'

'She has no right to touch my things!' Julia heard her answer, as she sidled out the door.

'These people are dirty, God knows what we would catch, if we allowed them to handle our belongings.'

Julia heard Miss Helen's laughter as she moved down the hall, her face flaming

'Big auld cow!' she mumbled under her breath - but the tears caught in her throat, a mixture of hurt and rage.

When Helen was in a good mood it was nice to clean her bedroom and pick up her clothes and Julia always liked to be sent upstairs. Some days she would pile up the bed-clothes and touch their soft folds and marvel at the feel of the dresses and silk chemises and gauzy stockings she sorted. She knew when the time was ripe to ask for favours. When Helen's sharp little face relaxed as Julia brushed and dressed her thin hair, she could be coaxed to read a page or two, normally a poem. She would continue until Julia, entranced by the words, paused transfixed, and forget her ministering. Then Helen would slap the book shut, call her a lazy, dozy girl and scold her for the rest of the evening, but it was worth it. Some day Julia would learn to read. Mama never had time to teach her and they never had the coins needed, to pay, to go to Mr.

Browne's school in the village. But some day, somehow, she would learn,

The sun had completely disappeared now and had sucked down with it every drop of colour from the landscape. The evening was rapidly turning to night and she had two miles to go still. Julia quickened her step, keeping close to the sheltered side of the ditch, she resolutely set out along the road to Leigh Court.

Chapter 2

Leigh Court, home of the Leigh family, stood on a hilly slope overlooking the Lane River, two miles to the south of Ballyleigh village.

The Leighs had owned this part of the County Wexford as far back as the seventeenth century. It was rumoured the first Leigh to settle here had come with the Cromwellian army in 1649 and had been granted title and deed to the lands by Oliver Cromwell himself for services rendered during the sack of Wexford town. As elsewhere in Ireland, property was taken from the old Catholic families and given to Protestant settlers. The Leighs from England had certainly been awarded a large slice of County Wexford and soon made their fortune from the land they had been granted and the trade across the Irish sea. In the 1780's they built the tall, restrained mansion house on the hill not too far from Wexford town and had its rooms decorated in the refined Adamesque manner of the period. With its walled gardens, conservatories, greenhouses and parkland, it sprawled like a colossus. Around its forty acres of garden and park, a village soon grew to service the Big House.

Major Leigh, the present occupant of Leigh Court, considered himself an Irishman, in the best sense of the word. Like most sons of Anglo Irish families, he had taken a commission in His Majesty's service and had done his duty for king (and in his case) queen and country in a far flung corner of the Empire.

The young Major had returned to Ireland with his wife and family when his father broke his neck while riding to hounds. The family blamed the high spirited stallion the old man was riding. The natives knew the spirits that killed him had been imbibed by the lord of the manor himself during the roisterous gathering of the days and nights prior to his demise. Never a man to flunk his duty, he had insisted on being helped onto his trusty steed, and had ridden off to his death with many jolly shouts of yoicks and tallyho before parting from his horse at the stone wall on the north side of Kerrigan's wood. The horse had decided to baulk the wall and his Lordship flew on regardless, the impact with the frost-hard ground had broken his neck and he died, most people allowed, as he would have had it, just as the hounds ran the fox to ground and started to rend him limb from limb a few yards away at the base of the old yew in Kerrigan's high field.

So, Major John Leigh had arrived fresh from India, with his bride, a pretty English rose, and his young family. Four year old John, the son and now heir. Helen, just three, and the baby Louise, born, by the mercy of God, just before the family left the shores of England.

The transition from father to son had made little or no difference to the inhabitants of Ballyleigh or the surrounding countryside. The estate went on as before, ably looked after by William Considine, the old man's imported overseer and manager, and the local labourers, whose jobs and homes were secure for life and for their sons' and daughters' after them, doffed their caps to the new Lord of the Manor and soon grew used to calling him Major.

Mick Whelan who had looked after the horses at Leigh Court since he was a child of seven and had helped his father, who was head groom since he himself was a young man, cared as little for his new master as he had for the old man.

If Mick was capable of caring at all, it was his horses who drew what little feeling he had from him. He knew horses. Boy and man, he had lived with horses and it was said that no man in the Baronies of Forth and Bargy was a better judge of horses, than Major Leigh's man.

His wife, Nan, had been in the kitchens of the big house since she arrived in the locality in the early eighteen fifties, working her way up from scullery maid to lady's maid to Lady Grace Leigh, the Major's young wife, who noticed the quiet spoken girl and took her under her wing. Indeed it was Lady Grace's kindness that had made Nan's life bearable over the years of her marriage to the brutish Mick Whelan.

Nan managed to look after his needs and rear her large family and still work as many hours as she could at Leigh Court, looking after her ladyship's wardrobe and being there to dress her hair and help her get ready for every big occasion. Nan dressed her own youngsters with discarded clothes from the young Leighs and fed them from the bountiful kitchens.

None of this went unnoticed in the house and the village women slighted Nan whenever they got the chance, talking in loud voices about her airs and graces and laughing slyly when the bruises her husband inflicted on her were too numerous to cover up.

Nan held her head high and walked to and from the big house until her strength failed and she could no longer make the journey, even by cart.

With the onset of her final illness, her one wish was to see Julia follow in her eldest daughter, Kitty's, footsteps and to be taken on at Leigh Court as kitchen maid. Nan had brought her daughters to the big house as soon as they could walk, and had set them to work in the kitchens at every opportunity as soon as they were useful for any chore, no matter how menial. Like a mother bird, forcing its young from the nest to fly alone. Her instincts were to remove them from their father's presence as soon as she possibly could. The boys would follow him into service as grooms and had to learn their trade at his side. There was nothing she could do about that, only pray that he would not break their spirits.

This evening, as Julia Whelan made her way along the frosty road to Leigh Manor, the family were assembled in the drawing room, all except John, who had left the day before to return to college in England.

The Major, a tall man with his father's florid complexion and penchant for fine wines and spirits was standing at the window looking out into the walled garden with unseeing eyes. His face flushed even a deeper red than usual was, as Nellie, the little parlour maid, told Mrs Walshe, the cook, 'like thunder over the bog,' and his fists were clenched at his side.

Lady Grace sat in her usual place, before the fire, concentrating on her needlepoint, and trying to keep calm so that the headache she could feel beginning at the base of her neck would abate. Helen was glancing through a sheaf of music and Lou-Lou was deep in an illustrated book about horses.

'Dammit Grace, the boy will have to see sense,' the Major burst out. 'No son of mine is going to carry a bag about and catch all sorts of diseases in some dreadful hospital. Medicine, in the name of all that's great and good! How can a Leigh study medicine? What's got into the boy? There is no way I will consent to it. No way! I have already secured his commission in the cavalry. I'd be the laughing stock of London. Only last month I was bragging in the club about how fine a horseman he is and Sinclare agreed that John is the finest horseman in his school, if not in the whole bloody South of England. No way. No! I refuse completely - he will have to change his mind. I won't hear of it!.'

The Major's blood pressure was rising with his voice and Lady Grace sighed and laid down her needlework. Helen turned a languid face towards her father, decided he was too far gone to be calmed and quietly made her way to the door. Louise put her fingers in her ears and continued her perusal of the book before her.

'Please John, don't upset yourself, you know what Dr. Cosgrove told you, calm down now. Of course we will see to it that John gives up this nonsense. Don't fight him, he will have forgotten it by Easter but you will have brought on an attack and you will be confined to your bed. Think of the shoot tomorrow - how would you like to miss that?

You know how you enjoy it. The best shoot in the county you, say every year - apart from our own, that is,' she added hastily.

Her husband's countenance relaxed a little and she spoke again, encouraged by his temporary silence.

'John is a good and dutiful son, he will do what you want eventually - you know he will.' She crossed to her husband's side and laid a hand over his clenched fist.

'Come on now - let us take a little stroll around the garden before dark, it will do you good, help you to relax before dinner.'

The Major nodded. Grace was right. He must not work himself into a rage, already he could feel the beginning of the tightness in his chest. He hated that feeling, it was to be feared and he knew it.

'Bless you my dear, what would I do without you - you are my rock of sense, as usual.'

He took her arm and they went into the hallway to wrap up before taking a gentle turn round the walled gardens. Lady Grace deftly turned the conversation to the horses and the journey her husband would make to the edge of the north slob the following morning, to the shooting lodge at Begerin and a week's sport with his peers. She knew in her head the battle was not over. Her son had the stubborn streak that had made his ancestors cling to these lands and survive in an alien country for two hundred years. He had carefully thought about his future and worked out the details, dropping the bombshell before leaving for England the previous day.

Now that he was nineteen it was time for him to join his father's old regiment, past the time really, and the Major had brought up the subject on John's last evening at home. The boy listened carefully to his father's plans and then announced in a low voice that he had no intention of joining the army.

'I want to study medicine, father - I have discussed it with Professor Holt and he agrees I have the brains for it.'

He continued on, disregarding his father's horrified face, and outlining his plans until the Major leapt up and caught him by the shoulder. Looking as if he was about to have an attack of apoplexy, the older man spluttered and coughed - shaking his son like a terrier with a rat.

'Medicine!' he roared again, 'I never heard such a thing. A Leigh to become a bloody servant!'

John managed to escape his father's clutch - although tall he was a slightly built young man and had none of the Leigh bluster. He stood his ground now and faced his father's anger calmly.

'Please father, you will do yourself an injury. This is why I did not discuss this matter with you during the holidays. I had intended making my plans known to you by letter when I arrived back in England. Please give the matter your consideration. I do not want to part with you on bad terms. We will say no more about it now.'

12

Major Leigh had dropped back onto his chair - his face was chalk white - which was more disconcerting to the boy than the bluster of the previous few minutes. He was gasping and seemed to be unable to catch his breath.

'My pills,' he choked, 'in the drawer.'

John ran to the desk and tore open the drawer. He grabbed the box of pills and opening them quickly handed two to his father who swallowed them and lay back closing his eyes.

'I will fetch Mama,' John said and when the Major nodded slightly he ran from the room to find Lady Grace.

This was what he had dreaded and why he had avoided a confrontation with his father. His mother had warned him, when he confided in her, that the Major would never agree to his wishes.

'He has reared you to follow in his footsteps - a career in the army and then home to take over Leigh Court when the time comes.'

She had always known something like this would happen. She loved her quiet, intelligent son, and often wondered who he resembled. Some distant ancestor on either side she supposed. Her own father and brother were scholarly men, but country men for all that, men who loved to ride and shoot. John could ride with the best of them but even as a young boy he refused to join the shoot. His preference was for quiet hours in the library, much to his father's chagrin. Over the years the Major had done his best to 'make a man of him.' He confided his fears and doubts about his only son to no one. Today his worst fears were confirmed: the boy was a bloody fop not wishing to take his rightful place, but talking this unutterable rubbish about becoming a doctor. Louise was more of a man than John. Why had she been born a girl? Her father often said it aloud, as she flew past him on the black stallion no one else but herself could ride. By God, if Lou was a man she would do him proud, he had no doubt about it.

The darkness was holding hands around the edge of the gardens, closing in silently and the air was still.

'Be lucky if we don't have snow before we get out onto the slobs,' the Major grunted. What more trouble could be wreaked upon him before the first month of this bloody new year was even over?

Chapter 3

The kitchen at Leigh Court was a vast room, stretching half way across under the huge entrance hall. It took up most of the space under the house, apart from the gun room and the wine cellars. Two large ranges ran along one wall. The centre of the room held two enormous wooden tables. Presses and dressers lined the back wall and two deep stone sinks were fixed to the end wall.

This was Mrs. Walshe's territory where she ruled with an iron will and an acid tongue.

To the best of everyone's knowledge there never had been a Mr. Walshe, but because she was head cook she was automatically given the honorary title of 'Mrs'. Her private life, if she had one, was kept strictly to herself. She had her own tiny sitting room off the kitchen, with her bedroom behind that again. These rooms were known to the other servants as the 'Holy of holies' and no one ever put foot across the threshold without a formal invitation. On her afternoon off she disappeared, in the pony and trap, with one of the twin Whelans driving. If she did not spend her time in Kerrigan's Manor House, at the other side at the village, with her friend, Mrs. Hayes, who held the same exalted position as herself as cook for the Kerrigan family; she went further afield to her married sister, who lived four miles past the village, on the way to the town of Ross.

Apart from these expeditions, the kitchen at Leigh Court was her world and one that she guarded jealously. She was good at her job, indeed she had such a reputation in the district that the gentry vied with one another for an invitation to eat at the big house.

A small round woman of indeterminable age, she bustled about her kitchen running it like clockwork and expecting full cooperation from the two scullery maids, the footman, Lonegan and the other servants. Indeed it was well known that her word was law with Lady Grace and that it was Mrs. Walshe who hired and fired the staff. Even the butler, Mr. Hynes, was in awe of her and did her bidding.

For all her temper, and she had been known to let fly with more than sharp words when under pressure, she was a fair woman and she looked after the staff, feeding them well. Her loyalty to the Leigh family was complete and it was said that Lady Grace was the only human being she took notice of; often declaring when in good humour after a particularly successful dinner party, that she would die for her ladyship if needs be. The Major she tolerated, as she did most of the gentlemen, being unable to boss 'them upstairs' as she could 'them downstairs.' But her views on the male of the species was well known, and often aired, as she went about her business.

'Men are useless' she was fond of saying, 'Useless nuisances'. When the previous scullery maid handed in her notice - journeying to Enniscorthy to marry a labouring man on an estate outside the town - she sniffed, wiped her hands on her voluminous white apron and announced to those present: 'Don't little girls be very foolish.'

Master John was the only exception to her rule and she doted on him from the first time she laid eyes on him, in the hallway at Leigh Court, when the family arrived from England. She refused to acknowledge the passing of time and continued to treat him like a small boy, serving up treacle pudding for dessert every time he arrived home. She had no time for his sisters. Miss Helen was dismissed with a loud sniff of disapproval and Louise was more or less lumped in with the men: Mrs. Walshe being of the opinion that one would have an attack of the vapours if she had to lift her skirts to scrub a floor or face a man, and the other one was half horse anyhow. Mr. Hynes hushed her and remarked: 'Not in front of the servants Mrs. Walshe,' when her tongue wagged too freely. This always reduced the maids to giggles and made Lonegan leave the kitchen in a huff, banging the door behind him and querying in a loud voice who and what the hell Hynes and herself thought they were.

'If the rest of us is servants what does that make them? I ask yiz.'

Today the kitchen seemed like heaven to Julia Whelan when she closed out the dark murky evening and hung her cloak on the peg on the back of the door. She quickly moved over to the glowing range to warm her dead hands and feet. Mrs. Walshe's face softened as she took in the girl's slight frame and her bare purple feet under the hem of her shabby skirt. She was fond of Julia, a great little worker and her mother's daughter. She had been sorry to say goodbye to Nan Whelan. 'That waster of a husband has succeeded in half killing her and the poor creature is too sick to drag herself to Leigh Court any more' she told Lady Grace a few days before, when advising her that Julia was now old enough to be taken on as kitchen maid. 'Sure hasn't the girl been doing the mother's work for the past few years anyhow - no harm to bring her to live in and get her away from auld Mick before he starts using her for a punch bag.'

Her ladyship agreed and Julia would be soon moving in to share the attic room with Katie Murphy, the other scullery maid and Nellie Flynn the tweenie.

Knowing Julia would not have eaten she told her to help herself to a mug of tea and some bread before she tackled the sink full of crockery and pots and pans.

'Hurry up my girl, we can't be waiting on you all day.' She spoke gruffly, but Julia smiled to herself; she knew the older woman's bark was worse than her bite.

'How is your Ma today alannah' Mrs. Walshe asked now, pausing to wipe her greasy hands on a cloth.

'Not too bad Mrs. Walshe, able to sit up today and she took a few spoonfuls of soup for Kitty at noon.'

'Huh, I suppose she did,' the cook sniffed under her breath, 'knowing that bastard of a husband of hers is about to go miles away and not come back for the duration'.

To the girl she said: 'Master John is gone again and a right to do we had here before he left.'

'What happened?' Julia asked.

'Seems he's told his Da he won't go in the army; wants to be a doctor, the poor child. I don't know where he got the notion, but I always knew Master John would never go in the army. Imagine wanting that angel to go off to them bloody pagan lands and fight all sorts of foreign armies. Why should my lamb fight for the bloody English, and he an Irishman? If he wants to go doctoring, well doctoring is what he should do.' But the last was delivered in less convincing tones. Even though it was Master John's wish to be a doctor, Mrs. Walshe was not too sure if this would be respectable work for the son and heir to Leigh Court. A soldier, definitely not! If he was not that way inclined, but a doctor, well that was another state of affairs entirely.

Julia nodded to herself. She was well aware that John Leigh was as different from his father as she was from hers. She had known John since she started to come to the house with her mother. He was a kind boy, gentler than her own brothers, and he had often spoken to the shabby little girl when he met her on the lower corridors or in the stables where she sometimes held the horses or cleaned out the stables.

'Will he have to be away for a long time then Mrs. Walshe?' she asked, as she hastily finished the bread and tea.

'How should I know? Come on my girl, enough of your auld chat, get your arms into that sink now, them bells will start to clatter any minute and me with the dinner only half ready and that lazy Katie Murphy still out in the garden getting cabbage - cabbage how are you,' she snorted, 'More likely down in the stables with Lonegan. That one is playing with fire and begod one of these days she will be burned bad. Burned bad I'm telling you.' As she swung the cleaver into the air and brought it down with a wallop on the joint of beef before her on the table.

Julia set to work. She was warm now and her stomach was full. She loved these times in the kitchen at Leigh Court when things were quiet. She could work away at something she was well used to and think her own thoughts, listening to Mrs. Walshe murmuring away to herself with the odd snort, or curse when something went against her. She could look forward to a good dinner herself later on tonight and then the prospect of helping Miss Helen get ready and being rewarded for her work with a pair of boots that would see her through the rest of the winter. She finished washing the dishes and pots and started to scrub the tables as Mrs. Walshe got the meat into the oven. When Katie arrived with the vegetables, looking flustered and out of breath, Mrs. Walshe caught her by the ear and squeezed until the girl started to screech.

'You'll be the sorry one me girl' she growled as she let her go.

'What d'ya mean ma'am?' Katie squeaked, beating a hasty retreat to the other side of the table rubbing the side of her head with a filthy hand.

'You know very well what I mean, you dirty slut. Get in and wash your paws before you come near my table and then get them vegges ready for the pot. Horrid dirty creature' she sniffed as Katie ran to do her bidding.

Julia laughed, she would feel sorry for Katie, but she knew her pity would be wasted. The girl was only half saved as Mr. Hynes would say, and she was only kept on because Mrs. Walshe was a distant relation of her mother and had promised to try to keep an eye on her, something she was coming to regret more with each day that passed.

It was well known that Lonegan the footman and general dogsbody in the kitchen and stables fancied himself as a lady's man and tried it on with every girl that came to work at Leigh Court.

'Rotten devil' Mrs. Walshe called him, wishing she could get him dismissed, but he was good at his work and able to butter the Major up and keep on his right side. All she could do was warn the young girls to stay away from him. But Katie was impervious to her warnings. Julia was well used to dodging his unwelcome attention and he usually left her alone, being a bit afraid of her sister Kitty anyhow.

Kitty herself now arrived at the back door, stamping her feet and shaking the frost off her shawl as she hung it up.

'Just in time to get the table ready and serve up' Mrs. Walshe said sharply as Kitty came up behind her and gave her a quick hug. 'Mind your manners my girl' she said gruffly, but Kitty smiled, knowing how fond the older woman was of her.

She winked at Julia as she put on her apron and cap. Kitty was a favourite with everyone in the kitchen, except Lonegan.

'You could depend your life on that girl' Julia heard Mr. Hynes tell Mrs. Walshe one evening as he sat smoking his pipe at the fire while the cook enjoyed a well earned rest after her day's work.

'Indeed you could Mr. Hynes, indeed you could, a good girl if ever there was one.'

Julia felt a glow of pride to hear her sister being praised. She was glad people knew how good Kitty was. Only for Kitty they would never survive at home, Julia thought to herself. No, life would be unbearable without Kitty.

Chapter 4

Helen Leigh sat gazing at her reflection in her dressing-table mirror. She turned the two side mirrors inwards slightly, so that she could view her profile, leaning forward and turning her head, first to the left and then to the right. She fluffed her hair up with an impatient hand and sucked in her cheeks, then tried a smile. No, if Helen was anything she was honest and by no stretch of the imagination could she pretend the face looking back at her was beautiful, nor even pretty. The jaw was too square, the eyes too small, the skin sallow the hair thin and oily. Why couldn't she have taken after her mother and not her father's scrawny sisters.

John was the only one with his mother's features and colouring, but then John was the charmed child, Helen thought savagely. Everybody's favourite, the golden son. Well maybe all that would change now that he had well and truly upset the apple cart and stood up to dear Papa.

Now Helen was really smiling, forgetting the perusal of her own face and remembering the furore of the previous day. The darling boy had really excelled himself this time, now maybe the parents would pay some attention to their second child, the obedient one. Helen had always done what she was told to do; outwardly anyhow. She never raised any serious objections, staying at home with that cretin of a governess when she too would have liked a real education. But her father had pooh poohed the tentative suggestion. Why in God's name educate a woman? Especially one with Helen's background and money. A good marriage with some well bred English gentleman would be in order, with this in mind she would be parcelled off to her Aunt Elizabeth in London in a few months time.

Elizabeth Brooke-Menton, the most presentable of the Major's three sisters, had married well and Sir Anthony Brooke-Menton, M.P. for South London ran an expensive Kensington establishment in the fashionable London suburb. Their own daughter, Antonia, was coming

21

out this season so it had been arranged that her plain Irish cousin could travel out into English society under her wing. Or carried on it, Helen thought cynically to herself.

'Damn the lot of them,' she spoke to her reflection, twin spots of anger lighting up her pale cheeks, 'I've a good mind to say yes to the Kerrigan lout and give them all something to talk about.'

Luke Kerrigan, the eldest son of Ned Kerrigan, who owned the Manor house and a couple of hundred acres adjoining their own land was hounding her as long as she could remember, spurred on no doubt by the old man, who would die happy if he could see his son married into the Leighs. The Major would probably horse whip both father and son if he had an inkling of their intentions, Helen thought. The Kerrigans were old Irish stock who got where they were by standing on the necks of their fellow Irish men for years, Old Kerrigan was referred to as the 'Grabber' by the locals because every acre he owned had been grabbed one way or another. Over the years he had, in the nearby town of Wexford, dragged himself up from the ranks of small traders. During the 'forties he bought every ounce of grain he could lay his hands on, not only in his own area but in the midlands where the great hunger was at its worst. This grain he had sold back to his starving country men at exorbitant rates. It was said that his heart, if he ever had one, had shrivelled up and in its place he had a swinging brick.

Helen Leigh laughed out loud as she remembered Nellie Byrne, the parlour maid's words, describing Ned Kerrigan and his brood.

'Scum' Nellie said, 'Scum and worse than scum; rats that fattened off the bodies of men and women, yes and children too, and stepped up, using the hardship of others as their stepping stones.'

Helen had no objection to the way Kerrigans had come by their wealth and the Manor House they now lived in. She had no love for the peasant Irish and allowed that if Ned Kerrigan was enterprising enough to make money out of a race of ignorant illiterates he was entitled to do so. She had never given Luke Kerrigan any encouragement. On the contrary, she mocked him and disparaged him at every opportunity, especially in public, until she managed to make him the butt of her caustic tongue and a laughing stock at every gathering of the young men and women of the area. Tonight Helen was in pensive mood. The row in the house earlier had given her food for thought. John would continue to defy his father, she knew them both well enough, neither would back down. If John continued to insist on studying medicine her father would never allow him to take over Leigh Court and as she was next in line there was a chance she could herself inherit. The only thing Helen cared deeply about was the house and lands belonging to the Leighs.

The stately house and its beautifully proportioned rooms and corridors fed a need deep inside her, a need she herself did not understand, but one that she ruthlessly meant to feed no matter what the cost. Her only real joy came from her gracious surroundings and her position as daughter of the house and part owner of the Leigh domain. She knew that even with her aunt's and uncle's patronage behind her she was unlikely to make any sort of good marriage in England. At best she would collar a second son in some remote part of the country and play second fiddle to her in-laws for the rest of her life.

She had no looks and even though her father was lord of all he surveyed in Ireland, she would be considered a poor catch on the London scene. She was under no illusions on that score and any ideas she ever had were dispelled in no uncertain manner by the young scions of British society who had accompanied her brother on school vacations. The Irish were mocked and looked on as ignorant and inferior by those across the water. The irony of it was that here in Ireland the Leighs and their like were considered to be English while in England they were dismissed as ignorant Irish.

Helen had no wish to suffer the indignity of hanging on to her English cousins' coat tails while husband-hunting in London, nor did she want to live in England, or anywhere away from Leigh Court. But the fact remained that to stay here she would need a husband, and if she had to have a husband at all why not one that she could dominate completely. Until tonight the idea of encouraging Luke Kerrigan would have been anathema to her but since she had allowed it to surface in her mind she was struck by the outlandish thought that maybe it was not such a ludicrous idea. Luke was an ignorant boor, but presentable enough in appearance. He was not a drunkard like most of the others around the area and he was as devoted to her as 'Lap sing,' her mother's pekinese was to Lady Grace.

What about her father? Helen bit her lip. He might be brought around to her way of thinking if she moved cleverly. He had no wish to spend too much money trying to marry off his plain daughter. The London season was Lady Grace's idea. Father would rather spend money on thoroughbred horses for Lou than on finding a thoroughbred husband for me, she thought. Then there was the Kerrigan land; the woods where the hunt usually ended up, her father had always wanted to own Kerrigan's wood - indeed he considered them his in everything but title. An alliance between herself and Luke Kerrigan would bring their lands together and not alone would she need no dowry but Ned Kerrigan would be prepared to pay any price to buy Helen Leigh for his son and heir.

Helen sat very still, her face sphinx-like as she allowed her mind to digest these thoughts. No price was too high for Leigh Court, she was prepared to do anything short of murder and in some of her wilder fantasies, even that had seemed not too wild a concept.

If she could only be sure that John would not return to take over the running of Leigh Court. Even if he gave up this medical nonsense he was ill equipped to look after their heritage.

He has too much love for the natives, he is too soft, a sentimental fool. Helen knew her brother lacked her strength of character. She prided herself on her unsentimental nature and looked on herself as a realist.

'If we are to go on as we are after father's time, it is my duty to take up the reins' she spoke out loud now, convinced that her plan was the only way forward for her. Louise would be easy enough to win over, just leave her the horses. Lady Grace was a little afraid of her eldest daughter. She, more than anyone, guessed at the depths of Helen's hard nature, and determined spirit, but then she would go along with her husband's wishes; she would have no choice. Her father would have to be convinced and now was a good time to begin, while his anger at John was still flaming.

Helen knew her father was worried about his health. She had watched him carefully over the holidays - noticing how he tried to curb his temper and how her mother's attempts to get him to rest were not always brushed aside.

Yes, now was definitely her chance and if she let it slip away she might never get another.

Helen smiled again at her reflection, but the smile did not reach her pale eyes.

A knock brought her back from her reverie and Julia Whelan put her head around the door.

'Yes, come in. Don't dally there' Helen said sharply as the girl came slowly into the room. Julia's face was flushed from the heat of the kitchen and the effects of a good meal and the long black hair shone in the lamplight. Helen Leigh looked at the young girl in front of her and thought how unfair it was. They breed like rabbits, live on scraps and have neither brains nor ability and yet some of them, like this one, have looks and figures that I could die for.

Her bitter thoughts made her even sharper than ever and Julia sighed to herself: Tonight would not be easy and if she put a foot wrong she would go barefoot for the rest of the winter. It would be hard to work this one into a good mood, but she would have to try. She picked up the silver backed hair-brush and set to brushing Helen's thin hair carefully. The older girl closed her eyes after a few minutes and Julia started to hum softly to herself. Sometimes Helen asked her to sing. She had a nice voice, so her mother always said and she had learned some of the old songs from Nora Crane, an old woman in the cottage down the lane from her home. Sensing Helen relaxing as she worked, she started to sing 'The bunch of violets' gently in her soft voice, Helen let herself sink into a pleasant stupor, only half listening to the young girl's voice. This one was different to the usual run of skivvies, there was something about her even though she could neither read nor write and was as unschooled as the rest of them.

It amused Helen to read a page or so for her now and then, laughing at her reaction to the words and there was no doubt that she could sing - she seemed to, have some sort of a soul, but how she came by it was a mystery. As she relaxed more and more, into a pleasant torpor, Helen Leigh became convinced that her plan was a viable one and could and might just work. She would begin tonight at the dance, she would have to take it slowly or people would notice too much. After all, up to now she had amused herself by ridiculing Luke Kerrigan at every tum, now she must be subtle in reversing her attitude. Subtle but firm, she must seize the moment, what was it old Armstrong was harping on about yesterday? Shakespeare - Julius Caesar: 'There is a tide in the affairs of men which taken at the flood leads on to victory.'

Helen laughed gently and Julia Whelan inwardly hugged herself, the brown boots were coming more within her grasp, it was looking hopeful again - very hopeful.

Chapter 5

The landing clock chiming the hour roused Helen from her pleasant reverie and she stiffened and sat bolt upright. Her face, which had softened slightly while she relaxed under Julia's tender ministries, sharpened again and the corners of her mouth turned down sourly as she looked at the reflection staring back at her from the mirror.

'Be quick girl' she said, twisting her head away from Julia's hands, 'I have only an hour to get ready. Dress my hair and get out my grey silk gown; I want to cut a dash tonight.' She smiled sourly, adding in her own mind: Do your best to make me look well.

Julia swept the older girl's hair up into a chignon and fixed a tortoise-shell slide at each side. She coaxed the thin hair into soft waves around Helen's sharp face and stood back to look at the effect, nodding with satisfaction.

Helen pinched her cheeks, trying to bring a little colour to her pale face and dabbing some perfume behind her ears, she placed a solitary string of pearls around her neck and stood up to allow Julia to lift the grey dress over her head.

Julia's fingers smoothed the beautiful gown into place, lingering over the soft material and lovingly fixing the folds that fell in abundance from the bustle at the back.

She handed Helen her fan and her gloves and turned to fetch the heavy cloak from the wardrobe.

Now is my chance, she thought as her eyes fell in the shoe press where Helen's footwear was kept. She would have to be careful; not too obvious; bide her time until the moment was ripe. Helen was turning around in front of the full-length mirror and she looked well pleased with herself. The new gown was very becoming, she was glad she had insisted on going to Dublin in November to choose the material and have it made properly. Tilly Lacey in Wexford was fine for day dresses and tennis clothes and even winter coats and capes, but for evening wear Helen liked to keep up with the London fashions, the word dowdy would never be applied to her, whatever else her smart London cousins might say. She touched the frilled collar and straightened her pearls.

'Yes' she said more to herself, than to the servant girl, 'That will do quite nicely I think.'

Julia helped her into the cloak and ventured a word: 'You look wonderful tonight Miss Helen, the new gown is so beautiful, quite the finest I have ever seen. There will be nothing at the dance tonight to come near it. Josie Kerrigan will be wearing the white taffeta she got for the New Year's Ball in Wexford and that wasn't a patch on your mauve silk. Everyone said so,' she added quickly, seeing the pleased look on Helen's face. 'The Moynihan girls only went to Tilly Lacey for their ball gowns this year, so Kitty told me, and Jane Green will have her usual frills and flounces - Nancy Porter told me she put on another stone weight over Christmas. Nancy says she weighs a ton now; at least.'

Helen laughed out loud at this last bit of information, she liked to hear the servants' gossip about the other young ladies of the locality, when it suited her.

'Good girl Julia' she said, turning to leave the room. 'Tidy up here please and wait up for me as usual. I should be back shortly after midnight. Papa made sure the roads would be safe before he agreed to let me travel tonight.

Just as Julia was plucking up courage to open her mouth and make her pitch for the boots, Helen turned in the doorway and said, languidly: 'You can take those boots I promised you, for God's sake wear them girl, I don't want you treading around my room with your dirty bare feet. God knows what you might have walked in.'

She slammed the door after her and Julia, grinning with delight swooped on the boot press and claimed her price.

The coach was already at the door when Helen descended into the hall. She drew in her breath sharply as the cold air hit her. Drawing the heavy cloak around her, she called Lonegan down to open the door and help her in. This he did grudgingly. Even Helen had little effect on Lonegan's surly manner. He hated his extra curricular activities which included driving her ladyship and the young ladies about when the Whelans were not there to do it. 'Cranky bitch' he muttered as he climbed back up into his seat and clucked at the horses. However it was a fine moonlit night, even if it was freezing cold and the roads white with frost. He might as well be taking this one to Kilrane as trying to dodge the auld hag Walshe in the kitchens. There was always the chance of a game of cards and a drop of porter in the stables with the other lads putting in their time waiting for their charges while they amused themselves prancing around like the eejits they were. Lonegan snorted to himself and shot a stream of tobacco juice out of the side of his mouth. The horses' hooves clanging on the frosty road rang out as they clipped along smartly and Lonegan urged them on even faster. The prospect of the drop he would get made him anxious to reach his destination.

Helen drew the heavy woollen rug around her and made a mental note to complain to her father about the behaviour of that surly brute Lonegan as she swayed from side to side. Last time he had driven her to a party in Wexford, before Christmas, he got drunk with the men servants during the party and she had to suffer the indignity of waiting while the other grooms held his head under the pump in the yard and sobered him up enough to drive her home. Her father had promised to take him to task, but he was as impudent as ever. She could see by his manner he had not mended his ways. Well this was his last chance; if he did not behave tonight she would take the whip to him herself. She stood up and knocked the top of the coach. The bloody fool would have them in the ditch if he did not slow down. Lonegan toyed with the idea of ignoring her knocking. He thought better of it and reigned in a bit. No point in provoking her, she would make right trouble for him with the auld fellah if he pushed her too far.

Helen settled down in her seat again as the pace slackened. She wanted to plan her strategy for the night - no point in being too obvious. She would simply let Luke Kerrigan get a bit closer to her; maybe dance with him a couple of times. No, even that would be too obvious - just one dance, towards the end of the night and then she would give him a little encouragement. No doubt this would puzzle him and it would take him some time to realise what was afoot. Plenty of time to work it all to her advantage and she would approach her father as soon as possible. She would have to get him on her side before time came to plan the trip to London. Once her father saw reason, her mother would have to go along with it. Yes, the more she thought about it the surer she became that her plan would work and she would end up mistress of Leigh Court one of these fine days. After all, John had made it quite clear he had no interest in his inheritance. He would end up thanking her for taking it off his hands and leaving him free to stay in London permanently.

Helen settled down into the folds of the travelling rug with a satisfied sigh. The beauty of the soft silver landscape, shining under the brilliant rays of a constant moon in a cloudless sky was lost on her. The silhouettes of the black trees and hedges standing out in relief and the soft coughing noises of the night might have drawn the attention of persons less preoccupied with their own affairs as Helen Leigh and her erstwhile groom as they travelled smartly over the country road towards their destination.

The tennis dance in Kilrane was one of the highlights of the New Year Season in the area. One would have thought that late January was a strange time to hold a gathering for tennis enthusiasts but the game of tennis was so popular amongst the local gentry that apart from getting together for matches all through the late spring and early summer, the man who was more or less elected to take charge of the local clubs had organised a New Years Ball in his home outside Kilrane during the first year of his presidency. It had been quite the most successful ball of the season. Now it was an annual event and not to be missed by anyone who counted as anything in the locality. Helen Leigh always attended, as did her brother John when he was in residence at Leigh Court. It was whispered that all the mamas and papas with marriageable daughters spared no expense fitting them out for the Tennis Dance and it was here that matches were set up and promises made by the young bucks from all over the county. Up to now Helen had curled her lip at all such talk, but tonight, much to her own surprise, her own match would be made, or certainly begun in the magnificent ballroom of Ballyruane House.

When Tom Lonegan reigned in the horses and turned into the driveway, the house was glowing with lights; every window seemed on fire and all along the curving driveway torches were blazing. The forecourt was already packed with coaches, unloading their passengers and the air was filled with the excited voices of young people with shrill bursts of laughter every now and then and the grooms and stable lads shouting instructions. As Helen descended from her coach she could hear the music swelling out from the open hall door, and with a last word of warning to Lonegan to watch his manners and his drinking and be there promptly at midnight to ferry her home safely, she moved swiftly across the threshold into the welcoming warmth of the ballroom. The dancing had begun and the eager beavers were already swaying to the tune of a waltz. Helen quickly appraised the gathering, noting that the Kerrigans, Luke and his younger sister Josie, were already present, standing at the far end of the long shimmering ballroom.

Toss Flynn, the owner of Ballyruane, a spare man in his forties who was as yet unmarried and who still considered himself one of the young set and an ideal catch, never stinted on anything to do with the Tennis Dance. He was proud of it and his reputation and fought hard to make the occasion more memorable each year. The room was decorated and lit to perfection and a full orchestra had been drafted in from the Capital for the night. Later on the buffet supper would be sumptuous, with food and drink of all sorts. Servants were drilled and warned to within an inch of their lives to overlook even the most crass bad manners of the more loutish members of the tennis fraternity. Indeed more than two thirds of the revellers would not know one end of a racquet from another and the closest they had ever come to a game of tennis was to ogle the young ladies delicately engaged on the court.

Helen joined a crowd of her acquaintances seated just under the balcony. Already the girls were filling in their cards and giggling and talking in high pitched voices. Helen hated this sort of behaviour and usually stayed on the outskirts of the crowd with a couple of her cronies; like minded young ladies who liked to think of themselves as too intelligent for such childish carry on, but were secretly mocked as wall flowers and "plain Janes" by the more outgoing girls. Emily and Florence Moynihan greeted her and Helen noted with pleasure that they were indeed wearing two of Tilly Lacey's more ambitious and less successful concoctions. The dresses did nothing for the gawky figures and plain features of the two and Helen could afford to greet them more effusively than usual. Since none of the young men seemed anxious to fetch for them, they decided to approach the punch bowl themselves and Helen agreed to accompany them when she saw that Luke Kerrigan was making his way in that direction. Better get it over with, she thought, as she glanced up and caught his eye. Luke who was used to being ignored by Helen or sourly put in his box if he made any attempt to fraternise, was surprised to see her face break into a smile as she approached. Hastily glancing over his shoulder to make sure the smile was directed at him, he swallowed and bowed slightly.

'Good evening Miss Leigh.' He waited for her to sweep past him in her usual imperious manner and was again surprised when she stopped in front of him.

'Good evening Luke, how nice to see you. isn't it a freezing night? I declare I could do with a glass of punch to warm me after the long drive.'

Helen heard the Moynihans' sharp intake of breath, but she pressed on regardless, taking Luke Kerrigan's arm and propelling the mesmerised young man towards the table where the punch bowls were standing.

Now that she had made her move, Helen was secretly enjoying herself. Luke Kerrigan was still not too sure what was going on; all he knew was, the object of his undying affection, who heretofore had treated him like a leper, and a particularly stupid one at that, was tonight for some reason singling him out for her undivided attention. The word had spread around the room and heads turned every time Helen and Luke came into view. Luke was afraid to open his mouth, he could not believe his luck and he was afraid to change it by saying something stupid. At twenty four years of age he was a fine man with broad shoulders and curly black hair, but a man more at home in the saddle, or working in the fields than dressed for the dance. Luke was a shrewd business man, his father's son, but in spite of the old man's efforts to make a gentleman of him, he lacked polish and had none of the social graces. His adoration of Helen Leigh was very real and totally sincere. He had fallen in love with her when he first saw her riding out to hounds when she was just sixteen. He had worshipped her from a distance since then, only daring to approach her now and then and putting up with her ridicule and obvious distaste for him. He had urged his sister, Josie to befriend Helen Leigh, but Josie too, was considered by Helen to be beneath her and so the young girl was discouraged from tagging onto Helen's entourage.

So, tonight Luke was tongue-tied. He stood at Helen's side most of the night, waiting to be dismissed and puzzled when he was not. He tried to ignore the titters of the other girls in the group and the amused faces of his own friends who stayed at a respectable distance. When supper was announced he expected Helen to flounce off but she turned and seemed happy to walk to the dining room beside him. More flustered than ever he walked beside her and, afraid even to eat, he watched her daintily pecking at her own supper. She asked if he was going to the shoot on the morrow, mentioning that her father's party were leaving shortly after dawn.

'Louise wanted to be allowed to go, can you imagine?' she smiled. Luke could well imagine the younger Miss Leigh wanting to accompany the men; she was one of the finest horsemen in the county and a fair shot to boot. He was on safe ground now and he ventured a few remarks about the Major's horses. He himself was not going to the shoot, he had business in Enniscorthy, he told her. Asking what day he planned to go to Enniscorthy, Helen intimated she might accompany him, as she had business in the town herself. Luke Kerrigan nearly swallowed the glass when she made her remarks, and ignoring his discomfort, she cocked her head sideways; 'Oh, the music is beginning again and it is way after eleven. I think you and I should dance a waltz before I leave' she said imperiously.

Luke could hardly believe his ears, but the shock cured his choking fit and before she might have time to change her mind he seized the moment and clutching her arm hurried her back to the ballroom. There to the amazement of all present, Miss Helen Leigh and Luke Kerrigan took the floor. Luke, although still looking slightly bemused was obviously fit to burst with pride and joy, and the older Miss Leigh had a look of determination written all over her face.

'My God, what do you make of that' whispered Flo Moynihan to her sister. Emma sniffed disdainfully: 'Well' she said, 'it looks as if Helen has picked a husband at last, and she is going for brawn, certainly not brain.'

The two girls watched open mouthed as Luke and Helen waltzed round the floor, seemingly oblivious to the stir they had caused.

Chapter 6

'**B**egod, that's a quare thing now.' Tom Lonegan pushed his cap back and scratched his head thoughtfully. He was standing in the avenue at Leigh Court looking after the departing trap in which Helen Leigh sat, wrapped to the ears and staring straight ahead of her. It was the sight of Luke Kerrigan's burly figure holding the reins in one hand and the whip in the other that drew the hushed remark from Lonegan.

He had heard talk in the kitchen alright; young Julia Whelan was full of it since the night of the tennis dance. He had not noticed anything on the way home, but then all his attention was focused on his own posture that night. It was hard to stay upright and look sober with a bellyful of good porter rattling around inside you. Lonegan licked his lips at the memory. He had collected that young sourpuss at the stroke of midnight and got them both back home safely. More credit due to the good team of horses, who kept to the road even when he dozed off himself, but no matter, herself must have been satisfied, because he heard no complaints then or since.

So here she was now, traipsing around the countryside in Kerrigan's open trap for all to see. What the hell is the bitch up to at all? Lonegan mused as he walked on up the drive. Not like her to have anything to do with the Kerrigans; thinks them too far beneath her and sure they are too! Auld Mick Kerrigan's da was a labourer at Edermine and his son was a cute hoore who made use of the peoples' need, to grow rich. They might not have the blood, but begod, they have the money. Talk had it that Kerrigan could buy and sell any of the gentry in these parts. But the Leighs had plenty, it couldn't be Luke Kerrigan's fortune she was after. What was it then? That wan was a dried up auld stick even though she wasn't yet twenty. It certainly wasn't romance she was after, Lonegan laughed nastily, his cess pit of a mind dismissing Helen Leigh. The young wan now, there was a goer for you, but she preferred horses to men any day, Lonegan laughed again and spat out of the corner of his mouth. Well she was up to something; time would tell. And what would the Major say when he came back from the hunt and heard about his daughter's gallivanting. Lonegan rubbed his hands together gleefully - he loved a bit of trouble as long as he himself was well out of it, and trouble there would be - the sparks would fly between the Major and his daughter, no doubt about it.

Julia Whelan was busy clearing up after Helen, she had been summoned hastily from the kitchen after luncheon and told to set out Helen's travelling clothes.

'I am taking a trip to Enniscorthy this afternoon, with a gentleman friend' Helen informed her, Julia knew it had to be Luke Kerrigan. The gossip about the tennis dance had spread like wild fire and Julia had it from Kitty the very next day. The Moynihan girls were full of it and their maid, Mary Ann Byrne, was Kitty's closest friend. Julia said nothing, waiting to see if Helen would elaborate. The girl's next remarks however nearly floored her.

'What do you think of Luke Kerrigan Julia? Come on girl, I won't bite you, tell me the truth, what do you think of him?'.

Julia's face paled and she took a step backward - what in the name of God could she say in answer to this question? And what was Miss Helen playing at anyhow? Everyone knew she had no time for Luke Kerrigan, even though the poor eejit was mad about her, Julia swallowed and tried to speak: 'Luke Kerrigan Miss?,' she stopped and swallowed again.

'Yes, yes girl, Luke Kerrigan. I want you to tell me what you think of him and don't do the dolt with me girl. I know how clever you are, so out with it now, the truth or I'll beat you soundly,'

Julia's mind was racing, trying frantically to think what the older girl might want her to say. But it was no use; Helen's pale eyes were boring into her and she felt like a fly caught in a spider's web, deadly paralyses setting in rapidly.

'Well, Mr. Kerrigan is a fine young man, yes a fine man indeed Miss, and they say he has money to burn and the pick of the ladies to choose from. His Da thinks the sun shines out of him, and he will own Kerrigan's fine house and all the land and property one of the day.' Julia's voice faded away and she looked at Helen hopefully: Oh Lord, I hope I said the right thing, her mind was racing. Helen continued to look shrewdly at the young servant girl - then as if making up her mind about something, she spoke: 'Well my girl, you might as well hear it from me; I'm sure it is common gossip around the neighbourhood anyhow, but I will confirm it for you: I intend to marry Luke Kerrigan; I have made up my mind to it and that's an end to it!'.

Julia was shaking with relief and she lowered her head so that Helen would not see the surprise in her eyes. What business of hers was it anyhow. Helen Leigh was a strange human being and if she had decided to marry Luke Kerrigan, well, that certainly was the end of it - but what a strange way for a prospective bride to talk about her intended nuptials.

'What have you to say about that?.' Her trial by fire was not over yet. Julia took her courage in both hands: 'I wish you the very best Miss, the very best and I am sure you and Luke Kerrigan will be very happy. When will the happy event be taking place? she added primly.

Two small red spots of colour glowed in Helen's pale cheeks and her eyes had a strange look in them, 'like ice gleaming under a harsh light,' Julia said later as she told Kitty about the conversation.

'Oh, there is nothing settled yet - nothing actually settled, I will have to think about the matter further and of course discuss it with my father.'

Pulling herself up as if realising whom she was talking to, she caught Julia's arm and squeezed it hard enough to draw a cry of pain from her. Drawing her closer she hissed: 'Now you had better keep what I told you to yourself or you will be very sorry.'

'Oh I will Miss, I will,' Julia promised hurriedly.

Mean cow, she thought, the sooner you move to Kerrigans the better, but God help poor Luke Kerrigan. I hope he knows what he's getting.

When Julia returned to the kitchen, Lonegan was drinking tea and Mrs. Walshe was slapping bread dough around, glowering at him as if she would have liked to apply her large hands to his ears instead of the mixture before her.

'Did you ever hear such rubbish' she said as Julia slid carefully along the wall, keeping well out of Lonegan's reach. 'This fellah is trying to tell me that Miss Helen has taken up with young Kerrigan - that will be the day now, when our young lady bothers with the likes of the Grabber Kerrigan's boy.' She sniffed disdainfully, wiping floury hands on her ample aproned girth. Julia stopped in her tracks, as if stuck to the ground. Mrs. Walshe looked up in surprise, then seeing the white face of the girl in front of her, she too stopped dead and narrowed her eyes. 'Come on Miss, why are you suddenly turned to stone? what's up? what have you heard?.'

Lonegan looked from one to the other and gave an evil cackle. 'I told you, this young wan knows the truth of it - sure didn't I see them with me own eyes - passin' by as jaunty as you like, clippin' down the drive a few minutes ago and herself done up to the nines in the new black hat and coat she got at Christmas, and Kerrigan, the big lug, with a stupid grin on his puss and he like a lamb being led out to the slaughter.

Wait till himself comes back and gets wind of it - then the fat will be in the fire.' He chuckled again and hugged himself at the thought of the fun the next weeks would bring.

Mrs. Walshe was still watching Julia, 'Out with it girl - what do you know about this business?' Julia looked back at her and clamped her mouth shut. Mrs. Walshe gave the dough a resounding smack and made a move towards Lonegan who rose and bolted out the back door like a scalded cat.

'Now that that little sleeveen is gone you can tell me what you know' she said and Julia shook her head: 'God Mrs. Walshe, she's after warnin' me if I say a word to anyone she will skin me alive.'

'If you don't tell me I might do a bit of skinning myself' the cook said, picking up the large meat knife and looking thoughtfully along the sharp edge.

'Well don't tell a soul then' Julia whispered, 'but she says she is going to marry Luke Kerrigan'.

'Well the curse of the seven snotty orphans on her' said Mrs. Walshe, collapsing onto the stool deflatedly, as if the wind had been let out of her suddenly and with a rush. Her red face was getting redder by the minute and Julia was afraid she was going to have some sort of turn. 'What can she be thinking of, disgracing us like that? and her poor father not even well, and my own lamb not here to talk sense to her. That one is a wicked, wicked girl!' and a large tear gathered in one eye. Julia watched, fascinated as the tear spilled over and ran down Mrs. Walshe's fat red cheek. She knew well the cook believed everything that happened at Leigh Court reflected on herself, whether good or bad, and the fortunes of the Leigh family were close to her heart, but she found it hard to understand why the news should have such a devastating effect on Mrs. Walshe.

'My ladyship will be destroyed with this news, and she planning to send Miss Helen to London for the duration so that she would get a fine husband; one of her own kind. The Major will never let her marry Kerrigan. Never! But that strap will make plenty of trouble for all of us. Auld Lonegan is right then.' She sighed and wiped her eyes with a floury hand, leaving a streak of white across her scarlet face.

'Come on now Mrs. Walshe, have a nice cup of tea and don't be troubling yourself; sure Helen could do worse than marry Luke Kerrigan. Isn't he the richest man around here. Look at all the land he owns.'

The older woman drew in her breath suddenly. 'That's it!' she said, 'that's what the little rip is at - she wants the Kerrigan land joined on here - that's how she'll get around the Major and wind her way into his affections. Oh, she's a clever puss, so she is, and a dangerous puss at that. Tea is it?' she said, rising ponderously off the little stool, 'it's something stronger than tea I want this day to help me get over that shock.

Helen Leigh and Luke Kerrigan! Well bedad there's matches for earwigs right enough, matches for earwigs,' she said again, shaking her head at Julia.

Chapter 7

The morning air was crisp and clear, and Julia felt as if she could see to the ends of the earth with just a little effort. Mrs. Walshe had told her to get on home to visit with her mother. Knowing that Nan Whelan's time on this earth was short she wanted her daughter to be there for her as much as possible and even though the other servants complained bitterly about all the time off the Whelan sisters were given, the cook's word was law. So every chance she got, she sent either Julia or Kitty home to be with their mother.

This morning Julia hadn't a care in the world. Her boots hung around her neck, she had carefully removed them as soon as she left the driveway of Leigh Court. Her heels were red and raw where the too-large boots had blistered them, but Julia was happy enough, her feet would soon get used to being shod again. She was as glad to be out of the big house as her feet were to be free of the hard leather boots and she laughed and did a little skip in the middle of the road. If Julia dreamed at all it was to be free, and her concept of freedom was to be out in the air and unfettered by rules and orders and able to follow where the fancy might take her. To follow that fat thrush for instance, which was cheekily singing its heart out right at the edge of the still, frost- white field beside the road. She eyed the bird now, willing it to stay and let her approach. She got close enough to see the little black currant eyes and the throb of the feathery throat, but then the bird flew, skimming the ground and landing again a few feet from her, looking back as if daring her to follow. Julia was caught now, and throwing caution to the winds she followed the little feathered pied pipes where it led; and where it led her was deep into Kerrigan's wood.

The spruce trees fanning the steel blue winter sky with dainty fringed fingers were huge over Julia's head and she gazed up at them and turned round and round in circles until she fell laughing to the ground, her head spinning. The thrush forgotten now, had passed on, busy with it's own pursuits. A flock of wood pigeons, disturbed by her laughter, flew up, making a loud swooshing noise and complaining in their deep throated old thick voices. Julia called back at them, flapping her arms, mocking their flight, they were like the fat old women at the back of the church, clucking at one another on Sundays after Mass, comparing complaints, heads together, deep in their black shawls. She moved oft the pathway and the moss was soft under her feet. She knew these woods well, every nook and cranny, every tree and space. All the Whelan children had hidden in Kerrigan's wood when their too hard life became unbearable.

Julia had climbed these trees as soon as she could reach the lowest bough. She had lain hidden under fronds of bracken, green in spring and brown and golden in summer and autumn and she had watched the moon, like a great drop pearl in the night sky when her mother thought she was asleep in the loft beside Kitty. Her mother was never surprised at her absences, only warning her in her gentle way, not to forget her chores or the jobs her father left out for her. She knew this daughter of hers was a free spirit; different somehow from the others who were Mick Whelan's children alright, but loved no less for that. Sometimes when she looked into Julia's, her youngest child's eyes, what she saw there frightened her. No one of their class had a right to such eyes. And such a soul, where in God's Name would it lead her? There was such a fire, such a hunger in those eyes; maybe that was why she never taught Julia to read, was it a strange effort to protect her? From herself? From what?

Nan Whelan knew it was an empty gesture, a futile effort, she should leave it to God. All she could do was shelter the girl as much as possible and keep her from crossing swords with her father. Nan had a feeling that Julia would die sooner than bend to anyone's will. She'll go to her grave with that spirit unbroken she thought, but God help her, I hope it won't be an early grave.

Julia was gone past the point of no return now. Her hair, flying out around her, she was part of the woods; like the wild fairy child her mother often accused her of being. The trees grew so closely and so thickly and it was so warm and sheltered, Julia could take her cloak from around her shoulders and leaving it on the floor of the forest with her boots she raced around the green turf like one of the young fillies at Leigh Court. She herself could never understand the feelings that took over when she was alone in the forest. Sometimes when she had exhausted herself with wild running and leaping, she grew afraid. She remembered Fr. Murphy's sermons about God and how women were to model themselves on His Holy Mother, who was white and still and pure like the snow and who never raised her eyes, let alone her skirts, to run mad like a march hare through Kerrigan's wood. What would God think of her? And if she died, would she burn in Hell with all the wanton sinners and fallen women and wild mad people. Maybe there was a devil in her; her Dada had cursed her once and told her there was a devil in her as big as a jackass, when he found her riding around the lower field on Pat Leary's jennet. She shivered now, her mad race over, as she lay stretched on the soft green sward, her head soaking, the morning dew and melted hoar frost mingling with her own sweat.

'Get down you young rip or I'll take the strap to you. Riding around like a tinker bitch, I don't know whose whelp you are, you're none of mine , you brazen hussy.'

Terrified she had leapt from the jennet's back and made off like a jack rabbit through the ditch into Kerrigan's wood. But she had to return home sometime and he had not forgotten. She still shook when she remembered the savage beating he had given her.

'I'll put manners on you, you divil's spawn.' he roared with every lash of the leather belt. 'I'll knock the divil out of you.'

'Is there a devil in me Kitty?' she had sobbed later as her older sister bathed her bruises and tried to console her. 'It's not you that has the devil in you alannah,' Kitty answered, 'but by God, the devil lives in the house all right.'

Julia shook herself now, pushing all thoughts of her Dada and the devil away enjoying the feel of the ground under her and the familiar noises of the woods. Then remembering she had to be back at the big house to clean up after the luncheon, she got to her feet and reluctantly retraced her steps. The pine cones were thick on the ground and Julia retrieved her shawl and gathered as many as she could carry in it. Mama would love to throw these on the fire and watch the coloured flames leap up. She could go the rest of the way home through the woods and only have half a mile of the back road to walk and she was wet to the skin now anyhow so it wouldn't matter if she had no shawl around her.

Nan Whelan looked up from the stool when her younger daughter entered the cottage, 'Well darlin', what a surprise to see you. Running wild in Kerrigan's wood again?' She smiled at Julia's flushed face and glowing eyes. 'Musha you're drowned' she said as Julia hugged her, 'take off that dress and put it by the fire and wrap that blanket around you before you catch your death.'

'Look what I brought for you Mama' Julia said opening her shawl, 'let me throw them on the fire and we'll watch them while the kettle boils and I'll make a cup of tea for you - Mrs. Walshe sent you a cut of lovely white shop bread - look I have it in my boot - don't worry' she said as her mother laughed, 'I have it well wrapped up - it's safe enough.'

Julia held her mother's frail hand and stroked her hair, noticing sadly how thin and grey it had turned even in the last few weeks. She told her all the news from Leigh Court - how Lady Grace had asked for her and how Mrs. Walshe had beaten Tom Lonegan over the head with the big soup ladle and chased him out of the kitchen. Then she whispered her most important news which was fast becoming an open secret up at the big house.

'Mama, you'll never believe what I am going to tell you now, but it's the truth, I swear on our Granny's grave - Miss Helen is going to marry Luke Kerrigan.

She felt her mother stiffen under her touch. 'Are you sure child? Who told you?'

'Miss Helen herself told me and she said that was an end to it.' Julia was delighted with the dramatic effect her news had. Nan Whelan sighed softly, seeming to shrink even more into herself. 'Faith and I'm sorry to hear that news; no good will come of a match like that; better for people to marry their own kind. The Major and Lady Grace will end up giving in to Helen, she always gets her own way and Kerrigan will turn heaven and earth to marry with the Leighs. Indeed he may have to turn heaven around to marry into the Protestant gentry. Ah well, sure it's nothing to do with us, the likes of us will have to do what we're told and whether its Helen Leigh or Mrs. Luke Kerrigan that gives the orders it won't make a posy odds of difference to us Julia girl.'

'I hope she doesn't want me to go with her to Kerrigans Mama, I want to stay at the big house' Julia said.

'You would be better to stay with her ladyship if you could at all child' Nan answered. 'But sure if the other one wants you to go you won't have much choice. But then, if it's Mrs. Walshe she's up against she may not get it all her own way.'

Nan laughed softly - 'We all know who rules the kitchen up at Leigh Court, and it's not the Master or Mistress of the House. Give us the tea now and a little bit of that nice soft bread. I feel a bit hungry today; I think I'm getting better.'

Julia bustled about taking down the little white cup Lady Grace had given her mother when she was leaving Leigh Court and, cutting the white bread into dainty fingers she spread it with a little honey from the jar Kitty had hidden away at the back of the press for her mother. She was delighted when Nan drank the cup of tea and ate a little of the bread. Her mother was better today - if the weather stayed fine and the snows stayed away she might be able to go out again before long. As if to give the lie to her thoughts, Nan bent over suddenly, clutching her chest and gasping with pain.

'Quick child, the bottle, get the bottle on the shelf there' she whispered.

Julia poured the drops onto a spoon and held it to her mother's white lips. She took them greedily and Julia helped her over onto the settle, laying her down gently and smoothing the hair back from her thin forehead which was wet with perspiration. With her eyes closed and the skin drawn taut across her cheeks she looked as if the life was gone from her already. Julia knew with an awful certainty that she was seeing the corpse her mother would soon become. She tried to stifle the sob that rose in her throat, but Nan heard her and moved slightly. Making an enormous effort she opened her eyes and tried to smile.

'Hush now child, sure it's just one of those old cramps, I'll be fine in a few minutes. Go back to the fire and warm yourself. Get that dress dry before you put it back on you and go and call Sadie - see if the poor lamb is well enough to get up and keep me company until Kitty comes this evening.'

She closed her eyes again, exhausted and Julia went to do what she was told, wishing Kitty was here already, to take charge. Thank God Dada would not be home for another few days, things were bad enough without having him to worry about.

All the joy of the morning had left her now and Julia felt as if the light had gone out of the very air, leaving her breathless and weary - with a terrible feeling squeezing her head like a physical hand and a fire of fear starting up in her head. She shook herself as if she could get rid of the darkness, as a dog coming from a pond rids himself of water.

Better to tidy up and do her mother's bidding and then get back to Leigh Court - Kitty would know what to do.

Chapter 8

The clear morning had left no traces as Julia made her way back towards Leigh Court. The early afternoon was already darkening and the sky was steely grey. Towards the east, the glowering clouds were banked down, shifting fitfully now and then as if eager to be off across what remained of the sky. Neither was there a trace of her own good spirits left and she pulled her shawl tight around her and lowered her head against the quickening wind. Her mother had looked so frail; lying on the settle where Julia had laid her and the looks of her sister Sadie had done nothing to cheer her heart. Mrs. Walshe's remarks to Hynes the butler that Sadie Whelan would never comb a grey hair had made Julia look at her sister with new eyes. She had always accepted Sadie as she was, sitting beside the fire, even in summer, never asking to come with her sisters and brothers when they went to gather frog-spawn in the early spring or fish for pinkeens in Kerrigan's pond later in the year. Julia never thought too much about it, her Mama had always had Sadie under her wing - but what would happen now? Mama was not going to get better; Kitty would have to spend more and more time at the big house now that she was moving upstairs to look after her ladyship when the new parlour maid arrived, and she herself would have no excuse to go home too often if Mama was not there.

Julia stopped dead in her tracks - she knew she would never want to go home if Mama was not there to greet her. What of the boys and Dada himself. They were fed at Leigh Court most of the time and Dada never went home nowadays anyhow, unless he was drunk and wicked and looking for someone to beat.

What about Sadie? Who would take care of her if Mama was gone? Julia never cried, she walked faster and choked down the pain in her throat. What was the use of thinking like this? Kitty would manage somehow, she always did.

The wind was getting stronger by the minute and the trees in Kerrigan's wood were no longer friendly or dreamy. They were murmuring angrily and the uppermost branches were whirling in confusion, whipped by the gale. Julia knew there was a storm coming - the crows at the White Cross were huddled together, what looked like hundreds of them in the branches of the big yew tree and the animals in the fields were bunched together in the shelter of the ditches.

The weather, which had been uncommonly mild up to and after Christmas, was going to turn fierce now and winter would get a grip on the land. Spring will be late this year, Julia thought. Poor Mama! If it snows now she won't be able for the cold.

Nan Whelan had never been too robust and the winter cold always took its toll, but now in her weakened state. . . Blast the weather, why couldn't it have stayed the way it was? But Julia knew she was being stupid, each season must come and have it's way with the land and the people on the land and then pass and make way for the next, that was the way of the world.

'What has the puss on you my girl?' Mrs. Walshe was not in good humour, this was obvious to Julia the minute she stepped over the threshold into the kitchen.

Katie Murphy was standing at the far wall with her apron over her head bawling like a jackass and the cook's florid countenance was puce.

'Stop that howling at once you wicked girl' she roared at the unfortunate Katie, 'and you Julia Whelan, get that puss off you and get your arms into that sink. I don't know what the world is coming to - no girls worth their salt to do a day's work and young ladies who should know better upsetting their parents and forgetting their place. I declare to God; I think it won't be long until the fire will come from Heaven and swallow us all'.

At these words Katie Murphy gave an almighty howl and Mrs. Walshe let fly with the iron ladle she was holding in her hand.

'Thank God it wasn't the cleaver,' Julia muttered as she tried to pacify the crying girl.

The worst of Mrs. Walshe's temper was spent now, once she threw something or slapped someone, she began to feel sorry. At heart she was a kindly soul, but much put upon as she liked to tell anyone who gave her a sympathetic ear. Julia did not want to know what had sparked this latest outburst, she guessed it was all to do with Helen Leigh's romance. She quickly despatched the still snivelling Katie to the gardens to collect the vegetables for tonight's dinner and hastily hanging up her cloak, she delved into the mountain of delph in the big sink. Mrs. Walshe sat down and mopped her face with her apron.

'God, that young one is useless, nothing but a lump of stupidity, taking up room in my kitchen. It won't be long before Lonegan gets her in the family way anyhow and then she'll be sent home post haste. I'm tired trying to watch her, and it's no use warning her; she won't be told'.

Julia secretly agreed, but she tried to calm Mrs. Walshe by changing the subject.

'When is the new parlour maid coming? That will make things easier, then Kitty can go upstairs full time and you will have someone who knows how to see to the dining room.'

Mrs. Walshe sighed lugubriously, not altogether convinced, but wanting to be mollified now that her temper had cooled.

'She should be here by the end of the week, and a good thing too. We'll have the shoot here at the beginning of February and now that your poor mother won't be here to help I'll have to go further afield. How is she today, then?'

'Not too good. I left Sadie looking after her until Kitty gets home, but she took an awful turn just before I left. She looks worn out'.

'Poor creature, she is worn out' the cook answered, pulling herself up from the chair. 'Well, time and tide waits for no man, here I go again. Herself only wants something light for dinner. There's only three of them, I thought one of my nice cheese soufflés, with that bit of mutton left over from yesterday, done in a nice potato pie.'

She nodded happily to herself, now that Julia was fast restoring order in her kitchen she felt better.

A good little girl that one, and a great little worker, tell the truth of her; a great little worker. Mrs. Walshe had a habit of finishing even her thoughts by repeating her final utterances as it to copper-fasten her remarks.

Kitty Whelan was finishing her afternoon chores as quickly as she could; if the new parlour maid would only come she would not have to go down and help in the dining room at meal times. It would take her all her time to get home now and coax a bit of broth into her mother and get her settled for the night before it was time to get back to work again. Thanks be to God, the auld fellah is away, at least I don't have to worry about him, she thought. But that won't last, he'll be back tomorrow and in a foul humour with a head on him and a thirst the Slaney itself wouldn't quench.

Kitty dumped the bed linen in the laundry chute and made her way down the back stairs. Not time to grab a drop of tea even. As she looked out through the long landing window on the lower corridor she swore under her breath. The sky had a metallic look now, a slight coppery tinge at the edge of the grey-black clouds. That's all we need now, a fall of snow to cover us in. She took the lower stairs in leaps and ran to get her shawl in the kitchen. Julia looked up from the sink and nodded, casting a warning glance across at the cook.

Kitty slowed down and took in the situation at a glance, but she would have to take her chances, no time to soft-soap Mrs. Walshe tonight.

'I'm off' she called, ..I'll be back well before dinner.' Not waiting for a reply she closed the door hastily and gasping as the wind caught her, she headed into the long driveway.

When she reached the cottage, the last of the weak touches of light had vanished completely and the sky was pitch black. The wind was moaning and howling now like a coven of banshees. Kitty had never been happier to reach the cottage door and she had to lean her weight against it to force back the wind and get it to close. The fire was nearly out and the room was bitterly cold. Her mother and Sadie lay together under the patchwork quilt on the settle. Neither of them opened their eyes as Kitty crossed the room and threw an armful of kindling onto the smouldering embers. She quickly fanned the flames and put some small pieces of turf on top. She would have to heat the place up quickly or they would have a double wake on their hands.

Rubbing the turf dust off her hands she took the lamp from the table and carried it over to the settle. Sadie opened her eyes and struggled up into a sitting position.

'Kitty, thanks be to God you've come; I can't wake Mama up, she went asleep shortly after Julia left and she was making awful queer noises. I shook her and shook her but she won't wake up.'

The little girl started to cry quietly and Kitty lifted her, as easily as you would lift a child and carried her over to the seat beside the now blazing fire.

'Hush, hush.' She quickly returned and looked down at her mother's still form. She bent down and listened for a breath and catching the thin wrist she felt for some sign of life. Her mother's face was waxen yellow and her eyes were closed. Kitty was sure she was dead until she felt a faint flutter under her fingers. Dropping her mother's arm, she ran to the dresser and fumbled for the little bottle Dr. Cosgrove had left in case of just such an emergency. Sweet Jesus, where had she left it? Here it is! Quick now girl. Lift her gently; hold it under her nose.

Kitty was shaking as she tried to revive her mother, she was waiting for this, she knew it was just a matter of time. It would be kinder to just leave her alone; let her fade away quietly. But she cried out with relief when a tremor went through the thin little frame and her mother's eyes fluttered open. But there was no recognition in those eyes and Kitty knew the moment she had dreaded was almost upon her.

'Mama' she whispered urgently, 'Mama, come on, wake up and take a little broth, look I brought it home for you from the big house; a lovely chicken broth.

But Nan Whelan was not to be recalled, not by the promise of broth, or even the desolation in her daughter's voice.

Kitty bent close as her mother's lips moved.

'What is it Mama, what? ' Nan's lips moved again and Kitty heard just one faint word: 'Tired'.

Now she could hear the rattle in her mother's chest and the thin hand closed on hers with amazing strength in its clasp.

'Sweet Jesus have mercy - Mother of God be with us.' Kitty was gabbling and she could hear Sadie behind her now, crying with fright.

A shudder passed over her mother's body and her eyes opened wide, then with a sigh she lay back into Kitty's arms and her hand fell limp onto the coloured rug. Kitty heard a high pitched keening cry and it was minutes before she realised it was coming from her own throat.

Julia Whelan was standing looking out at the trees lashing one another outside the windows of Leigh Court. The poplars in the drive were bent almost double and the branches of the huge oaks were like whirling dervishes.

Julia felt suddenly cold and she, who had not cried since she was a small girl, felt tears running down her face. Her whole body shook with sobs and she was powerless to do anything to stop them. She started to shake like the aspen tree in summer; the startled thought flashed across her mind. Then she was taken over by a feeling of such consummate loneliness, she felt as if she must be dying. Gasping, she turned to Mrs. Walshe. The startled woman opened her arms and the girl ran to her and clung to her like a drowning man clinging to a raft.

Slowly the shaking stopped and Julia lifted a tear-stained face. 'My mother is dead - I know it' she said in a quiet voice.

'For the love of God girl, don't be silly. You've caught a chill.' But as she looked into the huge green eyes, Mrs. Walshe too shivered, as if someone had walked over her grave.

Julia moved back to the window. The wind had suddenly ceased and the first flakes of snow were silently falling.

Chapter 9

Nan Whelan was buried in Ballyleigh as quietly as she had lived. Her sons and daughters stood silently watching as the pine box was lowered into the grave.

Her husband was absent.

A few of the neighbours stood at a discreet distance. There was no one from the big house except Tom Lonegan, cap in hand, standing just inside the graveyard gate.

The snow which had threatened on the night of her death had come to nothing and there was just a light powdering remaining on the ground and the tops of some of the ditches and trees. The sun was high in the sky this morning and Julia could feel the warmth of it through the thin black shawl over her head. January was over but Mama had not lived to feel the kindness of this St. Brigid's Day. Even if the harsh frost returned on the morrow, Julia would remember the benediction of this day, as if God was letting them know their mother was at peace. But Kitty would have none of this. When she tried awkwardly to tell her how she felt, the older girl pulled away from her and said in a hard cold voice: 'What God? Don't talk to me about God; I see no sign of any loving God in my life.'

Julia was horrified - she knew Kitty did not really mean those terrible words. She was black with grief and she could not be consoled. Julia said nothing; there was nothing anyone could do for Kitty - not yet.

The little band of mourners turned away and made their way back along the road. Life must go on and Sadie had to be looked after. Nan had not had much of a wake, they had done their best and the neighbours had been good to them. Lady Grace sent Lonegan down from the big house with food and drink and Kitty and Julia scrubbed the place from top to bottom. Nora Crane washed their mother's worn body and laid her out in the back room in what had been her marriage bed and the birth place of all of her children.

She looked like a young girl; her hair long and flowing over her shoulders and her face, in the candle-light, tinged with a colour she had never had in her life. Her one valuable possession, a mother of pearl rosary handed down from her own mother, was draped around her joined hands and a white crocheted shawl covered the old iron bedstead.

'She looks like a princess,' Sadie said, her eyes red rimmed from crying, wide with wonder as she sat in her usual place, as close to Nan as she could get.

Mick Whelan had returned with the rest of the entourage from the shoot at Begerin, to find his wife waked out. He showed no sign of sorrow, just stood over her for a few minutes, cap in hand, then pushing his sons out of his way he left the cottage and they heard the cart creaking and the horse's hooves as he headed down the back roads, going God knows where.

Markie Flynn's shebeen, Kitty thought, to drown his sorrows - What sorrows? What sorrows would Mick Whelan have? He never showed any human feelings in his life, why should he start now? His life would go on as before. He would eat and drink and tend the Major's horses and then drink some more. His children could go to hell as far as he was concerned, as long as they were there to wash his clothes and tend to his needs when he decided to come home.

Mrs. Walshe came to pay her respects to the dead and Tilly Lacey came all the way from Wexford to see her girlhood friend laid out. 'Wasn't it an awful pity,' she whispered to Mrs. Walshe as they sat together, keeping vigil over the corpse while the girls got the tea ready, 'Wasn't it an awful pity she ever married that pig of a man? Sure I couldn't believe it at the time - didn't everyone in the four parishes know what he was and his father before him and all belonging to him?'

'Sure her poor mother was desperate for a home for her before she went to her maker herself - God forgive her, she never knew what she let the poor crater in for' Mrs. Walshe sniffed, 'Where is he now, I wonder? Drunk under some ditch or sleeping it off in the stables up at Leigh Court. It's the like of him would survive and his poor wife gone to an early grave.'

'She's at peace now, well out of it I'd say. It's the poor girls I pity, with an invalid sister to look after and him to contend with. Oh God help us it's a hard life and no mistaking'.

The two women knelt as Nora Crane started the third rosary, and Kitty Whelan shut the door on the murmuring voices and continued to lay out the food to feed the mourners when the prayers were over.

Now the cottage was strangely empty - the hearth swept clean. Julia took off her shawl and knelt to light the fire. She stirred the grieshach and bending down she blew into the grey embers trying to get a spark going. This was the first morning she could remember the fire being so dead. Usually Nan or Kitty would bank up the ashes and throw a lump of turf on top to keep it going during the night; then in the morning they would stir it out and fan it easily into flame to heat the big black kettle and the black pot of stirabout before the rest of them stirred from sleep. Well that was then, she thought, and this is now and we will have to get on with it. Mama would be ashamed of this cold hearth and not a drop of tea to hand to anyone who might call. Before she had time to get a blaze going the door of the cottage flew open and Mick Whelan staggered in. His hair was matted and his face covered with dirty grey stubble. He looked as if he had been lying in the open over-night. He stood swaying on his feet; still obviously the worst for drink. His bleary eyes could hardly focus but he saw the black hearth and felt the cold in the room.

'Holy Jasus' he roared, 'are yiz all paralysed? Who let the blasted fire out? Bloody useless crowd of hoors - I'll kick yiz all out before this day is over - I should have done it years ago.'

He made a lunge at Julia and she side stepped. He caught the chair and lifting it, made as if to smash it against the wall. The door to the back room opened and Kitty stood in the doorway, her face a frozen mask of contempt.

'Put that down' she said in a low voice, 'put it down and get out of here - she's gone now and there's no reason for any of us to stay - if you want a home here, don't come back until you sober up.'

Mick Whelan stopped with the chair in mid air. His little red eyes blazing, he took a step towards Kitty. She stood her ground and stared him down. With an oath he threw the chair against the ground and staggered back out the door, kicking it to after himself.

By Christ - one of these days he'd do for that haughty bitch, he'd swing for her, but now he had to have a drink. His hands were shaking as he tried to pick up the reins and urge the patient old horse to move. He had half a bottle hidden in the stables if that bastard Lonegan hadn't got to it before him. Sitting up on the side of the cart he urged the horse on, in the direction of Leigh Court.

Kitty picked up the chair and set it against the table. They would have to work out some way of looking after Sadie. The twins were big and ugly enough to fend for themselves and herself and Julia were fixed up fine at Leigh Court, thanks to poor Mama. She did not know how much longer she could stand up to Mick Whelan. One of these days he would be just that bit too drunk, or her nerve would slip and that would be it. There was no doubt in Kitty's mind that her father was mad enough to do anything.

Whatever bit of a mind he had was completely eroded now by years of drunkenness and coarse living. She would have a word with her ladyship the first chance she got and see if there was something Sadie could do at Leigh Court. She was good at needlework, their mother had taught her to sew and mend and there was plenty of work like that to be done. But would Lady Grace take in another Whelan? Kitty thought not, even for her mother's memory. Her ladyship was kind enough when she wanted to be, but she would soon tell Kitty Leigh Court was not a charitable organisation if she was pushed too far.

'They are not like us' her mother used to say, 'They don't know how we live and they don't really care. Some day maybe we will have our own land back again and Ireland will belong to the Irish, the way it did in olden times.' Kitty often listened to her mother reading books for

Julia, about Fionn MacCumhaill and Cuchulain and all those heroes, filling her head full of nonsense, was Kitty's opinion. Julia was bad enough as it was with her strange notions and her dreamy way of carrying on - she'd put the fear of God into you sometimes with her strangeness. Better to keep your notions to yourself and your head down and learn how to work hard for your living. That was all the gentry appreciated. A civil tongue, a humble attitude and hard work well done. Ireland for the Irish, that went out with the Young Irelanders. She had heard the Major talking about the English Parliament and all that went on there. All he ever did was make a laugh of the Irish members. England would never let go of Ireland. Why should they when they could live off the fat of the land and have the likes of us to wait on them. Poor Mama is lying in her grave today and all her book learning did her no use. No! Forget about high notions.

Kitty had made up her mind years ago to take the boat for America, but there was always someone to look after. First Mama, now Sadie. Would she ever escape? Maybe not, but she would have a bloody good try if Mick Whelan didn't kill her first.

Julia watched Kitty covertly as she busied herself about the room. She loved Kitty with all her head, but sometimes when that black brooding look came over her face she looked so much like Dada, it was frightening. She put a cup of hot tea down on the table now and tried again to lift Kitty's spirits.

'Come on Kitty, drink that tea and we'll see to Sadie and get back to Leigh Court. The work will be piling up and Mrs. Walshe will be in sweet temper with Lonegan up to his old tricks'.

'Let the work wait' Kitty said coldly. 'It's not every day we have to go through what we went through today. Leigh Court will still be there in a few hours and so will Ballyleigh graveyard and our Mama's fresh grave. God Almighty! Even the likes of us should have a few hours to do our grieving before we put on our aprons again.

Chapter 10

Helen Leigh stood in the library waiting for her father. The Major had returned the night before, tired out but in ebullient mood after a successful shoot on the slobs at the north side of Wexford town. He would come here as he always did at this time in the morning to take a leisurely smoke before getting on with the business of the day and Helen had decided to beard the lion in his den. Better to get to him herself before the gossip reached his ears. She knew her father and her strategy was worked out carefully based on the premise that the best form of defence is attack. The only outward sign of any nervousness Helen might be feeling was the lace handkerchief she held tightly in her hand and dabbed to her forehead now and then in little quick jerky movements. Her face was no paler than usual and her jaw was set in a tight line. Once she was over this hurdle the way was clear before her. Luke Kerrigan was putty in her hands. Like a man bewitched, he would do her bidding no matter what she asked and to her own amazement, Helen found herself enjoying the experience. It was heady stuff, finding yourself the centre of someone's world and a totally new role for Helen, who had played a very second fiddle to her brother all her life. Helen had very few illusions about herself. She was plain in appearance, her personality did not exactly sparkle and if she did not take and shape her own destiny, her future was mapped out before her as the dull wife of some equally dull Englishman, tucked away in a backwater of the realm. Or worse again, an army wife trotted all over the globe, dealing with Hottentots or God knows what other low life form. No, Helen knew her own plan was the only viable one and this morning's interview was vital.

Major Leigh was surprised and slightly annoyed to find his eldest daughter waiting for him. It was unusual for Helen to seek him out, she preferred to keep herself to herself and go about her affairs in private;

even in secret. The thought annoyed him and he pushed it away hurriedly. Major Leigh had to admit he did not like his daughter Helen very much. There was only one woman in his life and that was Grace, but then Grace was like no other woman, marrying her was the best thing he had ever done, apart from leaving the army. John Leigh would not have admitted the latter, even under torture, but he had never really liked the army. He had done his duty - what else could one do? - and followed his own father into the cavalry when the time came. He had soldiered and won distinction, bringing honour to the family name. But when it was time to come home to Leigh Court, he had done so with great joy and thankfulness. Now his own son was falling down in his duty and the Major could not understand it; had the lad no back bone? No sense of family? He shrugged the unwelcome thoughts away and sighed. Helen turned and took in his appearance at a glance. Papa was failing, he was growing old she realised with a start. Well all the more reason why she should press on with her plan, before it was too late.

'Papa' she said without preamble. 'I have something to say to you. Something very important and I want you to hear me out. Please sit down.'

Major Leigh smiled wryly; Helen always managed to take the initiative, no matter who she was dealing with, she would have made a good officer. How strange that his two female children had all the characteristics of good army material that his son lacked. He sat down, noticing that Helen remained standing, putting him at a disadvantage. She was a shrewd young woman, he thought, not for the first time. He sat back and gave her his attention, pursing his lips as she began.

'You know mother wants me to go to Auntie Elizabeth and come out with my cousin Antonia this season? Well, I have no wish to go through that frippery. I have thought it out well and let me speak plainly Father. At best I would make a mediocre match. I don't want to live in England, my life is here at Leigh Court, surely you can understand that. I can be of great help to you, especially now that John has indicated that he wants to stay away for God knows how long.'

Her father's brow darkened, but she pressed on regardless: 'I have decided to marry Luke Kerrigan'. There, the bombshell was dropped. The Major sat forward in his chair, a look of total astonishment on his face.

'Marry Luke Kerrigan? Have you lost your mind completely girl?' he spluttered.

'Listen to me Father, hear me out.' Helen had expected just such a reaction and her ammunition was at the ready.

'The Kerrigans have more money and property than any of those jumped up second sons on the market in London. Luke is prepared to be married in our church and make a fine settlement on me; also his father is prepared to sign over the Kerrigan land to be joined to ours on his death, and my sons will inherit everything. Seeing John is disinterested, it would do no harm to have the inheritance secure and I will keep the name Leigh on my marriage.'

Helen stopped now. She had shot her bolt. She knew her father's pride in family, his feelings for the local land owners, but she also knew he was above all a shrewd man and a realist like herself.

Major Leigh was speechless. He sat staring at Helen, an amazed look on his face. After what seemed an eternity to the waiting girl he spoke: 'So Helen, you have worked it all out to the last detail. What a mind you have, pity you were not a man. I could have put you in charge of my affairs.' His tone was sarcastic but Helen's thin smile of pleasure told him she felt complimented by his remark.

'This is quite a revelation to me, you understand, but I have no intention of getting upset; my doctor has advised me against the wisdom of entering into combat with anything bigger than a fox,' he added drily. 'A year ago it would have been out of the question for me to even think of your marrying into the Kerrigan family. But events of the last few months make me believe I should give this matter some thought. You have spoken plainly to me, now I will do likewise.'

Helen sat down opposite to him, it was her turn to be amazed. She had never foreseen this, in all her rehearsals of today's conversation. She had seen herself using every argument in her power to even get her father to listen. This reaction on his part was beyond her wildest dreams. The major continued: 'My own health is not what I would like, as you are well aware. You also know what passed between your brother and I before he left, and this absurd wish of his to become a doctor. What you don't know, indeed nobody except my manager and I know, is that we are hard pressed for money.'

'Yes' he added as Helen's head shot up in surprise, 'Leigh Court has been draining away at the family fortunes for generations, and my late father was an extravagant man. He neglected the affairs of the estate and I am afraid I inherited many of his debts along with the title and land. It would do us no good if this got out. As you can imagine, we are depending on our good name for our business concerns, both here and on the mainland. We have been singularly unfortunate with the horses over the past while and we have to buy in new blood. What we need is an injection of capital and I had planned to go to London soon to try to raise a large sum. However, if you are determined to marry young Kerrigan and knowing you, my dear, I am sure you have thought it out well, maybe our little problem can be solved in quite a different manner to that which I had envisioned'. He finished speaking and looked across at his daughter's shocked face.

For once Helen Leigh was rendered speechless. Whatever she had thought would happen, this was unbelievable. She would be instrumental in saving the fortunes of the family. She would keep her beloved home from ruin. Her mind racing, her pale face flushed, she struggled for self control. Major Leigh watched her silently.

Helen spoke, her voice high with excitement: 'It is settled then Father. I will announce my engagement at the Hunt Ball next month.'

He could see that she felt more was needed and her effort to show him some form of warmth was pathetic.

'Thank you Father, I am grateful for your understanding and support. Luke Kerrigan will call upon you formally when I tell him.'

The Major inclined his head slightly. I am sure he will, he thought, Luke Kerrigan will do whatever you say for the rest of his life or suffer the consequences. Well, no matter, it was what the Kerrigans had been after all their lives. They could go up no higher now, without an alliance with one of the families around and why not aim for the top. They had reached the top of the pile in every other walk of life. Major Leigh knew from his own business dealings that Kerrigan owned half the town of Wexford as well as most of the land around here that was outside the Leigh estate. Grace would not be pleased, but he would talk her round and Helen would be happy, if that was possible, ruling the roost in the neighbourhood and ruling the Kerrigan clan too. He had no doubts about his daughter's ability in that direction.

When Luke Kerrigan called to Leigh Court the Major realised the young man was prepared to sell his very soul to secure the match. He saw to his intense surprise that Luke was in love with his daughter. He had thought the old man, Luke's father, the instigator of the alliance and even still he had no doubts that Ned Kerrigan was the prime mover. When he cast his eye over the papers Luke proffered he knew he was right. The settlement was generous, the terms ample, but this was to be an alliance between the two families and Ned had no intention of obliterating his name and line, no matter how much he wanted his son to marry into the Leighs. His lawyers had copper-fastened the agreement. In return for moneys and title to Kerrigan's vast properties, which with his death would pass to his only son, by insisting that Helen take the name of Kerrigan along with her own, Ned was ensuring that his descendants would bear the name Leigh-Kerrigan, with rights and title to the Leigh estate.

The major smiled grimly, the wily old fox had checkmated him all right and he wondered how much of his business was known to Kerrigan already. Young Kerrigan might be love sick but his father would look after his interests for him.

'You understand, no doubt, I must have my own people look over this document' he told Luke, who looked uncomfortable and extremely awkward, poised as he was on the edge of a chair facing him. The young man nodded eagerly.

'Of course, Sir, of course'

'However' the Major added 'you may consider yourself free to call on my daughter, with my permission.'

Kerrigan sprang to his feet, sticking out his hand as if to shake the Major's, then thinking better of it, he backed away hastily coughing to cover his embarrassment.

'Thank you Sir, thank you and may I say Sir, you won't regret it, I love Helen and I intend to look after her. You have made me the happiest man in the county of Wexford, yes in the whole country. Indeed you have. I will withdraw now Sir, with your permission and go tell Helen' he said stiffly, almost falling over himself in his enthusiasm.

How young and vulnerable he looked, the major thought as Luke turned and almost ran to the door. Poor young man, how true it is that love is blind, he thought to himself cynically. But by God in this case he would wager the saying of the local people would prove true and marriage would be an eye opener.

Chapter 11

Helen Leigh and Luke Kerrigan were married in the Protestant Church in Ballyleigh on the twentieth day of June, just four months after the announcement of their engagement at the Hunt Ball in Leigh Court.

The happy couple had spent some time in London with the Brooke-Mentons, where the bride-to-be purchased her wedding gown and her trousseau. The big house had been at fever pitch in the ensuing months and weeks with presents arriving every day and preparations for the wedding reception vying with work on the house and gardens.

Lady Grace, her initial dismay abated, set to with a will helping her daughter to plan her forthcoming nuptials and to draw up her guest list. Helen had turned amazingly good humoured and the family and servants were beginning to hope that life with Luke Kerrigan was what she really wanted and would change her nature permanently.

'A leopard don't change his spots,' Lonegan insisted whenever Mrs. Walshe began to talk fondly of Helen, saying the child was not too bad at all, bless her, and maybe they had all misjudged her.

Julia kept her own council, hoping she would not be asked to accompany Helen to her new home. However her mind was set to rest on that matter a few weeks before the big day when Kitty and herself were called to the drawing room for an interview with Lady Grace.

Julia found it hard to be at ease in the big room. She had never been inside the doors except on one occasion when she had to clean out the fire when the downstairs maid was ill. Now she stood before the mistress, her head down and her hands clasped in front of her. She was glad Kitty was beside her. If there was any talking to be done, Kitty would do it. Julia had never spoken directly to Lady Grace in her life. Now her ladyship was talking about Helen; saying she was anxious to bring a personal maid from Leigh Court when she took up residence in her new home.

'Mrs. Walshe tells me that you are a very good girl and quite a promising cook Julia.' Julia's head shot up in surprise; Promising cook?, she had never been allowed to cook anything in the kitchens of Leigh Court even though Mama had always got her to make the bread at home.

Lady Grace was still talking.

'She wants to keep you here and would like to take you under her wing and train you to assist her in the kitchens. I have agreed to this, even though my daughter also requests that you be allowed to go with her. You are quite a popular girl' she smiled at the little figure in front of her and noted the red tide seeping over her pale face. The child was as timid as one of the forest creatures. How odd that both Helen and Mrs. Walshe were engaged in an almost tug-of-war to secure her services. 'I have decided that Kitty would be much the better choice to accompany Helen, though I don't want to part with her myself.' This time she favoured Kitty with a brief smile. Kitty was not too happy herself at the thought of moving to the Kerrigan household. Helen was a much harder woman to work for than her mother, but she knew she had no choice in the matter. Her ladyship had put it to her when she approached her about giving Sadie work at Leigh Court. Lady Grace had agreed to take the little girl on, and to give her board and lodging in return for her services as needlewoman. The sting in the tail came when she informed Kitty that she wished her to accompany Helen to the Manor House when she went there as Luke Kerrigan's wife.

What matter, Kitty thought now, Sadie will be looked after and Julia wants to stay here. She will get her chance, Bridie Walshe will teach her all she knows and she may end up running the kitchens at Leigh Court. Wouldn't Mama love that now? There was only one thing worrying Kitty, her little sister could not read or write and neither her ladyship nor Mrs. Walshe knew this. She would have to be able to do both if she was ever to become a cook. Julia is as smart as a tack, she said to herself, she will learn somehow.

Lady Grace was dismissing them now; knowing full well they would both do as they were told.

'You may go now girls, I trust my arrangements are to your satisfaction.'

Julia and Kitty both nodded obediently and she smiled again, turning away to look out through the window. The sisters backed away and escaped thankfully out into the hallway. Julia caught Kitty's hand and looked sharply into her face.

'Are you sure you don't mind leaving Leigh Court Kitty?' she asked anxiously.

'Not a bit of it chick, you and Sadie will be grand here and you heard what she said, you're going to work with Mrs. Walshe. Do you know what that means?'

Julia shook her head.

'Well chick, if you do what you're bid and work hard you could end up ruling the kitchens here some day.'

Julia's eyes widened and she stood still in the hallway. You're foolin' me now Kitty,' she said, her face even whiter than usual.

'Bedad I'm not, play your cards right now and you're made up. Mrs. Walshe always had a soft spot for you and she was always telling Mama what a light hand you had when she tasted your soda bread. Of course Mama was careful to tell her it was your bake. Poor Mama was always looking after us in every way.'

Julia's eyes filled with tears and Kitty give her a push, 'Go on now, back to the kitchens and not a word to Walshe, wait for her to speak. Just get on with your work as usual.

So the months passed. The grass began to grow on Nan Whelan's grave and her last daughter moved into the attic at Leigh Court. The cottage was nearly deserted now. The girls rarely visited except on their evenings off when they went home to clean and wash their father's and brothers' clothes. They stayed well out of Mick Whelan's way and he seemed to have forgotten their existence. The twins came to Kitty for advice and counsel as they had done to Nan when she was alive and they too avoided their father outside of the time they had to spend in his company in the stables at Leigh Court. Jem was to be made under-footman on his eighteenth birthday and he was already walking out with Nellie Flynn, the little parlour maid. Kitty approved of this. Nellie was a nice little girl and her ladyship did not mind her servants fraternising. Jack, the stronger of the twins, confided in Kitty that he wanted to join the army, he had hoped to go with Master John, but now that John had changed the Major's plans on that score he still wanted to go and intended to ask the Major about it as soon as the wedding was over. Kitty knew it was useless to try to dissuade him and anyhow maybe he would be better away from Mick Whelan who would spend his paltry wages for him and beat him around the place whenever he felt like it.

The wedding day was bright and clear and the staff of Leigh Court were up at the crack of dawn. Tables were groaning under the weight of food and the piece de resistance; Mrs. Walshe's wedding cake; a huge concoction, iced and decorated with meticulous care; had pride of place in the entrance hall for all to see and admire as they entered the dining room. The flowers were magnificent in the big house, and in the church.

Helen Leigh was pale and appeared nervous as Julia dressed her hair for the last time and helped to pin her fragile veil of Limerick lace in place. As she descended the main stairway at Leigh Court, the train of her beautiful satin gown spread out around her, she looked resplendent, a worthy successor to all the Leigh brides who had gone before her over the years. Lady Grace, looking up from the front hallway realised that for once, her plain daughter looked almost pretty her face flushed with excitement, a soft wreath of wax flowers holding the filmy veil in place, her hair soft around her features.

'Darling, you look radiant' she said, and Helen smiled: 'I feel radiant Mother, this is a happy day for me.'

'I'm so glad' Lady Grace moved forward to embrace her daughter, but Helen held out a hand, saying sharply: 'No Mother, don't crush my veil, and shouldn't you have left? Papa and I should be the last to arrive at the church.'

Lady Grace stepped back and nodded, 'You are right of course Helen, how sensible you are as usual.' And she turned ruefully and made her way out to the waiting coach to join her son and her younger daughter.

The June night was warm and close. Indeed it hardly seemed to be night at all in Kerrigan's wood. The moon was riding high, secure in the knowledge that this was its time to rule the sky and there was no trace of cloud to mar its splendour. There was a translucent light over the world as if the gods had spread a blue gauze to dim the brilliance the moon was making. Julia Whelan had slipped away from Leigh Court when all the work in the kitchens was finally done. She was exhausted but she knew she would not sleep tonight. Julia never slept well when the full moon was high. Mama used to laugh and say it was because her fairy kin were calling her out into the moonlight. For whatever reason, she had long ago contented her mind to lying awake until the early hours on nights such as these and sometimes she made her way to her favourite place in all the world, the dark pool in Kerrigan's wood. Now she lay on the soft mossy bank, her hands behind her head, staring up into the sky. There was just one star, like a solitary diamond winking overhead and the night was so still it seemed to be holding its breath. The water was warm to the touch, shining with a phosphorous glow and Julia could resist it no longer. Kicking off her boots she quickly stripped and lowered herself gently into the water. It closed around her like velvet, soft and caressing and she swam silently out into the centre of the pond. Turning on her back she floated blissfully and feeling the tiredness flow out of her body she let the gentle ministering of the water take her over completely. After a while and reluctantly, she swam back to the edge and pulled herself up onto the mossy bank. She stretched her hands over her head, standing on tip toe, reaching for the moon, she laughed out loud feeling the joy rise up in her, drunk with the beauty all around her and the freedom of her own secret world. She turned round and round until dizzy and intoxicated with the sights and smells of the summer night she fell down onto the soft ground and stretching full length pressed her face into the damp moss.

John Leigh had left the revellers at the hall. He was happy for his sister, though God knows what had prompted Helen to marry Kerrigan. She was a strange one, always had been and there was no way John could ever hope to understand her motives. But then who could ever understand a woman's motives anyhow? His mother was the one woman John Leigh loved and respected and even Lady Grace baffled him most of the time. But she had stood with him against his father and he appreciated how difficult that was for her.

John was anxious to get back to his studies. Medicine was his consuming passion. As a child he had always felt that he would never fit in to his father's world and it had worried him. Then when he went to England to school he was shattered to find that he was not welcome. This was not his home either and he had suffered unmercifully from the bullying meted out to him at the hands of his English peers, who looked on him as an ignorant Irish clod. His feelings of isolation increased when, during the holidays, the local youths, those he had known and grown up with, backed away from him now, treating him like an Englishman. How ironic, John thought as he walked through Kerrigan's wood in the moonlight. At home I am not Irish, in England I am not English. I am not a soldier for my father, not a gentleman for my mother. Why is it that I always feel in the company of others as if I am on the outside looking in? But medicine now; there was something he could give his heart to. To be able to do something positive. Make some contribution to the world.

John Leigh was a deep thinker, in another family, or given another set of circumstances, with the proper stimulus, he might have given himself up completely to intellectual pursuits. As it was, he was a dreamer, a lonely young man, caught between many worlds. The fact that he had stood up to his father showed him to be a man of deep conviction and courage, but he did not see it that way, only that he was a disappointment to his family and a failure in his own place. So, tonight, he found himself alone and enjoying the beauties of the night, deep in Kerrigan's wood instead of being in the middle of the merrymaking at Leigh Court.

John stopped suddenly hardly able to believe his eyes, he drew back into the shadows. In the clearing beside the deep pool a young girl was standing with her eyes closed and her arms extended to the heavens. She was stark naked and her skin was white and luminous. Her face cut crystal in the moonlight. The trees that sheltered her, scattered a lightly moving pattern across her arched back. He could not take his eyes away. It was as if he too was being caught and held by the moonlight. He felt no sense of the erotic, there was no voyeurism in the fascination the scene held for him. This was not earth, or it was all of earth, she was all the beauty he had ever seen or even dreamt of. The gods themselves had set this tableaux and he must not disturb it. Quietly he moved back into the trees, hardly daring to breath, leaving her to her magic world. As he turned he heard her laugh, the sound like no sound he had ever heard. It held all the joy, all the freedom, all that he had ever longed for and he stood listening, his head on one side, until the laughter stopped and the night was still again. Then he walked back along the path, carefully, like one leaving a holy place.

Chapter 12

Leigh Court was basking in the after-glow of a job well done. A general feeling of well being, lassitude even, permeated the house and gardens. In the kitchens the staff were in holiday mood. Mrs. Walshe, still flushed with success, was holding court as one by one the other servants stopped by to drink tea and relive particular moments of the festive day before. They were all well aware that Helen Leigh's wedding would be the talk of the county for years to come and having had no little part in it, the staff of Leigh Court would share in the reflected glory.

The story was fast becoming the stuff of legend, a fairy story in the best tradition. And what if the central characters were hardly prince and princess material, small faults that could and would be overlooked when the drama was told and retold for the entertainment of people whose lives were drab in the extreme.

The happy couple had departed the evening before and taken the boat for England on the first leg of an extended honeymoon tour of the continent. The house was still in festive mood, meals leisurely and relaxed and good humour the order of the day. The remaining guests could be fed with little effort and those who had not joined the various expeditions to the local beauty spots were playing croquet on the front lawns or sitting about on the terrace, enjoying the morning sunshine and sharing their own thoughts on the previous days' events, or planning their activities for the remainder of the weekend.

John Leigh was anxious to be away but Lady Grace had prevailed on him to stay over until the following day.

'We so seldom see you now John, it is such a joy to have you home for a few days. Please don't rush away yet.' She was secretly hoping for a reconciliation between father and son.

The Major was in expansive mood. He had married off his daughter and solved the problems at Leigh Court and all without any effort on his part. He planned to go to the midlands to look at horses within a few days; taking Mick Whelan with him of course.

Louise was begging to accompany him and maybe he would bring her along. Yes, why not? She was a damn good judge of horseflesh. She would be an addition to the party and no trouble. Louise never gave the Major any trouble. They understood one another, it was about time he let her take a more active part in the doings of the estate. John was obviously adamant to go his own way. The Major knew when to cut his losses, no point flogging a dead horse, and no point having bad blood between father and son.

John had always been a disappointment to him if he admitted it, so best to let him have his head and when and if he tired of his studies, he could come back with good grace. If not, well be damned to him, he would never be fool enough to let his inheritance fall into the hands of his sister and the Kerrigan clan. Anyhow, that would be another day's work. For the moment the Major was well satisfied to have Helen off his hands and not only to be solvent again but to have the coffers filled with Kerrigan wealth. He could afford to be generous in his forgiveness of his son and it would make Grace happy to see them reconciled.

John Leigh made his way to the kitchen to see his old friend, Bridget Walshe. As a young child it was to the kindly Mrs. Walshe he went with all his problems. She wiped his tears, mopped his bloodied knees and fed him tit bits to console him in all his childhood sorrows. He knew he was incapable of wrong doing in her eyes and was always welcomed in her parlour.

Today she was beaming all over and welcomed him with open arms pressing him to eat some of the special ginger cake she always kept on hand for his visits. John never had the courage to tell her his taste for ginger cake had departed around the same time as his baby curls, so he dutifully sat and drank tea and managed to put away a slice of the dreaded cake.

'You've lost weight Master John' she said, clucking worriedly as she looked him over. 'Working too hard at all your studies and going into all sorts of terrible places. You're too soft hearted' she said smiling at him lovingly.

John knew it was useless to do anything but agree with her so he nodded wordlessly, while she launched off into a series of reminiscences about his childhood. Her memories of times past grew rosier with each year and John let it wash over him, knowing she was happily running on and there would be no need to add anything except the odd discreet murmur now and then, when there was a lull in the conversation.

The room was quiet and stuffy in the afternoon stillness, and John closed his eyes and relaxed into a pleasant drowsy state, tired after the excitement of the last few days.

Suddenly there was a tap on the door and Mrs. Walshe looked up, annoyed to be interrupted in her monologue.

'Yes, what is it? she asked. 'Come in'.

The door opened and a young girl entered: 'Excuse me, Mrs. Walshe. How many will there be for dinner? I want to send Katie for the vegetables, I'm sorry to interrupt you' she stammered when she saw John Leigh was present, 'But I thought you would want me to begin work'.

'Yes, yes, we will have twelve. Her ladyship wants it kept simple after all the heavy food yesterday. Tell her to get plenty of salads, go on now, don't dawdle'.

Julia was glad to escape, she was aware that the young man's eyes were on her and she kept her head down, not daring to look in his direction.

John Leigh was sitting bolt upright now, wide awake, his torpor forgotten. By all the gods, the little scullery maid standing before him, dressed in a coarse black dress, worn boots, her hair knotted up in a bun at the nape of her neck was his vision of the night before, his Diana of the Moonlit Grove in Kerrigan's wood. He would know that face anywhere. She left the room without even a glance in his direction.

'Who is that girl?' he asked Mrs. Walshe, his voice quick with interest.

'Girl? That's my scullery maid, Julia Whelan' Mrs. Walshe answered, looking at him in surprise. 'None of them can do a tap without asking me. Now, where was I? Yes, that little black puppy the Major gave you for your seventh birthday, remember how he ran away with my best cock pheasant after the shoot and we chased him down the back avenue to rescue it before the Major missed it?'. She laughed so hard the tears ran down her plump jaws, not realising she had really lost her audience this time. John Leigh was back in Kerrigan's wood in the moonlight staring at a vision out of his dreams.

Julia was elbow deep in water when he eventually took his leave of Mrs. Walshe. She was bent over the big stone sink at the far end of the kitchen, her hair escaping from its bun and hanging in damp tendrils around her face.

She's only a child, John thought, last night was a trick of the moonlight, a cruel trick. He sighed slightly and Julia looked up, startled, blushing when she saw him in the doorway, staring at her intently.

She may be young, John thought, but by God she has the face of a Botticelli angel. He nodded and she smiled tentatively and then ducked her head shyly. John stood watching her for a few second then he turned and left, closing the door gently. What could he say to her? I saw you last night in Kerrigans wood and you were a water nymph, a wood sprite, a renaissance Madonna, who will fill my dreams for the rest of my life. Poor child, he would probably frighten the life out of her. Better to leave her alone and keep his dream intact.

Julia bent over the sink, her face flaming. What a strange young man Master John was. He surely was beautiful, so pale and handsome with all that lovely black curly hair, not a bit like the Major, more gentle like Lady Grace. Imagine him looking at her in such a friendly way, almost as if he wanted to talk to her. Julia laughed to herself, Kitty would give her a good shake if she heard her talking like that, she always said the gentry never ever see the likes of us, we all look the same to them. Julia couldn't fathom how the latter could be true but Kitty was usually right about these things.

Katie Murphy came in, her arms laden with vegetables and Julia promptly forgot about the young master and concentrated on the work in hand.

Mick Whelan was lying drunk in the stables. He had not been sober now for two days and nobody had noticed his absence the day before. Mick was seldom sober these days and his sons were finding it harder and harder to cover up for him. He was beginning to wake now from his drunken stupor, but he was reluctant to come round and only his terrible thirst pushing insistently at him forced him to open his eyes and try to make out his surroundings. The last of the sun's rays through the dusty glass were shining on his face, adding to his discomfort. He sat up, raking his hands through matted hair and trying to focus his eyes on his surroundings. He could barely make out the figure of his son Jem, bending over the bales of hay at the far end of the long building. He coughed harshly and spat, rubbing his hands over his dry caked lips.

By God he would have to get a drink somehow. He tried to think, willing his fuddled head to remember if he had any drop left around the place. There was an empty bottle beside him in the straw. He tried to drag himself up, but failed, his legs were too weak to hold him. He sat back, gasping, holding onto his head in an effort to keep the floor from spinning.

'Jem' he tried out his voice, but nothing emerged but a feeble croak.

'Jem!' he tried again, mustering all his strength. This time he succeeded in making enough noise to attract his son's attention. Jem Whelan looked up fearfully, then seeing his father's slumped figure, he made as if to turn and leave. Mick Whelan felt his anger rise, giving him strength and he pulled himself up, leaning against the wall of the stall behind him.

'Jem!' he roared this time, 'come here you waster.' The youth turned back and came a few steps towards him.

'Get me a drink before I die from the drought' he said, 'quick now, go out and find Tom Lonegan, tell him I sent you. Hurry on, he'll be up at the house.'

Jem went reluctantly. He knew better than to argue with the old man. There would be hell to pay if he did not get more drink, and hell to pay if he did.

Lonegan grinned wickedly and handed Jem the bottle: 'What shape is he in? Bad huh?' he said when he saw the young man's face. 'Best give him this and try and get him to eat something. The Major is bound to miss him soon. Go on, try and get him straight before he goes looking for him'.

Jem took the bottle and headed back to the stables. Mick Whelan was still leaning against the wall and he lurched forward when he saw Jem coming. 'Gimme that!' he growled, grabbing the bottle and putting it to his mouth.

'Dada, for God's sake let me get you something to eat, the Major will be looking for you.'

Mick drank greedily until the bottle was nearly empty. Then he lowered it and shook himself twice. He drew in a great shuddering breath and eyed his son blearily: 'To hell with the Major and to hell with you!' he roared, the alcohol giving him temporary strength.

'What do I care about any man, what did I ever get from any of you? Only hard work.'

'Come on Dada.' Jem took a step closer, trying again to talk his father into sobering up. But his efforts were futile. Mick Whelan put the bottle to his head again and lowered the rest of the contents in long gasping gulps. Then he threw the empty bottle against the far wall, where it smashed to pieces and fell amongst the straw. He shook himself again and straightened up. Jem watched anxiously. He knew his father's ways only too well. His little eyes were red now, he looked like one of the Major's bulls, pawing the ground angrily, his back to the wall, looking for some way or someone to vent his spite on. Jem backed away hastily as his father fixed him with a baleful eye. His foot caught in a fork buried in the hay and he tripped, falling heavily to the ground. Mick Whelan was on him in a flash, flaying with his fists and cursing and swearing angrily.

'Waster! Good for nothing bastard' he roared, flaying and kicking at his son who had got to his knees, his arms over his head trying to defend himself.

Jack Whelan heard the noise as he approached the stables. He knew what was going on before he got to the door, but the sight of his twin brother on his knees fending off blows and kicks from his deranged father made him see red. Grabbing the hammer from the anvil inside the door, he ran forward swinging it as he ran. Mick Whelan heard the noise behind him and half turned his head, the hammer connected with his temple and he toppled soundlessly, like a felled tree and lay motionless on the ground.

'You've killed him Jack.' Jem gave a strangled cry and sat back on his heels, his face white. Jack stood over the recumbent figure, the hammer hanging at his side, his chest heaving. He bent down and looked closely at the crumpled form on the ground, feeling for some sign of life, but finding none. There was a ferocious noise in his head and he felt as if he was going to faint. Jem crawled over on all fours and stared down at his father's body. There was no blood to be seen, just a bluish black mark on his temple which seemed to grow larger before their horrified eyes.

'Oh Jesus, he's dead alright, what are we going to do?'. Jem started to cry.

'Shut up,' Jack made an enormous effort to pull himself together, trying to think. There was no doubt about it, his father was dead all right and he was not going to swing for it. The bastard deserved it. God knows he had asked for it often enough.

A loud whinny rang out. Miss Louise's black stallion in the end stall was getting anxious. He was an ugly brute at the best of times. The loud voices had disturbed him and he was growing more restless by the minute. Even as Jack Whelan got to his feet he could hear the bang of the horses hooves against the walls of the stall.

'Quick Jem, give me a hand.' He caught hold of his father's feet and started to drag him along the floor of the stables. 'For the love and honour of God, what are you at?' his brother said, his white face glistening with sweat.

'Catch his arms and do what I tell you' Jack said.

Used to obeying Jack, Jem did as he was told and together the brothers dragged Mick Whelan's body towards the end stall. Opening the gate, Jack rolled his father's body into the stallion's stall and shut the door. Grabbing his brother's arm he motioned him to move swiftly and together they crept to the back of the building and out, ducking as they ran for the cover of the small copse at the rear of the stables, the high pitched screams of the stallion ringing in their ears and the thud of his hooves as he reared and stomped in anger.

Mick Whelan's battered body was found in the stallion's stall at Leigh Court stables at midnight on the night after Helen Leigh's wedding. Nobody could understand why Mick Whelan had entered the stall. The general consensus was that he had been too drunk to know what he was doing. The body was battered nearly beyond recognition by the blood crazed horse and Dr. Cosgrove did not bother to give it more than a cursory examination.

Jem and Jack Whelan had to be summoned from their beds in the home place and Mick's daughters came from the big house and stood at a distance, watching, dry- eyed, as the body of their father was carried from the stables, covered in a horse blanket.

People resented the accident, following as it did, on the heels of the festivities of the last few days, it cast a gloom over the area.

Louise Leigh worried in case it would have a lasting effect on her beloved horse.

Mick Whelan was buried a few days later after a verdict of death by misadventure was brought in by the hastily convened coroners jury. His sons and daughters went back to work at Leigh Court and Major Leigh set about finding a new groom. He was deeply annoyed to lose such a good man, especially now that he needed to replenish his stock.

Julia Whelan tried to think a kind thought about her father, but she failed.

When she tentatively broached the subject to her sister, Kitty said the best thing they could do for Dada was to forget him and leave him to God and get on with their lives.

Julia thought Kitty was probably right, and did as she was told.

Part 2

Chapter 13
1895

The sun streaming through the library windows transformed what could be a gloomy room, turning it into something quite beautiful. The dark mahogany furniture glistened and gleamed, highlighted by the sun's rays and the prisms of light reflected from the elegant cut glass lamps.

The young woman standing by the long window cast a practised eye around the room, and touched a fold in the heavy velvet curtains, smoothing it down, her hand lingering lovingly on the soft material. Then satisfied that all was in order she moved briskly across the carpeted floor, pausing again for a last quick glance before closing the door gently and moving off towards the back hallway of Leigh Court.

She loved these rounds; taking almost sensual pleasure from the sights and smells of the morning household. A slight, ethereal figure in her severe dark dress, her hair swept up into a modest chignon, Julia Whelan had changed so much in the five years since her parents' death as to be almost unrecognisable. Still small of stature, just over five feet in height, her manner and bearing made her appear taller. In her trim uniform she looked as if a strong breeze could blow her away, but her appearance belied the strength and toughness in the compact little frame. Her tiny hands and feet and her pale skin and black hair added to the air of delicacy, but when one drew close enough to be caught in the clear gaze from her green eyes, huge in the narrow heart shaped face, one was left in no doubt of the strength of the personality of the young girl.

The years had been kind to Julia as if compensating for the hard childhood she had endured. Since the night of Mick Whelan's death his young family, especially Julia and Kitty, had gone from strength to strength. Kitty moved to the Manor House a few miles away to help Helen Leigh settle into her new state. Bridget Walshe took Julia under her wing, confident that she had a young girl who would more than repay the trust she was conferring on her. Indeed this was the case and Julia had repaid that trust a thousandfold.

Miss Armstrong, governess to the Leigh girls and more or less redundant after Helen's marriage and when Louise was allowed to accompany her father on his business trips and around the estate, was inveigled by the wily Mrs. Walshe into giving Julia lessons in reading and writing.

Appalled at first by the task thrust on her in return for the cook's favour, the governess soon discovered that teaching Julia Whelan was pure joy. The young girl's quick mind and agile brain was hungry for knowledge and soaked it up as parched ground takes in water after a long drought. Miss Armstrong, grudgingly at first, but soon falling under the spell of Julia's gentle nature, began to look forward to the times spent with Julia and to grow fond of her. Julia soon moved on from the simple readers, poring over the books Miss Armstrong gave her, with what seemed an insatiable lust for learning. From poetry to history, to novels and plays, Julia devoured the written word until the governess knew the pupil had outstripped the teacher and she herself looked forward to hearing Julia's opinion of the latest books she was reading. With nearly as much eagerness she applied herself to learning her trade in the kitchens of Leigh Court, making herself indispensable to both Lady Grace and Mrs. Walshe and even Hynes the butler trusted Julia, knowing her discretion and competency was total and complete.

The years had not dealt as kindly with the owners of Leigh Court themselves. The Major's head condition had deteriorated, especially during the severe winter of the year before and Lady Grace's delicate looks were beginning to cause unease amongst the staff. Severe influenza had carried off both Ned Kerrigan and his wife in the winter of 1892 and now Helen Leigh-Kerrigan was running the Manor House as well as interfering with affairs at Leigh Court as often as she could. Mrs. Walshe was not getting any younger, as she constantly told the kitchen staff and over the last few months more and more was thrown onto Julia Whelan's slim shoulders. Since Lady Grace's last bout of influenza she relied on Julia to see to the smooth running of the Big House. Though nothing was said, it was generally accepted by both family and staff that Julia was not only assistant cook but unofficial house-keeper at Leigh Court, despite the fact that she was just twenty years old.

Julia loved her life. She had been given a little room of her own at the back of the house on the second floor. It had been a box-room, cleared out to make temporary space for her to be close to her ladyship during the nights when her fever was high and Julia was the one she cried out for.

When Lady Grace recovered she had intimated that Julia could stay where she was. Little by little the room had taken on the appearance of a study, filled as it was with books and charts, many loaned by Mrs. Armstrong and some purloined from the Major's collection, read hungrily and returned without his knowledge or consent.

She spent all her time at Leigh Court now, with hardly a break, except for excursions to her old home to visit her brother Jem's young family.

Jem had married Nellie Flynn shortly after his nineteenth birthday and already they had two fine little sons. Sadie, unable for the life at the Big House, had returned home to help look after the babies and she was happy to resume her place at the fireside in the little cottage. Transformed now out of all recognition, it was a happy place, filled with the sound of Nellie's singing. The children's voices had exorcised the memories of Mick Whelan's evil temper and loud drunken rows.

Julia often took her book and something to eat and spent her afternoons off deep in Kerrigan's wood in her own particular spot by the pool. She never took the children here, they would find it in time when they were hardy enough to move from the cottage, just as she and her brothers and sisters had done.

Jack Whelan had disappeared a month after his father's death and they had heard nothing from him apart from one brief note, written in

England a year later, telling them he was safe and well and had joined the British Army.

Today, Julia wanted to make sure everything was in order, John Leigh was arriving on the mail Boat this evening to spend a brief holiday with his father and mother. Dr. John Leigh he was now, with a distinguished record of scholarship in medicine already behind him, he was fast making a name for himself in the London hospital to which he was attached. His visits to Leigh Court over the years had been rare and brief. A day or two at Christmas, a brief visit during the summer, he rarely went out, spending all his time at home with his mother or walking the estate in the evening with the Major. Now and then he rode out in the early morning with his younger sister or took dinner at the Manor House with Helen and Luke Kerrigan. Julia often saw him walking in the grounds or disturbed him in the library where he spent some of his time, deep in a book. He spoke to her on these occasions, his deep voice gravely courteous and, as the years passed, losing the shyness and awkwardness of youth. She learned to answer his polite questions and even linger for a moment or two in his company. She had no interest in the young men of the locality, answering Kitty when she joked her about her single state by saying with sincere surprise that she had no time to think of such matters. Kitty herself had not married, though there were a few young men in Ballyleigh and even two or three fine Wexford men who were willing to change that situation. The sisters spent what spare time they had together. Kitty was immensely proud of Julia, watching her progress at Leigh Court with delight and amazement. She secretly thought her little sister was getting more like one of the gentry every day and she poured scorn on the catty remarks of the village women who resented Julia's quiet ways, liking her to her dead mother who in their opinion had had notions beyond her station. Julia was oblivious to all this. The days were never long enough for her. So little time and so much to do, so much she wanted to learn and do, her life would never be long enough.

Julia opened the kitchen door now and the smell of coffee greeted her. The Major took coffee at mid-morning now and Mary, the little kitchen maid was getting the tray ready. Mrs. Walshe was busy at the big table and Tom Lonegan was drinking tea, perched on the wooden stool at the range. He looked up when Julia came in and then cast his eyes down hurriedly. Lonegan did not know what to make of Mick Whelan's daughter. By God, she was a smart one all right. Running the whole shootin' gallery almost single handed and she only a slip of a girl. Even so he had to admit she hadn't got too big for her boots. She was an obliging young wan and good to the rest of them, even managing to check auld Biddy Walshe's worst excesses. Still, who would have ever thought that a daughter of auld drunken Mick Whelan would end up in a position like this young wan had. Begod, life was strange, no doubt about it.

Mrs. Walshe smiled at Julia: 'Everything ship shape then Julia?' she nodded happily.

Tonight, himself would be home, the poor lamb, and she would have a chance to feed him up a bit for a few days anyhow, before he went back to that awful hospital or wherever it was he spent most of his time. Humming tunelessly, she thumbed through her recipe book, wondering what would be best for afters; the treacle pudding or the spotted dick. Master John loved both, but which would he prefer first? she wondered, or maybe she should do one of each. Julia smiled at the older woman's bent head. She knew John Leigh would try to tackle the ghastly rich pudding, no matter which one Bridie decided to make. He was too kind hearted to tell her the truth, how much he hated the meals she set before him. She herself wouldn't dare to interfere, it could be what her life was worth to say a word on the matter. Best to leave it between them.

Tom Lonegan looked up now with a sly grin.

'How is your sister Kitty this weather?' he asked Julia.

With some surprise Julia turned to Lonegan.

'Why, she is very well, very well indeed' she answered.

Lonegan was looking at her slyly, his eyes half closed.

'That's not what I heard the last time I was down at the Manor House, I heard she was poorly'

'What do you mean?' Julia was startled now, something in Lonegan's manner sent a shiver up her spine.

Mrs. Walshe banged the heavy book shut and glowered at Lonegan over her glasses: 'Have you nothing better to do than sitting in the kitchen talking with the women? Get on with your business now before I am tempted to wipe that grin off your ugly puss.'

Lonegan got up hastily and left the mug on the table. He made his exit, but not before firing a parting shot at Julia: 'Tell Kitty I was enquiring for her health the next time you see her' he said, slamming the door loudly.

Julia stood staring after his retreating figure. 'What was that all about, I wonder?' she said uneasily.

Mrs. Walshe sighed to herself. Some things never change. For all her book learning and grown up ways Julia Whelan was still as innocent as a newborn babe. What would happen when she found out what the pig Lonegan was hinting at and what was being talked about in the four parishes? God help us, was she going to have to be the one to tell the poor creature that Kitty, her sister, was carrying Luke Kerrigan's child, and that it wouldn't be long before Helen Leigh found out about it?

Chapter 14

John Leigh strode down the gangplank of the Mail Boat at Ballygeary Harbour. He breathed deeply, filling his lungs with the clean salt tanged air. Then, his step jaunty, he set out to find Lonegan who would have been despatched to fetch him home to Leigh Court. He smiled, nothing changes, Lonegan, the Major's man, would not seek him out, John never knew whether to be annoyed at Lonegan's thinly veiled insolence or to admire the blackguard.

God, but it was good to be on Irish soil. The thought caught him by surprise and he smiled again wryly. What would his colleagues think if they knew some of Dr. John Leigh's secrets? Here he was again, panting to be back in a place where, yearly he became more and more a stranger. Longing for a glimpse of a girl who did not notice his existence, for whom he had little or no existence. What would Professor Molloy, or Dr. Denton, or the nursing staff whose nickname for him was the iron Man, say if they knew he had waited for nearly five years for a young woman to look at him and see a man and not a master.

Stupid, stupid man, he said now, reprimanding himself and pushing the thought out of his mind. I am here to see Mother and Father and have a well earned rest,nothing more.

Lonegan was lounging against the wall outside the little hut on the quay, pretending not to see John's tall figure approaching.

'Ah, Lonegan my good man, look after my bags and be quick, there's a good fellow. I am anxious to get home before we lose the light.'

'Yes Sir, welcome home Sir..' Lonegan was all servility now, making a great show of putting out the pipe he was smoking, but doing it very slowly.

John walked on down the long pier, his eyes impervious now to the sight of the evening sun touching the little rippling wave tops, hungrily raking the landscape ahead of him.

It was a glorious May evening, soft and sensuous, the sun still setting in an almost cloudless blue sky. He paused to enjoy the sight of the sandy cliffs before him and the wide sweep of the harbour on either side.

'A pet day Sir,' Lonegan spoke softly, coming up silently on his heels. 'Only a pet day, we'll have the rain before morning,' He coughed harshly and spat over the side of the wooden balustrade, trudging on in front, carrying John's two small bags, managing to give the impression of a man heavily laden. John smiled again, he was home all right.

Lady Grace sat at the front window of her bedroom watching the broad sweep of the driveway with its army of poplars standing sentinel on each side. Surely they should be here soon. She hoped the boat was on time. It could not take more than an hour to get here. That brute Lonegan was probably dawdling along, the man was never sober. How tiresome that she had caught another chill, when she really wanted to be downstairs to welcome John home. Maybe tomorrow she would feel strong enough to venture down. It would be too bad of her to expect John to sit in a stuffy bedroom and keep her company. There they were. She sat forward eagerly as the carriage swung into sight around the corner. If only she felt strong enough to be at the door to greet him, but she knew her husband would be there. These days he looked forward to his son's visits almost as much as she did. Grace Leigh paused, how time changes everything, time and age, she thought ruefully. The Major's habits had changed drastically over the last year or two. She suspected he found it increasingly difficult to keep up with Lou-Lou and his dislike of Helen was becoming more and more apparent. Maybe he understood John a little better now and appreciated his gentle and scholarly nature; things that had irked him so much before his own health had begun to fail. 'What a pair of old invalids we are becoming'. She spoke out loud, then pausing and holding her head to one side as she heard the beloved footsteps approaching the bedroom door.

'John, John, how lovely.' Lady Grace held out her arms and her son ran the last few steps and fell to his knees in front of her chair, wrapping her in his embrace.

My God, how frail she has become. His doctor's eye had taken in his mother's appearance at a glance and now as he held her in his arms he had to make an effort to control his face. He sat back on his heels and looked at her hoping she would not see the concern in his eyes: 'Mother, its marvellous to be home. How are you? Another chill Lonegan tells me. What am I to do with you at all? You are not taking care of yourself. Worrying about Father, I suppose.'

Lady Grace smiled, patting his cheeks, tears of joy standing in her eyes.

'Don't scold me my darling. I will be out and about in a day or two now that I have you here to look after me. How was your journey? Did you have a good crossing? Are you hungry?' Her pale face was flushed now and John stood up and laid a finger across his lips. 'Shush Mother, no fussing. I'll make a bargain with you; I'll promise not to fuss if you will too. Now I'm going to my room to remove some of the stains of travel. When I have some supper I will come back and we can have a chat. I will tell you all my news and you can bring me up to date on the local scandal'.

Lady Grace laughed. 'Since when were you interested in local gossip; but do hurry back; I want to hear all the news from London. I'll take a little rest while I wait for you' and she sat back against the cushions and closed her eyes.

John left the room, closing the door gently behind him. He had come home expecting to find cause for worry in the Major's deteriorating condition, but he knew even without a cursory examination, that his father would be here long after his mother's passing. What the hell was Cosgrove thinking of? Damn the man, couldn't he have sent for him before now, or at least let him know what the situation was like. He would seek him out tomorrow and have strong words. Even if he was a country doctor, and an old fashioned one at that, the man had eyes in his head, hadn't he?

John made his way to the dining room where his father was already seated, having waited to dine.

'Well my boy, how does she look to you? A bit peaked after the winter d'ya think?' he asked, an anxious look on his face. 'I was thinking of taking her away for a while. Italy maybe, or the South of France. Buck us both up. What do you think?'

John shook his head, not wanting to alarm his father by saying that Lady Grace would not be strong enough to undertake such a journey, he said he would have a look at her tomorrow and have a chat with Dr. Cosgrove before he would give an opinion. The Major's face relaxed. 'Needn't tell you how good it is to have you home. Missed you, my boy. Your mother and I not getting any younger, you know.' He was embarrassed now, his relief at having his doctor son here to look after his beloved wife, making him speak foolishly. John laid a hand on his father's arm and squeezed it gently. 'Thank you Father, it's good to be home. I wish I had longer, but I have made arrangements to take my vacation in August and I will be here then for some weeks' he lied. He had made no such arrangement, but he would do so immediately he got back to London. If they could do without him even sooner than August, he intended to take a protracted leave of absence. He was needed here now and this was where he would make it his business to be.

Later on, that night as John Leigh was quietly leaving his mother's room he saw a small figure approaching along the top corridor. He stood waiting as she approached, his eyes taking in the swept up hair, unruly now at the end of the day and escaping in little tendrils curling around her face and the nape of her neck. She was deep in thought, rapt in a world of her own and she had not noticed his presence until she was almost past him.

'Good night Julia,' he murmured and she jumped.

'Master John, I never saw you there in the shadow, you startled me'. Her hand had flown to her throat and she laughed, a soft tinkling sound in the semi-darkness. She made as if to pass on and he spoke quickly, keeping his voice low: 'My Mother is not well, I am quite distressed at her appearance.' He had her total attention now and she stood stock still in front of him, her pale face seeming to glow in the darkness.

'Dr. Cosgrove says it is another chill she has caught, because she is still weak after the influenza. But she will be better now that the weather is improving, it was a cold damp spring'. She paused, looking at him anxiously. 'She will be alright, Master John, won't she?' Her soft voice was beginning to sound alarmed and John shushed her hurriedly, moving away from Lady Grace's door, he drew her after him, catching her slim arm. This was the first time he had ever touched her, the longest conversation they had ever had since she was a little child and he had known her only as one of Whelan the groom's brats. Would to God it was happening under happier circumstances. She was looking down at his hand on her arm, surprised. Hastily he withdrew his hand and let his arm fall to his side. 'My Mother is going to need constant care. I plan to talk to Dr. Cosgrove tomorrow. I will have to go back to London in a few days but I will return as soon as I can and take over her treatment myself. Until then I am relying on you to keep me informed of how she is progressing. Can I do that Julia? Will you look after her for me?'

Julia nodded, trying to get over the shock of what she was hearing. She knew Lady Grace had grown frail over the last while but she had no idea her condition was as grave as it must be to have Master John so obviously upset and talking this way to one of the servants.

'Indeed you can count on me Sir' she said now, her voice shaking.

'Good girl, we will talk again tomorrow. Goodnight now' John said stiffly as he turned and walked away. Julia stood looking after his retreating figure, thoroughly alarmed and worried by his words.

'Your Mother was always a delicate lady, her present state is only to be expected after such an attack of influenza.' Dr. Cosgrove, annoyed at young Leigh's manner, tried to hold his temper. This young whip was going to tell him his business, just because he had come back from London with a whole lot of new fangled ideas. He thought he knew it all. John Leigh interrupted. 'My God man, her lungs are in a terrible state and her heart-beat is so faint it is nearly impossible to hear. Even her pulse is like a thread. What have you done for her? She should have been sent to hospital months ago. I would take her back to London now, but I fear she would not be able for the journey. However I am going to prescribe medication and care and I will be back to look after her as soon as I can possibly get away. I want you to keep an eye on her and if you see any sign of deterioration send for me immediately. Do you understand?'

Dr. Cosgrove's face was flaming now and his voice shook with rage: 'I understand one thing, you have no right to address me in such a manner. I have looked after the Leigh family, three generations. I have taken care of Lady Grace's health since she came here. Do you not think I didn't advise her, and the Major, of the seriousness of her condition. I begged your father to send her to Dublin, or at least to send her to a specialist, weeks ago, but neither of them would listen. I have done my best for her, making her rest, trying to get her to eat. How dare you, Sir!' he finished, his voice breaking.

John Leigh was horrified, he should have known, how could he have been so crass?

'My dear Doctor,' he said, 'forgive me for such a rash judgement. I should have known you were doing your best, I have been out of my mind with worry since I arrived here last night and when I looked at my mother this morning, my worst fears were confirmed. Please forgive me, I should have known the Major would not want to hear what you had to say and she would never have him worried, no matter what.' He sat down, his head in his hands and the older man moved to his side, looking down at him pityingly.

'I understand John, it is always like this when one has to treat one's loved ones. Especially at the beginning. You are young my boy, but you are a fine doctor. Between us we will look after your mother and do our best for her.' He did not add that that would mean keeping her comfortable and happy for as long as they could. His anger forgotten he laid his hand on John Leigh's shoulder and looked down sadly at his bent head.

Chapter 15

The weeks flew by after John Leigh's return to London. Lady Grace's health seemed to improve slightly as the warm summer days followed one upon the other. She let Julia help her to dress most afternoons and came downstairs for an hour or two. Even venturing out onto the terrace once or twice, to the Major's delight. Julia watched over her like a mother hen, remembering her promise to John. She hesitated to put pen to paper though, the thought of writing a letter was formidable enough, let alone to write one to John Leigh, so when she arrived down to the kitchen one morning to find an envelope with her name on it her heart leapt into her mouth. With shaking hands she lifted the letter from the table hardly believing what she read there:

Miss Julia Whelan
Leigh Court,
Ballyleigh,
Co. Wexford,
Ireland.

Julia had never received a letter in her life, had never seen her name written except when she wrote it herself. She held the letter in her hands wonderingly and then hurriedly placed it in her pocket when she heard Mrs. Walshe coming. Reluctant to let it go, she kept her hand in her pocket as if releasing it might make it disappear. All morning the letter seemed to burn through the material of her dress until she could physically feel the heat of it on her thigh. It was late afternoon before she got a chance to examine it again. Then on her way to see to Lady Grace's room she paused on the upper landing. She drew the letter from her pocket and examined it closely, turning it this way and that, holding it up to the light. It had come from England, she could see the mark, there was only one who could have written it, she could hardly allow the thought to settle in her brain. Her face flaming, and with trembling hands she took her small scissors from her pocket and carefully slit the top of the envelope. There was just one thin sheet of paper. Julia tried to read, but the words danced before her eyes. Steadying herself by leaning against the wall she read:

Dear Julia,

I write to thank you for your constant care and for the kind and diligent nursing you are giving my mother.

Dr. Cosgrove keeps me informed and he is well pleased with her progress. He mentioned you particularly, saying how invaluable your presence in the house is to her well-being.

Julia paused, her hand to her flaming face, then she read on:

I trust you are, yourself, in excellent health and enjoying the beautiful weather. Indeed I hope to be in Leigh Court myself before the end of July, when we will talk again.

Gratefully,

John Leigh.

Julia read the letter over again. She touched the thin parchment sheet, amazed at its fragility. The writing was just what she would expect from John Leigh; firm and strong, yet small and neat, but why should he write to her and discuss his business, and thanking her for doing her work, work that she was paid to do. What a strange gentleman the young master was. Julia folded the letter, placing it back in its envelope, she put it gently back into her pocket, careful not to crease it. She felt excited now and even a bit fearful. Imagine getting a letter, Kitty would be amazed when she showed it to her. But could she show it to anyone? Even Kitty? She would have to show it to Kitty, ask her what she thought his reasons for sending it might be; whether she should talk to him as he said, and if so what should she say? She hadn't seen Kitty now for weeks. Indeed she had not had any time off for two months now, she did not want to leave Lady Grace for any length of time. However Mrs. Walshe had suggested only the night before that she should take the following Sunday off and go and visit her family. She would send a note to the Manor House when Lonegan next went over, asking Kitty to meet her. She was sure Kitty could take the time, because Miss Helen and her husband were away at the moment. Luke Kerrigan was in London on business and his wife had accompanied him. Maybe she would persuade Kitty to come to Rosslare for the day. Julia was dying to take a trip on the train ever since Jem had taken his young family for an outing a few months before and regaled her with stories about the journey. She had determined to do the same before the summer was out. Now she made up her mind. After all it wasn't every day a girl received a letter all the way from London. It was time she spread her wings. She had money enough to pay for both of them. Yes, Kitty would have to come, she wouldn't take no for an answer. Patting her pocket happily, Julia moved on into Lady Grace's room, her step light and her head high.

On Sunday morning after Mass in the village, Jem Whelan drove his two sisters into Wexford in the pony and trap. Julia could barely contain her excitement. The day was as fine as she had hoped, the sun bursting out from the misty morning heat - haze, shining brilliantly in an almost cloudless sky. Just a few little puffy white cumuli lazing overhead, like fat faced cherubs. She wished she could cheer her sister up. What a job she had persuading Kitty to come, she had to nearly go on her knees and in the end she had only given in when Julia told her she had something very important to discuss with her.

Kitty was pale and angish, Julia thought now, watching her covertly. Her face had grown thin, she looked older somehow.

Julia's heart constricted with fear; God, if anything were to happen to Kitty . . .

Perish the thought. She's just tired, the day at the sea will do her a power of good, put the roses back in her cheeks, Julia straightened her straw bonnet and raised her parasol, feeling like a queen as they travelled along the road to Wexford. The pony's hooves played a little tune on the road and the smart leather trap creaked as it swayed gently from side to side. The sun dappled the road under the hands-joined branches of the overhanging trees. Julia had her black bag with all they would need for the day. Freshly made corn beef sandwiches and thick slices of Mrs. Walshe's best plum cake. An apple for Kitty and a peach for herself from the garden at Leigh Court. They could get a cup of tea in Kelly's refreshment rooms, newly opened on the strand road. Jem had bought tea for himself and Nellie and lemonade for the boys and he said the prices were quite reasonable, all things considered. Anyhow it was their day out so you could expect to have to pay out some money.

The station was quite crowded already when they arrived and Julia grew anxious as she joined the queue at the ticket box. What if it was full up before it came to her turn? But the man behind the counter didn't even look up as she asked for two return tickets to Rosslare, just handed them over and took her money. Julia felt she would have to remove her gloves, the heat was making the perspiration break out all over her. She could feel it trickling down between her shoulders. She should have worn her other dress, it was lighter than this black bombazine. My God, they would bake if they had to stand out in the sun for much longer. Already her feet were sinking into the melting tar and there was a shimmer over the train tracks as if the air was all crinkling up and wilting like themselves. Mothers were holding on to their children, terrified to let them near the edge of the tracks and the children themselves were hopping up and down, like horses champing at the bit. Julia was nearly sick with excitement. Kitty was as cool as a cucumber, but then she was well travelled, she had even gone as far as Gorey last summer with Miss Helen.

Suddenly a stir went through the crowd, moving from the front where the people could crane their necks and look down along the track.

'She's coming! She's coming . . . Here she comes!' Everyone surged forward and Julia gathered her belongings, urging Kitty on.

'Calm down, calm down,' Kitty caught her arm, laughing. 'There'll be room enough for everyone, don't get hurt in the rush and watch yourself climbing up there, don't let your foot slip off the step, it's quite high'. Julia was shaking as she clambered on board, a young man gave her a hand up and she thanked him nicely.

She sat down at the window, Kitty sitting opposite, and straightened her bonnet. A shrill whistle sounded and there was much shouting and banging of doors. Some of the younger children were crying shrilly, terrified of the huge dragon-like monster spewing steam at every orifice. Julia couldn't blame them, she was more than a little scared herself. The train was huge and it went very fast, she wondered was it really a safe way to travel. My God, the way it had hurtled into the station at break neck speed. Maybe it would be slower now that it was filled with people. It was moving; definitely moving - it seemed to be going backwards . . . but no, with a stomach wrenching lurch it took off and they were certainly moving forward now. Julia had to stop looking out the window; as the station receded she felt a rush of panic and her stomach turned over. She closed her eyes and clutched the edge of her seat tightly and when she opened her eyes she saw Kitty's grinning face opposite and she smiled herself, apologetically. Kitty leaned over and patted her knee:

'You're all right chicken, it's safe enough. Don't look out the window until you get used to the movement. Your stomach will go back where it should be after a few minutes.'

Julia nodded, her face tight with effort. She was determined to enjoy every minute of this day but she wasn't sure if she would ever want to ride in a train again.

By the time they arrived at the little station in Rosslare, Julia was a seasoned traveller, sorry the journey was over so soon. She was sitting forward, pointing out the sights, her face flushed with excitement.

She's only like a child, God help her, for all her learning, Kitty thought as Julia feverishly gathered her belongings before they shuddered to a final stop. They followed the crowd down the station road and as they came over the brow of the hill, got their first glimpse of the sea. 'Oh, Kitty! Did you ever see anything so beautiful?' Julia was standing still, her bag clutched to her chest, her eyes like saucers.

'Come on will you; you'll be walked on,' Kitty gave her a chuck. 'Don't go all dreamy on me now, we have a long walk ahead of us. Put up that parasol or we'll both be like red Indians before much longer.' Julia walked on, as if in a trance, her eyes fixed on the vision ahead of her. She stopped again when they came to the corner, making as if to cross the road to the sandy beach.

'No. We want to get a bit of privacy, come on, it's worth the walk to go further down. Jem and Nellie walked a mile or so down this road and found a little lane-way leading onto the beach. He told me where to find it.'

Julia tore her eyes away from the sea and reluctantly followed Kitty down the road.

Jem was right, it was worth the walk. Seated at last on the scorching golden sand, their weariness forgotten, the girls sighed with pleasure as they removed their boots and stockings.

'See, what did I tell you? There's not a soul about, they all stayed up at the other end, we will have the whole place to ourselves down here, we could even paddle our feet in the water.'

'Oh, Kitty, do you think we could.' The very thought was making Julia's mouth water.

'Of course we can, come on,' Kitty didn't hesitate, hitching her long skirt up she walked into the little wavelets at the edge of the ocean. Julia sighed with pleasure as the cool water lapped over her sweating feet. Kitty linked her arm in hers and together they walked along the deserted beach.

At four o'clock the girls made their way to Kelly's Refreshment Rooms and chose a table at the wall. They ordered tea for two and unwrapped their sandwiches. They had eaten the fruit earlier, too hungry and thirsty to wait. The waitress brought a tray with cups and saucers and a little silver tea pot for each of them. Julia thought she had never tasted such tea, it was like nectar of the gods, not that she knew how nectar tasted, but it couldn't taste any better than this. Kitty laughed at her again: 'You and your poetry!' but she looked at her lovingly.

'You look better now Kitty, you have a bit of colour in your cheeks. Now you're glad I persuaded you to come.'

Kitty nodded, looking down at the plate in front of her. She hated spoiling Julia's day, hated to have to wipe the joy off the little face opposite, but now was as good a time as any. She would have to tell her before it got to her from someone else. It was a miracle she hadn't been told already, since half the bloody county seemed to know. Oh why had she ever opened her mouth to that bitch of a Maggie Halpin? She should have known that one would spread it to the four winds. But she had been sick with worry and needing to confide in someone.

'Julia,' she said now, 'I have something to tell you.'

Julia looked at her sharply; something in the other girl's voice sending a sharp dart of anxiety through her.

'There's only one way to say it and that's straight, without embroidery: I am going to have Luke Kerrigan's child.'

Chapter 16

In later years, when she looked back on that day in Rosslare, Julia Whelan knew it was the turning point in her life, the end of innocence. She could never remember the rest of the afternoon, the return journey, the days and weeks after Kitty's words to her across the table in the little tea room. But the moment of revelation was etched on her memory forever. The still brilliant sun splashing the modest room with golden highlights. The crisp white cloth on the table, the silver tea pot, the dainty blue cups and saucers, a half eaten sandwich on Kitty's plate, Kitty's face, framed by her thick reddish hair, copper-burnished where the sun caught it, and her own feeling of happiness and well being shattered instantly, like a hammer blow laid to glass. The other occupants of the room, indeed the rest of the world faded and dissolved and they were caught, the two of them, suspended, gazing with agony into one another's faces. All the joy and life drained out of Julia and she felt as if she was smothering.

She tried to speak, but no sound came. Kitty reached across the table and caught her hand, shocked by its coldness.

'Oh, Julia, don't look like that, its going to be alright, honest to God it is. Please, please don't look at me like that.'

But Julia could do nothing else but sit as if turned to stone, staring into Kitty's face, her eyes tragic in a white face. 'Come on, finish up your tea and we'll get out of here and go for another walk.'

Julia stared like a sleep walker coming out of a trance. She lifted the cup obediently and drank the tea.

'Eat your sandwich' Kitty urged, but Julia shook her head:

'I'm not hungry.' Her voice sounded strange, even to her own ears.

'Oh, Kitty, say its not true, you're trying to cod me,' but even as she spoke she knew how ridiculous her words sounded.

'What are you going to do? How did this happen, did he force himself on you?'

Kitty shook her head impatiently, her voice low and urgent in the still afternoon air. 'I'm not ashamed of what happened. I am more to Luke Kerrigan than that marble statue he is married to. I have loved Luke for a long while and he loves me too.' She looked defiantly, her eyes daring Julia to contradict her. But Julia sat, as if turned to stone listening without expression.

'When I told him the way I was, he said he didn't care about Helen, he said he wanted a son and she is never going to have children. Its plain to see she has even given up hope now. All the fuss she made when they were first married, wanting a son just so she could have Leigh Court when the Major dies.'

Julia was horrified: 'Kitty, Kitty, for God's sake what are you saying, how can you talk like this? Luke Kerrigan is Miss Helen's husband.'

'He says I am more of a wife to him than she ever was. You don't know the life they have been leading. You haven't heard the fighting and the way she treats him. He means no more to her than any of the servants. She is a cruel, mean natured woman, but you do know that, surely your memory is not that short.'

Kitty paused, looking into Julia's face for some crumb of reassurance and seeing only the younger girl's confusion. 'We are going away together, to America, just as soon as the baby is born. Oh Julia, tell me you understand, tell me you don't think badly of me.'

Julia shook her head: .'I don't understand all this Kitty. How can you go away with Luke Kerrigan? What will you do in America? What will happen to the Manor House and all the Kerrigan land? There is nobody else to look after it if Luke goes away. He'll never leave Miss Helen and his home, how can he?'.

'He will Julia, he will, he promised me. I am going to stay with Jem and Nellie until the baby comes and then, when I am strong enough we are leaving Ballyleigh for good and all. Julia, I want you to come with us. You are wasted at Leigh Court. You'll spend the rest of your life looking after people who don't care a damn about you. You are so clever, you could do anything you want to in America. Please, oh please, say you will come.'

Julia's head was spinning , she was trying to make some sense out of what Kitty was saying, but she just could not control her brain. It was as if her whole world was breaking apart and she looked on, powerless to raise a hand to stop it. She was paralysed as if in the midst of some awful nightmare.

'Kitty, I am going to faint.' She pushed back her chair and rose hurriedly, rushing towards the door, heedless of the flurry her headlong flight across the room was causing, Kitty quickly gathered up their belongings, fumbling for coins to pay the anxious looking waitress who appeared at her elbow.

'My sister is not well, needs fresh air' she mumbled, thrusting the money into the surprised girl's hand. Then she hurried out to find Julia, leaning against the outside wall, her face still white, her hands to her throat.

'I'm sorry Kitty. I got an awful shock listening to you. Please let me clear my head. Let's walk a little way down here before we go back to the station.' Kitty nodded, silent now, waiting to hear what Julia would say. They walked a while in silence before Julia spoke.

'Kitty, you know you have always meant everything to me, especially since Mama died. Only for you Dada would probably have killed half of us and certainly me! He always seemed to hate me more than anyone else. I don't know how I will survive if you go to America. I don't understand much about love, but I know Luke Kerrigan is a good man. But I could never leave Leigh Court, its everything to me. I'm happy there, happier than I ever thought I could be. I have so much, all my books and Miss Armstrong to talk to about them, and my job. Lady Grace trusts me so much and I have to look after her.' Julia stopped short, she would not mention John Leigh, or her letter, not now.

She turned suddenly, throwing her arms around Kitty: 'I love you Kitty, please be alright. Don't go away. Stay with me. We can look after the baby between us.'

The sisters stood locked in a fierce embrace as the sleepy little sandy village slumbered in the afternoon heat, an unlikely venue for such depth of passion and anguish.

Julia went through the next few weeks in a daze. She carried out her duties in her usual meticulous fashion, but Mrs. Walshe, who knew her so well, shook her head sadly, knowing she had at last been made aware of he situation at the Manor House. She was kinder even than usual to Julia, encouraging her to take things easy, but hesitating to infringe on her privacy, waiting for Julia herself to speak. Julia said nothing to anyone. Her face a tight mask, she kept to herself, barely answering when spoken to. Lady Grace noticed the young girl's withdrawn manner and hoped Julia was not gong to succumb to some sort of illness. She was not herself, that was quite obvious. One evening, Bridie Walshe came across her sitting in the darkened kitchen at twilight, staring straight ahead of her.

'My God, girl, you frightened the heart out of me, I thought you were a ghost sitting there so white and still.' She flopped down beside Julia, her hand clutching her ample bosom, her voice breathless and husky with tiredness after the day's effort.

'I hate this dead heat, its too much for my old body,' she moaned, fanning herself with her apron. Julia looked at her, her eyes distant, like someone surveying a faraway landscape.

'What ails you alannah, can't you tell your old friend?' Mrs. Walshe touched Julia's sleeve tentatively and waited. The kindness in her voice made Julia draw in her breath.

'Oh Bridie, what am I to do?'. Her voice, heavy with grief, cut through the stillness like a knife, sharp with anguish.

'You know about Kitty, don't you?' Not waiting for a reply she continued: 'I don't know what to do or where to turn. I feel as if I am going through some sort of nightmare, but it won't go away and I can't wake up.'

Her voice was ragged with pain and the tears caught in Bridie Walshe's throat as she listened.

'Hush crater, nothing is ever as bad as it seems. When you get to my age you know the golden rule; life goes on regardless. There's nothing you can do for Kitty now only be there when she needs you, and by

God she is going to need you, poor lamb. Ask God Almighty and his blessed mother to look after her, she's not the first girl to get herself in that state and she won't be the last. She won't be the last. Sorry part of it is that it should happen to such a good girl. Aye a good girl. Kitty's heart always let her down, it's too big so it is, too big and too soft. Kerrigan is not the worst in the world, he'll see that she is provided for, that's if the other wan don't get wind of it.'

Julia knew she meant Miss Helen.

'That wan was too ill to ever have a child, or maybe if it could be done without the help of a man she might have managed. I'm not making excuses for Luke Kerrigan, but begot a man would have to look for a bit of comfort elsewhere if he was married to Helen Leigh. . . I think you and I will make a nice cup of tea now. Put the kettle on to the heat there and boil it up, there's a good girl and don't be tormenting yourself. When you've ploughed all I've harrowed, you'll know what I'm telling you is the plain truth, there's no point letting anything in this auld world get you down. Come one now, Julia Whelan, you are going to have to weather this for yourself and for Kitty.'

Julia stood up to make the tea, she knew Mrs. Walshe was right. Kitty had always looked out for her, now it was her turn to do the minding.

Luke Kerrigan was drunk. He had been drinking all evening, trying to stop thinking of Kitty Whelan and the dilemma he was in. He had never meant it to get out of hand, never. In the beginning, when Helen and himself were first married, he had made excuses for her. After all she was a high born lady, gently reared, she knew nothing about life or men. He had been patient with her, waiting for her to want him to love her. But over the years, the painful realisation had been borne in on him; Helen Leigh did not love him, indeed she could barely tolerate him. She gritted her teeth and allowed him into her bed only in the hope of conceiving a son to bear her name and secure her rights to inherit Leigh Court. As time passed and she did not become pregnant she made it abundantly clear that she had no time for him, either in her bed or out of it. The love he felt for his wife slowly corroded until he felt as much revulsion for her as she did for him. He drove himself like a man possessed, working or playing. Luke Kerrigan took no rest. His drunken exploits were legend in the county and most people felt more than a little sorry for him, especially the servants at the Manor House who suffered under his wife's shrewish temperament, nearly as much as he did himself. Kitty Whelan looked after Luke from the earliest days after his marriage, often waiting up for him when he returned late at night, to induce him to eat something, or just to pull off his boots and cover him with a rug where he lay, too drunk to go to his bed. She remembered her own father's drunken state and she knew this was different.

Luke Kerrigan was a good man, kind hearted and gentle even when the worst for drink, there was no fight in him, he stumbled like a confused, hurt child. Luke began to rely on Kitty, talking to her and looking forward to seeing her waiting when he returned home. His drinking lessened. He spent more and more time in her company until one night he took her in his arms. Kitty did not turn from his embrace but was the willing recipient of all the pent up passion, indeed her own deep need for love and acceptance answered his. They found a happiness in one another that had up to now eluded them both.

But now she was going to have his child and he was going to have to let her go. Luke groaned, his head in his hands, he went over the scene earlier on in the evening when Helen had confronted him:

'You will get rid of your whore. Don't think I care what you do, but you won't drag my name through the muck. If I ever lay eyes on your bastard, I will not be responsible for my actions. Get rid of her before she drops it under my roof.'

She stood before him, the ice maiden, laying down the law as usual and he saw red.

'I'm leaving you, you cold headed bitch. I love Kitty and I am going away to America with her when the child is born.'

Helen had not batted an eye, just laughed at him, if the sound she made could be called a laugh: 'You are going away together? How quaint. How do you propose to support yourself and Kitty Whelan, not to mention the whelp? Do I have to remind you of your father's will. Every penny we own is in both our names and tied up so tightly you can never get your hands on any of it without my consent. Not alone will you not get that, but I will use the Leigh name to ruin you wherever you go.'

Luke knew she meant every word she spoke and he appealed to her: 'For God's sake Helen, why can't you let me go, you don't love me, you don't even want me here. Let me go and I will only take what I need to get a start in the new country, you can have the rest.'

'But I have it all now, including you my dear husband. You forget, you are just that: My dear husband. I have no intention of parting with any of my belongings. Now I am tired of this conversation, remember, do as I tell you or it will not go well for you or your fancy woman. Get out of here, I am sick of the sight of you.'

Luke made as if to strike out at her and she smiled her tight lipped smile and turned her back on him. Her disdain was so complete, she did not fear him in the least. Luke knew he was beaten, she was always too strong for him. That had been hours ago, he had lost track of time. He had to drink himself into a fit state to tell Kitty it was over. She would have to leave the Manor House before his wife found some way to injure her and the child.

Chapter 17

The lovely summer days slipped by, almost unnoticed, as Julia divided her time between Lady Grace and Leigh Court and her sister Kitty. Any time she could slip away from the big house she made her way down the road and through the leafy pathways to Kerrigan's wood, her head bowed and her ears deaf to the calling of the birds. The light had gone out of her own life and she mourned for and with Kitty, whose spirits were so low it seemed those close to her would never see her smile again.

Luke Kerrigan drove her to the cottage with her few belongings and left her with hardly a word. Kitty took to her bed, her face to the wall and spoke to no one. A worried Jem Whelan went to Leigh Court that evening to see if Julia could get away.

'Honest to God, Nellie and I don't know what to do with her. She won't speak, she won't eat, just lies there in the dark; if she keeps this up she won't live to bring the child into the world. Jesus, I feel like going after Kerrigan and horse whipping him, but sure where would that get us. I'd be walking the roads looking for another position and Nellie and the children could go hungry. There's no justice for the likes of us.'

'I'll come with you in a little while. Let me talk to Mrs. Walshe' Julia hushed him in case his angry words would be heard inside the house.

'Go quick alannah and stay the night with her, I'll look after her ladyship until you get back. No, no, don't fret yourself, I won't tell her a thing, just that one of your family is sick and needs you. God knows that's no lie.' Bridie Walshe almost pushed Julia out of the kitchen door, while Lonegan, who was in his habitual position at the end of the table, mug in hand, cocked his head, sensing the atmosphere and hoping for a bit of gossip.

Julia opened the door and walked across the darkened room, looking down at the still figure on the little narrow bed. She sat down and put her hand on Kitty's back, feeling it cold and unyielding under her touch. Julia could find no words to say. She sat as the darkness deepened trying to pray but unable to bring even those familiar words to mind with any sort of conviction. She felt for some sort of hope or courage in her own spirit but her mind kept darting away from her, seemingly determined to dive into the blacker inner darkness. She talked to her mother: 'Mama, if you can hear me, please tell me what to do to help Kitty, I don't know what to do. I have no words to say.' She remembered the times of greatest sadness in her own life when she ran to her beloved Mama. Mama would put her arms around her, dry her tears, stoke up the fire and give her something to eat. Suddenly Julia bent down and put her arms around Kitty, hugging the cold still body to herself, murmuring the words Mama used to say:

'Hush alannah, hush my darling little one, dry your eyes now and give me a kiss. Everything is all right, sure I'm here with you amn't I?'

She kept on murmuring, hardly knowing what she was saying, rocking Kitty in her arms like a child. Suddenly Kitty's body shook and her arms went around Julia. Great racking sobs shook her and the tears coursed down her face, splashing onto Julia's hands like great drops of stormy rain. The sisters clung to one another until little by little Kitty's sobs became quieter. Julia wiped her eyes gently and disentangled herself. She lit the candle beside the bed and kneeling down smoothed the hair back from Kitty's wet face.

'A nice drop of tea and maybe a little bit of soda bread' she whispered.

'Don't leave me Julia, never leave me,' Kitty's voice was hoarse and insistent.

'Only to ask Nellie for the tea, then I'll stay the night, I won't be far away until you are feeling better.'

She crossed the room hurriedly, opened the door and signalled to Nellie and Jem who were huddled at the table.

'A drink of tea Nellie and a bit of bread.'

Jem looked at Julia relief spreading across his face: 'Thanks be to God!' he said. 'Thanks be to God!'

Kitty and Julia talked long into the night, Kitty pouring out her heart, all the hurt and torment she felt, all her worries about the coming weeks. Now and then she broke down again and clung to Julia, weeping uncontrollably. Julia let her cry, she knew instinctively that tomorrow they must pick up the pieces but tonight was for grief and mourning.

The first light of dawn was fingering it's way into the little room before they slept the sleep of exhaustion, their arms around one another in the narrow bed they had shared as children and which was now too small to accommodate them in any sort of comfort.

Nellie tried to keep the little boys quiet but their voices woke the sleeping girls a few hours later. Julia rose and pushed Kitty down onto the pillow. 'You rest yourself now and I'll go and get us both a bit of breakfast. I'll have to get back to Leigh Court in a while. But not yet,' she added as Kitty's face darkened.

When she brought the bowl of stir-about, Kitty ate it hungrily and Julia echoed Jem's prayer of the night before, thanking God that she was over the worst of it. They would manage. Nellie and Sadie and herself would look after Kitty and the child when it came and then they could make their plans for the future. Before she left the cottage, she helped Kitty to get dressed and made her promise to sit out in the sunshine later on. 'How long before the baby comes?' she asked her so that she could be prepared.

'Not long' Kitty answered. 'I reckon it should be about the end of August.'

Julia nodded, making up her mind to keep all her time off until then.

As she walked back through Kerrigan's woods, she lifted her head, pausing to let the peace of her surroundings soak into her tired body and soul. The sun was high overhead but the trees filtered most of its heat and the glade where she stood was dappled green and gold. The earth was cool and clean as if newly laundered and the sounds and smells of morning seemed so achingly beautiful to Julia's bruised spirit that she felt her soul swell up and rise, taking her over completely. She was sure she must leave the ground and float up among the lofty tree tops and on and on to touch the very dome of heaven itself. Julia was powerless to fight what was possessing her, nor did she want to. Surely her whole body was about to disintegrate and she, Julia, would cease to be, would become part of the universe itself. Suddenly it became too much and she drew back, afraid. Gradually the feeling ebbed away and she was left alone and tiny, standing on the mossy floor of the woods, while around her the universe shrank back too, just touching her longingly with lone shards of outstretched sunlight as if reluctant for the experience to end. Julia bowed her head, she was weak now, all feeling drained from her, but she was at peace.

John Leigh came home the following day, looking tired and drawn but his delight at seeing the improvement in his mother's condition made him happy. The Major was in fine fettle and Louise, home at Leigh Court for once and not travelling with the horses to some unpronounceable venue, was delighted to have her brother's company on her morning rides. John had made his mind up, he was approaching his thirtieth birthday. It was time to sort out his future. He would know where he stood before his extended holiday was over, he would know what his future held. Or if he had a future at Leigh Court. It would depend on Julia. He would declare himself to her the minute the opportunity presented itself. He had sought her out once or twice during his first few days at home. She seemed more at ease in his company, looking straight at him for a change not seeming as if to dart off at the first chance. She was quieter herself though, almost solemn, and John wondered what could be worrying her. She had an abstracted air about her as if her mind was elsewhere.

On the Friday evening as he took the air after dinner, walking slowly along the terrace, enjoying the afterglow of evening and the scent of roses borne on the breeze, he stopped at the trellis over the little gateway at the side of the house, struck by the beauty of the luminous white blossoms tumbling in such profusion there. He heard a light step approaching. Julia, lost in thought had almost passed by before she noticed his still form.

'Mr. John, I never saw you there in the shadow' she laughed softly, ashamed of the nervous start she had given when he moved.

'Julia, what an evening this is, I don't think I even noticed those white roses before; how beautiful they are.' He fell into step beside her, walking back along the terrace. Julia was curiously relaxed, normally she would have felt awkward and ill at ease in Mr. John's company, but tonight it seemed quite reasonable for him to walk at her side.

What a nice man he is, she was thinking, not for the first time, when John Leigh spoke again: 'Julia, I can't help wondering if there is something troubling you. Please don't mind me asking, but I am concerned about your well being,' he added hastily as Julia looked at him in surprise.

'Is there anything I can do to help, you must know how fond I am of you'.

Julia had stopped in her tracks, a look of utter amazement on her face and John Leigh cursed himself silently for his awkwardness. There was no backing off now, he would keep going: 'Dear girl, I have wanted to speak so many times but had not the courage. My dearest wish is that we should get to know one another better,' If the situation had been less fraught, John Leigh would have laughed out loud at the sight of Julia's face.

She was staring at him in dismay, her mouth open in a round O of astonishment, her eyes wide with disbelief at what she was hearing. God, he hoped he had not put his foot in it completely. Never one to know how to talk to a woman, John was growing more and more nervous by the minute. We are two babes in the woods where matters of the heart are concerned; the thought struck him and he closed his mouth and stood looking at the young girl in front of him, neither of them knowing what to say or do next.

To say Julia was surprised would have been to put it mildly. She was thunderstruck! Hardly able to believe her ears. She had never walked out with a young man, never been courted in any way and here was the young master, declaring his feelings for her, if she was hearing him correctly; and he did not appear to have drink taken.

'Please think over what I have said and we will talk again soon.' John Leigh lifted Julia's hand to his lips and kissed it quickly. Then, turning, he walked away leaving the astonished girl gazing after him,

Chapter 18

For a week after her meeting with John Leigh on the terrace, Julia hardly left the house, except to slip away in the evening to pay a brief visit to Kitty. She was terrified of meeting John on the corridors and took to scurrying from one room to another, pausing to check for his familiar figure before venturing out of the kitchen at all.

Mrs. Walshe was too busy trying to cope with the stifling heat in the kitchen to notice Julia's odd behaviour. She missed the help of Katie Murphy who was away having her fifth child. Lonegan had married her eventually when Fr. Murphy brought pressure to bear on him, threatening to denounce him from the pulpit for living openly in sin with poor Katie who now shared his small cottage on the estate. People turned a blind eye on their doings over the years, mostly forgetting that Katie and himself had neglected to have their union blessed by the church, but the persistent priest had worn Lonegan down, so now Katie was his long suffering wife and his children were legitimised.

The staff at Leigh Court had diminished over the years. No replacement for Kitty was hired and Julia and Helen Gleeson, a young local girl, together with Bridie Walshe and Katie, looked after the house. Nellie worked when she could and her husband Jem and Lonegan worked with Jeremiah Roche, the groom who replaced Mick Whelan in the stables. There were two gardeners employed on the grounds surrounding the house and William Considine looked after the estate and the workmen and tenants who farmed the surrounding property.

Helen Leigh-Kerrigan had taken more and more control of the family business as the Major's health deteriorated and he confined himself to dealing with his horses, leaving all the travelling to Lou-Lou who had no other interest in the world apart from her beloved horses.

The Major and Lady Grace did very little entertaining and even the annual shoot had become the property of Helen and Luke Kerrigan.

Louise had no time for socialising and neither had John Leigh when he was at home.

Lady Grace watched her son's profile as he sat with her in the library. His face pensive, he had not spoken for nearly an hour. She was content to sit quietly in the drowsy afternoon light, watching the different expressions flit across his sensitive features. Now she broke the silence: 'If I did not know better, John, I would swear you were love-sick' she said gaily, amused at his startled reaction. His reply was so unexpected, it took her by surprise.

'You could say that Mother, though I am amazed at your using such an expression'

'John! You have met someone?' Lady Grace was delighted, she had almost given up hope of her son ever choosing a partner: 'Do tell. Who is it? Is she a local girl or one of your English friends?'. All animated, she leaned forward, her face flushed.

John Leigh, looking back out the window, continued to view the lawn with what seemed like total concentration. He knew his mother would not be fobbed off. But what to tell her?

'Come on dear boy, don't keep me in suspense; tell me all'.

'I can only tell you that there is someone I would dearly love to spend my life with,' John spoke earnestly not looking in her direction, his gaze still firmly fixed on the view from the window: 'I cannot say more at present, until I find out what her feelings for me are.'

'You have not spoken then?' Lady Grace's voice was anxious.

'Yes, in a way I have, but I don't know if she will have me, or even what she thinks of me, it is all rather complicated. Trust me Mother, you will be the first to know when things are settled one way or another.'

'But, how typical of you John; of course she'll have you. Why, any girl would be proud and delighted to be your wife. Now, who is she?' She paused as John rose from his chair and started to pace up and down the room.

'Please Mother. Don't press me. I have said all I am going to say.' Then, looking at her disappointed face, he walked over and caught her hand. 'Yes, she is an Irish girl and one that I'm sure you will come to love quite easily when you get used to the idea. But you must understand, it is a very delicate situation and I must tread carefully. Can't we leave it at that for the moment?'

Lady Grace nodded, drawing him down and kissing his cheek fondly. 'How intense you are, always so sensitive, even as a little boy. I hope this girl is worthy of your love. She must be rather special. Very well, John, I will just hope and pray that all goes well for you, although I am sure in my heart it will. But bear in mind, I will wait impatiently to hear the outcome. Go on now' she laughed, 'go out and get some fresh air, it's such a lovely evening, I may just take a turn round the gardens with your father before dinner.'

Later that night, Julia and Bridie Walshe sat in the kitchen, cool and quiet in the deepening darkness. Happy with each others company, they had not bothered to light the lamps. Suddenly there was a loud rapping on the door, shattering the calm peacefulness.

'My God, who can that be at this hour?' Bridie Walshe said with alarm as Julia hastened to open the door. Jem Whelan burst into the room, clearly in a very upset state: 'Julia, you'll have to come quickly, it's Kitty, the child.'

'Oh my God!, so soon' Julia had not expected this summons for another couple of weeks at least. With a quick word to Mrs. Walshe, she took her shawl from the door and followed Jem to the waiting cart.

'She's been bad all day, but she wouldn't let me come for you. Nellie and Nora Crane are with her, but Nellie said to get you. She says she doesn't like the looks of things. It's not going right at all'.

Jem urged the horse on and Julia had to hang on with both hands as the cart hurtled over the pitted ground, swaying and creaking frantically. For all their speed it seemed an age before the cottage came into sight. Julia jumped down and ran, trying to calm herself before she got to Kitty's side. No sense in alarming her. Jem was probably over reacting. Nora Crane had helped bring them all into the world, as well as most of the children at this side of the town of Wexford. She would know what to do.

115

When she entered the back room, she knew immediately she was wrong. Kitty was lying on the little bed, twisting and moaning, her face and hair wet with sweat. The old woman bent over her looked up as Julia came in: 'The child is the wrong way round and I can't get it to turn. I don't know what to do; she's exhausted as it is.'

Nellie was standing at the top of the bed holding on to Kitty, her face strained and anxious.

Julia took in the scene at a glance, then she turned and ran back out to the kitchen where her brother was standing: 'Quick Jem, go to Leigh Court; ask for Dr. John, tell him I want him to come. Go. Go!' she pushed the protesting Jem out the door.

'He won't come here Julia, you must be mad.'

'Just do what I tell you; quick now, he'll come all right. Quick, quick! There's no time to waste arguing. Go!'.

Jem turned the horse and headed off into the night and Julia went back inside.

'Talk to her, keep her calm, try to quieten her down.' The old woman was out of her depth, she had seen this once or twice and she had little hope for the outcome, but they would have to do their best.

Kitty was groaning now, her eyes glazed, her lips white with pain. Julia took the cloth from Nellie and wringing it out in the basin of cold water, held it to her sister's sweating brow.

'Kitty, Kitty, can you hear me' she tried to keep her voice calm. 'Don't push, don't force yourself, the baby is not ready to be born yet. Hold on alannah, there's help coming. Just hold on.'

Kitty turned her wild eyes to look for Julia, clutching at her hands. Julia had seen the same wide eyed terror once before when she helped Mick Whelan to deliver a foal many years ago in the stables at Leigh Court. It was the only other birth she had ever seen. She wished she knew more. If only there was something they could do.

Kitty was screaming, her teeth clenched and flecks of foam on her lips. Julia held her, murmuring and praying. 'For God's sake Nora, isn't there something you can do?'.

'I'm trying girl, but she's bleeding something awful' the old woman answered.

'Oh, my God!' Nellie shoved her fist into her mouth to keep from crying out, the child would be smothered and Kitty would bleed to death, that's how her own mother had gone.

'Kitty, Kitty, listen to me now, try to hold on' Julia put the wrapped cloth between her sister's lips: 'Bite down hard on this; good girl, it won't be long now and you'll be fine.'

She lifted her head; thank God, the noise of the horse and cart returning could be heard by everyone in the room and suddenly John Leigh was there, pushing up his sleeves as he came and calling for water to wash his hands. Without a word he knelt down and took in the situation at a glance. Not waiting for water, he set to work with deft hands and total concentration. Kitty was moaning now in a high unnatural voice. Julia held her shoulders and said the Hail Mary, over and over, every fibre of her being willing it to be over and her sister safe. After what seemed hours, but could only have been minutes, Kitty gave a loud shriek and slumped back, her body still and Julia heard a faint mewing sound. It took a few seconds for her to realise she was listening to a baby's cry and she turned as John Leigh handed a tiny red squirming form to Nora Crane.

'It's a girl, a little girl, God be praised' the old woman said.

John Leigh continued to minister to Kitty, who lay still now, her skin stretched taut across the bones of her face, her eyes closed. Julia bent down, terrified, 'Kitty, Kitty' she whispered. John Leigh spoke for the first time: 'Leave her be; let her rest.'

Julia drew back, kneeling beside the bed.

At last John Leigh rose and nodded to Nora Crane. The old woman waddled forward, laying the little bundle down on the bed beside Kitty. John beckoned to Julia who hurried after him into the other room. 'I've done all I can' he told her, 'I think I've managed to quench the bleeding; the next few hours are crucial. We can only wait and see.' Julia's white stricken face made him long to put his arms around her but instead he said: 'I think we could all do with a cup of tea; what do you say?' Julia nodded blindly, moving to the fire to check the old black kettle.

John Leigh sat at the table in his shirt sleeves, drinking tea from a thick white mug. Jem and Nellie could not raise their heads to look at him. Julia and Nora Crane kept vigil at Kitty's side. Around midnight Kitty's eyes flickered open and she smiled wanly at Julia.

'It's a little girl' Julia said, squeezing Kitty's cold hands gently.

'Estelle'. Julia could hardly make out the weak whisper. 'Estelle; call her Estelle. Mind her for me Julia, promise you'll mind her, never let her go.'

'Don't say such things Kitty. You'll mind her yourself, we'll mind her together.'

Kitty shook her head: 'Too tired Julia, tired' she said softly. Julia felt the chill starting in her chest and her whole body began to shake. As the tears started she cried out: 'No Kitty. Oh God, please no!' Her cries brought John Leigh running into the room and as Kitty closed her eyes, Julia turned and walked blindly into his outstretched arms.

Estelle Anne Whelan was baptised the day before her mother's body was carried to Ballyleigh churchyard to lie beside Nan and Mick Whelan. Julia stood on both occasions, as if carved from stone, with John Leigh at her side. When he took her arm and walked with her from the graveside, nobody remarked on the significance of his presence beside her. For once the people of Ballyleigh were sorry for Julia Whelan. Her grief had melted even the stoutest heads.

Chapter 19

This year the blazing colours of autumn, the brown and golden leaves, the misty, sun-shafted mornings and rolling scarlet sunsets, left Julia's senses untouched. Kitty was dead and her heart was unable to feel anything but a leaden despair. Even her mother's passing had not had this effect, but then she had never dreamt that Kitty would leave her alone in the world. She slept little and when she did it was a storm-tossed sleep, full of dark dreams.

When morning came at last she was reluctant to acknowledge it, except to be glad the long night was over. Her first waking thoughts were of Kitty and then she had to take up the terrible burden again and try to carry it for another day. She was feverish with sorrow and a kind of dread. A white heat was searing her brain, an unbearable pain worse than any physical suffering she had ever endured. Her tears were an endless river until she could feel the furrows they were making down her cheeks. Then there was the shaking. During the night and now and then during the day her whole body would start to tremble uncontrollably and she was powerless to stop it. The bed shook under her when she was lying down and during the day when the terrible shaking overcame her she had to hide herself away until the storm passed over, leaving her weak and breathless. She could not eat and nothing held her interest.

She went from day to day terrified of the fear and dread that seemed to posses her, wishing she too were dead. Sometimes the thought of taking her own life presented itself and seemed to her a most inviting prospect; but she lacked the courage to take the step. I can't live and I am afraid to die, she said to herself as she stood staring out over Kerrigan's pond, with unseeing eyes. There was no yesterday no tomorrow, just this awful now, where her dead body moved heavily through a cold fog of unfamiliarity and her brain ached and burned out through her trembling head. This must be what hell is like, she thought abstractedly. This is why we are told to pray for poor sinners. And she did pray, but not as she had ever done before. It seemed to the distracted girl that there was a hole where the top of her brain had been, there was no lid, no check on her thoughts any more. The state of fear she lived in now was so ferocious, so all consuming, that all the little fears of her previous life ceased to matter. She coldly pondered all that she had ever been told or read about God and the universe. Little bits of sermons and essays floated around in her brain all made a nonsense now by the hugeness of what was happening in her mind. There was nothing but blackness, a darkness, vast and all consuming. She felt she had fallen through into some other dimension, some other world, and thought the ordered world of her existence up to now was still there around her, it seemed as if she was separated from it by a great wall of glass or ice.

Yet in the awful place where her spirit wandered, lost and terrified, she spoke to someone or something, begging for some relief or an end to her suffering.

John Leigh watched Julia, powerless to help. He knew the girl was on the verge of some sort of mental collapse. She moved through the days like a grey ghost and nothing seemed to affect or touch her in any way. He saw her in the kitchen at Leigh Court, looking down at her hand as an ugly red weal spread where scalding water had fallen. Mrs. Walshe cried out, but Julia just stood soundlessly staring at the hand, disinterested, devoid of feeling, as if it was not part of her body. John got up from the table where he was deep in conversation with Mrs. Walshe. He caught Julia's hand and plunged it into the cold water, then he told her to wait while he fetched something to dress the wound. Julia hardly looked at him, her eyes dead and lifeless, stared over his shoulder.

When he arrived back with salve and a bandage she had not moved from where he had left her. He caught her shoulders and shook her gently, 'Julia, Julia, what am I going to do with you?'

Bridie Walshe watched the little tableaux as she had watched John Leigh's treatment of Julia over the days and weeks since Kitty's death.

As God is my witness, she thought, that man is as much in love as I have ever seen a mortal man.

The startling fact of John Leigh's feelings for Julia made her shake her head in wonder. Where will it all end? she thought. First Helen Leigh and Luke Kerrigan, though there was no love there, Helen Leigh was not capable of loving anyone, not even herself. And poor Kerrigan was destroyed as everyone had known he would be. But John Leigh was another matter. Mrs. Walshe could not have loved John more if he had been her own flesh and blood. And as for Julia Whelan! Sure the girl was more to her than she could ever say. But a match between the two of them? Bridie Walshe shook her head again sadly. It would bring nothing but misery to them all.

'Oh God help us, where will it all end?' she said, speaking the words out loud, without realising what she was doing.

John Leigh looked around at her, his face grim: 'You know how things are. I see by your face you don't hold out much hope for us. Well I have made up my mind to marry Julia, and marry her I will, but first I must get her well. Her sickness is one I don't know how to deal with. However I am going to start by taking her away from here for a holiday . . . No, don't say anything' he held up his hand as Bridie opened her mouth. 'I am relying on you to get her ready, I am taking her back to London with me. If the journey does not raise her spirits, there are colleagues of mine I can take her to see.'

Bridie Walshe could only nod her head, her face anxious and tormented. 'Something has to be done for her Master John, she can't go on like this much longer.'

They both looked at Julia, who was still standing, staring out the window, obviously deaf to the conversation going on a few feet away from her.

John Leigh left Leigh Court with Julia Whelan early on a blustery October morning to take the boat for England from Ballygeary Harbour. Not since his departure years before, when he had defied his father and returned to London to study medicine had there been such an upheaval in the big house. The Major was totally nonplussed. He thought John's behaviour had ceased to amaze him, but this latest was beyond belief. Declaring his intentions to marry one of the servant girls, albeit a decent young woman and a particular favourite of his wife's, was tantamount to madness, and would probably be the death of his mother. Then to pack the girl in question into the coach and depart with her for London. . . . The Major was so incoherent with shock, he did not take in half of what John was telling him. Apparently, the girl had suffered some sort of brain storm or something after the death of her sister and John was taking her away for the good of her health. Louise had laughed and said John would come to his senses and bring her back when he did, or else get her employment with one of his friends' families in England. In the meantime, they would have to get someone to take over the household. Julia Whelan was a jolly good servant and would be hard to replace: 'Dashed unkind of John to take her; and who will look after mother in the interim' she complained to the Major.

Major Leigh was afraid to go up to Grace's room after John's departure. How would she react to this madness?

Lady Grace was sitting in her usual chair before the front window when her husband entered her bedroom that evening. She did not turn her head and the room was in semi-darkness, though a cheerful fire blazed in the hearth.

'Is that you darling' she spoke softly. 'Come and sit with me for a while. No, don't light the lamp yet, I am enjoying the view.'

He was surprised at her calmness, but then Grace never ceased to surprise him. He sat down in the window seat and looked out. The trees on the lawn and down along the drive were moving gently in a stately arabesque as the autumn wind partnered them and the rooks were rising in a dark cloud over Kerrigan's wood. The evening was drawing to a close and night was waiting impatiently in the wings.

'Winter won't be long coming' the Major sighed tiredly. Lady Grace looked at his drawn face. How to console him she wondered; he had borne so much disappointment over the years. John and Helen; and now John again. Such awful children. But she could never compare John to Helen. No, their son was a strange one, no one could argue with that, but he was, for all that, a fine man, a man to be proud of. If only she could help his father to see that, as she did. It had taken her days to think clearly about his wish to marry Julia Whelan and even now it did not sit easily on her mind. But John was John, he never took the path laid out before him, always went the difficult way.

'Things are changing Mother, we are on the verge of a whole new century. The old ways are going, mankind is moving into a different era. Why, in England, already working people are demanding a new way of life. Old fashioned mores are dying, soon we will have a new society based on principles as yet just guessed at. The dignity of man has to be recognised and upheld and it will mean change. great change, but it will be all for the better. Maybe Julia and I will be breaking new ground, but I love her and I know I am doing the right thing. Please tell me you understand. You know Julia, you know her worth. She has a fine mind and a beautiful nature. She is so kind, so good and gentle. Oh Mother, I know you are going to come to love her in time and to cherish her as a beloved daughter and companion.'

Lady Grace held him to her bosom, patting his bent head as he knelt before her. She could find no words to say even when he looked into her face beseechingly. She tried to smile at this, her only son, and to hide the fear in her eyes. But in her heart she was crying out to him. Oh, John, John, do you know what you are taking on, not just a little girl from the servant classes, but a whole section of society, with ignorance and prejudice on both sides.

Now she tried to console the Major, as she had done all their lives together. 'This is hard for you to bear, my dear, but you have always known John is no ordinary young man. Remember how you felt when he wanted to become a doctor and yet it has worked out well and brought him great happiness. I know Helen's marriage is not a success and she did not find happiness, but then would Helen have ever found happiness with anyone? Let us be honest, our daughter is not a person to be content in any role. But John is different, he has always known his own mind. If he believes this girl is the companion for him, then we must trust him. He was never bothered by convention and I think he knows what he is doing.'

She paused, looking at the Major.

'I hope you are right my dear, I sincerely hope so. If John brings this girl back here and makes her his wife it is going to prove difficult for all of us. You spoke of Helen; well let us consider Helen for a moment: How will she react to this? You know as well as I do, she has her heart set on inheriting Leigh Court. I think she always hoped John would marry and settle in England. She never let herself believe he would ever come home. However he tells me he plans to live here and practice medicine in Ballyleigh. He feels he will be of more use here than in London where there are many doctors. I must face the fact that for my own purposes I led Helen to believe she, or at least her heirs, would inherit, but I never had any intention of taking Leigh Court from John . . . I always hoped he would come back. You see the dilemma I now find myself in? I can tell you I do not look forward to my next encounter with our daughter.' He lifted a hand to his brow with a weary sigh. Lady Grace was silent for a moment. Then she spoke again in the same calm tones:

'We have never had any great grief to contend with and you could say we have been singularly blessed during our lives together. We must not allow ourselves to be distressed. This too will pass and our lives will go on. You have looked after your inheritance to the best of your ability and done your duty to your country, and your family. You will leave Leigh Court to your son and he must do his best to preserve it and look after it for his son. That is how it has always been'.

Major John Leigh nodded: 'You are right as ever dear heart.' He patted her hand and rose to light the lamp and draw the heavy curtains against the dark night.

Chapter 20

Jem Whelan did not know what to make of John Leigh. He had lost his oldest sister because of Luke Kerrigan and now here was another rich man trying to tell him he would look after Julia. Jem was totally confused, he tried to talk to Nellie and Sadie, but they were no help. Then there was the child, Kitty's child. Nellie would have to care for it along with their own two. Sadie was good with the children but she needed looking after too, if the truth were told. All those mouths to feed and things getting dearer every year. Now Julia was sick and God knows what would happen if she lost her position at Leigh Court. He couldn't take Julia in as well, there was just no room in the cottage. With all this worry on his mind, Jem was in no fit state to deal with the talk in the village and at the big house itself.

John Leigh seemed like a decent man. He had come to see them every day after Kitty died and he sat at the table as if he was one of their own kind. But wanting to marry Julia? Jem had never heard anything so preposterous. A Leigh of Leigh Court marrying a servant girl. There was enough upheaval five years before when the Helen one married Kerrigan; and look where that ended. Probably when he had his way with her he'd throw her to one side and leave her to fend for herself like poor Kitty. Jem didn't know what to do about Julia. If she was sick so as to need nursing, they would do their best for her but she was like someone in a trance since her sister's death. There was no use talking to her. Well then, let Leigh take her over to see his fancy doctor friends, there was no other way out of it. Let Julia take her chances. As to him marrying her . . . well that was another matter. Julia was always a sensible girl, if she could shake off the state she was in she would be able to look after herself.

Jem made up his mind to keep his mouth shut and say nothing to anyone. He was well used to putting up with jibes and taunts, he had done it all his life. 'Sticks and stones may break my bones, but words will never hurt me' his mother used to chant the rhyme when the children came home in tears from the village. They had soon learned to turn a deaf ear to the cruel treatment meted out to drunken Mick Whelan's brats.

The whole neighbourhood was talking about John Leigh and Julia. They were seen at the funeral and on the days and weeks after it, walking and driving quite openly around the countryside. Now they were gone off together. Tom Lonegan was delighted to carry every bit of tittle tattle he could to the local shebeen and anywhere else he found an open ear.

It never occurred to Jem to wonder what the family at Leigh Court thought, nor did he care. Those people would be all right, didn't they always come out on top no matter what? Well he would keep his head down and do his work as he always did, there was nothing else he could do.

Major Leigh's interview with his daughter Helen came sooner than he expected. The very morning after John and Julia's departure, the door of the library flew open and Helen Leigh rushed into the room, looking, he said to Lady Grace later, like someone possessed. The Major was taking his usual morning smoke when she arrived.

'Is it true?' she shouted at the surprised man, her voice loud and shrill. 'Has my brother really gone off to England with the skivvy Julia Whelan?' Before he could open his mouth she rushed on, her voice growing wilder by the minute. Not for the first time the Major wondered if Helen was not slightly deranged. Her behaviour this morning was not that of a sane, rational woman. She began to stride up and down the floor, beating the side of her long skirts with the crop she held in her hand. Literally frothing at the mouth, she castigated her brother, using words no gentlewoman should know. She stopped in front of the desk now, her face livid: 'He will never get his hands on Leigh Court. Never! No matter who he marries or what spawn he produces with the slut. You have no excuse now Father, you must sign everything over to me before John destroys us completely. Surely you see you have no option but to do what I say.'

She paused, her eyes like coals, red rimmed and staring.

Her father was shocked as much by her appearance as by her outburst.

'Helen, for God's sake calm down and we will discuss this matter quietly.'

'There is nothing to discuss.' Helen's voice rose again and she brought the crop down with a crash on the rosewood desk. 'Leigh Court is mine, it was always mine and if you try to keep it from me I will destroy you, all of you!'

'My dear child . . .,' the Major was seriously alarmed now, rising to his feet he tried to reach out to Helen, but she backed off until her back was pressed against the wall.

'I am not your dear child, I never was, don't try to get round me. I mean every word I am saying. You sold me to Kerrigans so that you could keep yourself in money and Lou-Lou in horses. Well, I did what I did for Leigh Court and it is time for my payment. I warn you Father,' and the ominous low voice sounded even worse than the shrill tirade, 'I will have the place, one way or another'. She stood facing her father, and he shrank back before the look in her eyes.

Pulling herself up to her full height, she straightened her hat, the gesture so unexpected it threw the Major completely off balance.

Calmer now, she spoke again. 'You had better see to it Father, before this business with John goes any further. I will call again in a few days.'

With that she turned and left the room, closing the door carefully, leaving the stunned man staring after her.

'I tell you Grace, the girl is definitely unhinged.' the Major and Lady Grace were walking in the walled garden that afternoon, getting the last of the watery sunshine between squally autumn showers.

'Helen was always a headstrong and wilful girl, best leave her for John to deal with. No doubt she will present herself again as she said, you will just have to be firm with her. Tell her you have no intention of listening to her threats. Next time you will be ready for her. After all dear, you were able to deal with a whole regiment of men, your own daughter should not be too difficult to handle.'

'You did not see or hear her Grace, if it had been a man I would have had him locked up until he came to his senses.'

Lady Grace paused in her stride. 'Well darling, you can hardly lock Helen up, but you can refuse to see her if she insists on carrying on in such a fashion. Tell the servants she is not to be admitted to your presence without your permission. They won't find it strange, I don't think anything that goes on in or around Leigh Court would cause a stir any more,' and she smiled wryly. 'However we had better return to the house' she said as the rain began to spatter down from a leaden sky.

Luke Kerrigan was tired listening to his wife's strident tones. His head was aching and he longed to be drunk. He was seldom sober now, since Kitty Whelan's death, he had been in a near constant state of drunkenness. He knew she'd had a daughter, and that John Leigh had saved the child's life, but he couldn't save Kitty. He could not bring himself to go to see the child. He would not be welcome anyhow, he had no interest in it, even if it was his own flesh and blood and the only child he would ever have. Now Helen was going on with some cock and bull story about her brother taking off for foreign parts with Kitty's younger sister. Luke vaguely remembered Julia Whelan. A pale little creature with great startled eyes, not a bit like any of the rest of them, Helen had wanted to bring her here with her when they were first married. Pity to God she hadn't and then Kitty might still be alive. Tears of self pity filled his eyes and he got up, and kicking the chair back lurched towards the door.

'That's right, go off and meet your dreadful friends and get drunk. That's all you are good for.' Helen's voice followed him out into the hall and he swore under his breath. Some day he might muster up the courage to strangle the bitch and put them both out of their misery. But for the moment he would go to Ballyleigh and get drunk.

Chapter 21

On a bright, crisp morning in early December, John Leigh hurried along Oxford Street, his head high and his step jaunty. He wanted to collect a brooch from the jewellers. Julia had admired it so yesterday. It was not an expensive piece, just a cream cameo, with a lady's head in profile. John had noticed many such brooches pinned to the ladies' gowns. He would surprise her with it this afternoon, she was so easy to please. He looked forward with anticipation to the way she would accept the little parcel, her head bent, she would open it so carefully, saving the wrapping paper and string and taking her time before opening the box, savouring every moment. Then the quick smile would kindle in her eyes first, then light up her whole face. He would help her pin the brooch to her gown and she would lift her face to his, like a child, waiting for his kiss. John shook his head in wonder. He still found it hard to believe Julia was the same sad waif he had ferried away from Ireland such a short time ago. She was a different person now. Shy still, timid even, with anyone other than himself, but growing stronger and surer with every day. Soon it would be time to tell her his plans for the two of them. Yes, very soon now he could broach the subject of their return to Leigh Court.

John's step grew slower as he remembered the day they had left the house, the coach tearing down the driveway as if pursued by demons. Julia huddled like a lost soul, those huge sad eyes staring blindly and he, his arms supporting her, hoping against hope he was doing the right thing. Then the sea journey, long and arduous, with hardly a morsel of food passing her lips. It was when they got onto the train for London that he had seen a change in her demeanour. When they walked onto the rainy platform, the smell of the steam engines and the loud clatter of unfamiliar noises and accents ringing in the air, Julia halted and looked about her. 'Are we going on the train' she asked hesitantly.

'Yes, we must take the train to London' he answered, hardly able to believe she had spoken; since she had shown absolutely no sign of interest during the voyage. She approached the train almost eagerly and stepped up into the carriage. As the whistle blew sharply and they shunted forward, she spoke again: 'I went to Rosslare on the train once. Kitty and I. What a lovely day it was.' She was suddenly animated and then as he watched, her whole face crumpled and great tears began to course down her cheeks.

'Kitty, oh Kitty,' she sobbed wildly, clutching at him as he moved quickly to her side. John held her as he had on the night Kitty died. Then she had cried quietly with hardly a sound, but now her grief was wild and terrible. She battered his chest with her fists, crying and shouting, in an uncontrollable frenzy of anger.

John made no effort to stop her. He let the anguish pour out over him, waiting and watching, letting her do and say what she liked.

Little by little the tearing sobs grew less violent until she was lying in his arms, crying quietly now, her awful anger spent. He stroked her hair, saying not a word; just waiting.

As the train sped through the gathering darkness, she fell asleep in his arms, worn out by the strength of her emotions and John looked down at her ravaged face, growing more peaceful with the passing hours.

That night Julia ate some supper in the little hotel in Knightsbridge and as John left her in the comfortable bedroom, she said she thought she might sleep, she felt so weary. Then she shyly reached up and kissed his cheek. 'Thank you John, you have been so kind to me, I don't deserve it.' She started to cry again, softly, but John touched her lips with his finger and shushed her gently. 'Rest my dear, I believe you will be able to rest now and tomorrow we will talk.'

Indeed they did talk, on the morrow and over all the following days and weeks, Julia Whelan talked as she had never done in her life. She poured her heart and her life out to John Leigh. All the sadness of her childhood, all the grief she had buried when her mother died and all the terrible agony and desperation she was still feeling when she thought of

Kitty. She confided to him her guilty feelings of anger against her sister, how she had felt on that day in Rosslare when Kitty told her her secret. Her terrible confusion about God and all of life itself and the dreadful mind bending fear that rose up and threatened to suck her in and drown her in its dark belly.

John listened, hour after hour, the distant murmur of traffic outside the hotel the only reminder that there was another world outside the quiet room where they sat. He said very little, just held her in his arms when the shaking took over her thin frame. Held her and gave what comfort he could, stroking her long dark hair with his gentle sensitive fingers. Inside he was rejoicing. He knew the healing process had begun and Julia would be well, indeed she would probably be better than she ever had been, able to face life and all its vicissitudes. Little by little Julia came to terms with her grief. Her joyous nature started to reassert itself and she smiled for the first time in what seemed an eternity, tentatively at first and then, to John, it was as if he was watching a glorious sunrise after the bleakest of nights.

'Today my dear, I think we will venture out to see the sights. After all we have been in London for nearly three weeks now and you have not even seen the inside of a shop or the outside of a building. What do you say to a grand tour of the city?'

Julia smiled again. Feelings that she thought had gone forever were welling up inside her. Excitement, eagerness, happiness even. Imagine, here she was, Julia Whelan from Ballyleigh, going to be shown around London by the dearest friend anyone could have. John had long ceased to be Master John Leigh, now he was the person who mattered most to her in the world. This new world she was slowly being born into. She clapped her hands now, her pale face flushed with excitement. 'Do you think we could? Oh John, can we really go out and see the great city of London?'

'Indeed we can, my girl, every inch of it if I have my way,' and he hugged her to him, giving silent thanks to God for the miracle he was witnessing.

Julia's head was in a whirl, there was still no yesterday, but today was enough. She was totally overcome by the immenseness of the city around her. They travelled by coach and John pointed out the famous landmarks: Trafalgar Square, Buckingham Palace, Marble Arch, The Strand.

They walked down Oxford Street, in and out of the marvellous shops. John insisted that they go shopping and Julia was handed over to a very smart lady who whisked her off into an Aladdin's cave. Such clothes! Julia had never seen such clothes, even in Helen Leigh's or Lady Grace's wardrobes. A young girl helped her into the beautiful dresses and made her walk out to where John waited, sitting on a little gilt chair. Julia was too excited to worry about the rights and wrongs of the situation. She was like a child in a sweetshop, this was part of her new life. The old one was left like her dress and the coat borrowed from Louise Leigh, discarded on the floor beside her worn boots. She emerged from the portals of the exclusive establishment a few hours later and nobody who had known her would now recognise Julia Whelan. In her new dress and coat, with a smart hat to match, her feet and legs encased in high button boots of the softest kid leather, her face glowing with pleasure, she was the picture of elegance and quite the most beautiful girl in all of London, or so John assured her.

That night they went to the opera, Julia in a plain white silk gown, her hair swept up in a soft chignon, a single string of pearls shining against her white throat. John watched her profile as she sat forward, rapt in wonder as the music swelled and the glorious voices of Signor Caruso and Madam Melba filled the huge auditorium. How could anyone who saw her now, doubt that she was a fit mistress for Leigh Court.

Why he would be the envy of all his contemporaries, whether here or in Ireland.

They floated back to the hotel, Puccini's beautiful music still echoing in their ears. Julia had cried at the ending, as the heroin lay dying and John squeezed her hand comfortingly. When the curtain fell and the singers appeared to take their bows the house rose in a standing ovation and Julia clapped and clapped until her hands stung with pain. 'I don't think I will ever come down to earth again' she told the amused John, who had been in two minds as to whether to bring her to Covent Garden in the first place, thinking she might appreciate Mr. Gilbert's and Mr. Sullivan's offering at the Savoy Opera House more.

'Could we go again. Oh could we John?'

'Of course, my dear, as often as you wish.' John Leigh did not tell her he had resigned his post in the London hospital, sending a letter to his superiors the week before, explaining that he must now return to Ireland for very pressing personal reasons. He would stay here with Julia until she was strong enough in mind and body, and then they would both return to Leigh Court.

John was surprised and delighted when Julia returned his kiss that night, putting her arms around his neck and lingering in his arms. 'Don't leave me John, don't ever leave me' she whispered. 'You are my life.'

He stood with her, hardly daring to believe what he was hearing, his heart bursting with joy. 'Oh Julia, my darling, how long I waited to hear you say those words.'

'How long John?' she asked.

'A lifetime my dear, since once long ago on a midsummer's night, I followed a will-O'-the-wisp a long way from here and came across a vision in Kerrigan's wood, a fairy child, made all of moonlight. A silver water nymph who stood before me paying homage to the night and stole the heart out of my body.'

Julia drew back, trying to see his face in the gloom. 'Was it me then? I often swam in Kerrigan's pond in the moonlight. I never saw you there, were you watching me?'

'I didn't know it was you, Julia, not until the day I saw you in the kitchen at home, and you like a little timid fawn out of the forest. I could hardly believe you were my angel of the night, but you were, the very same, and so I waited all these years. I knew we would be together some day. I always believed you would be mine eventually. It took all this sorrow to bring us to this place, but no matter, we are together now and nothing is ever going to separate us.'

Julia drew his face down to hers and kissed him gently at first and then as she felt his passion she responded willingly. They stood together in the darkened room and the darkness became a river to drown in.

John and Julia were married quietly in a little catholic church in Eton Square on the second week in December. John's friend and colleague, Dr. James Marshall and his wife acted as witnesses and then they withdrew for supper at the Ritz. Dr. James had worried about John when he first heard what he planned to do, but the sight of his friend transformed and the obvious joy of the couple, when he at last met John and Julia, had utterly convinced him that John was doing the right thing. He could shake his friend's hand after the ceremony and honestly say: 'You are a lucky man John and may you both have all the happiness you deserve in your life together.'

John was happier than he had ever thought possible. 'I have Julia now, I have come home' he said with such utter conviction that James Marshall found himself envying him. . . It is not given to many men to find such happiness, he thought, I so hope it will last; knowing John Leigh, I think maybe it will.

Chapter 22

Mr and Mrs. John Leigh arrived home at Leigh court one week before Christmas to a mixed reception. The servants were assembled in the front hall to welcome the new bride as was the custom.

Lady Grace had decided that this would be done. She wanted to set a precedent; Julia was now John's wife and her daughter in law and as such was entitled to be obeyed and respected by the staff.

The Major was ill at ease, not knowing how to deal with the situation that was about to present itself under his roof.

Louise had gone riding as usual, nothing short of an earthquake would keep her from exercising Hero, her new horse. She told her parents it would hardly matter to her who her brother married. As a matter of fact, if John came home with a Fuzzy Wuzzie, it did not effect her life. She had her own business to attend to and had no time for this romantic lark.

The happy couple were on time, the crossing smooth and uneventful and the drive home along the dry frosty roads taking little more than an hour. Lonegan met them at the boat, his usual deferential mood tinged with impudence, but even he knew when to draw back and one look at John Leigh's face put him firmly in his place. Tom Lonegan had to admit the change in Julia Whelan, or Julia Leigh as she was now, was amazing. The shy girl was gone and in her place; a stylish young woman. But then, Julia had always had an air about her, as if she considered herself a cut above the rest of them. Well we'll see how she conducts herself now, and he grinned wickedly to himself, remembering some of the talk he had heard in the village and at Leigh Court. Then there's the Helen wan, begod, she won't have an easy time when the Helen wan gets hold of her. Lonegan chuckled to himself, rubbing his hands together in anticipation of the time ahead.

'I am glad go see you in such good spirits Lonegan, but please load the luggage, I don't want my wife waiting about in the cold.' John Leigh helped Julia into the coach, wrapping the rug about her and smiling reassuringly into her eyes.

Julia was afraid. When John told her of his plans to return home before Christmas, her heart pounded so loudly, she felt he must be able to hear it. John, watching her carefully, noted the sudden pallor and the fear springing up in her eyes. Here in London, Julia was safe and happy. In this environment she felt she was born again, born into a new world. Complete with a new personality, a new name, she was a different person. But to go back to Ballyleigh, to Leigh Court to a life and an identity that had broken her in the first place, she did not know if she could face it. What if the darkness came back to drown her? What if the terror, the shaking, the inability to live returned again? She clung to John, pouring out all her worries and foreboding.

'Julia, my dear, you will never go back to what you were. You have faced the noonday devil, nothing could ever effect you like that again. Kitty's death and all that ensued, made you face yourself and your life and instead of destroying you it made you stronger. You chose life my dear, and life as my wife. We go back to Leigh Court as man and wife, together. I am here at your side to support you until you learn to stand alone. And learn you will, I know my Julia. Come on now, cheer up, you have a lot of packing to do.'

Remembering his words Julia took a deep breath and with her head held high she entered the door of what was no longer her place of work but her home in every sense of the word. They were all there. The Major and Lady Grace at one side, the staff on the other. Lady Grace moved forward, her arms outstretched. She approached Julia and hugged her warmly: 'Welcome home my dear, and you John, how well you both look.'

John took his mother in his arms and held her gently. 'Thank you Mother' he whispered, so that only she could hear.

The Major nodded gruffly, 'Yes, yes, very well indeed, very well'.

Julia turned and looked at her former friends who were standing awkwardly, not knowing how to behave. Her eyes fell on Bridie Walshe and she rushed forward, throwing her arms around her, laughing and crying at the same time. Bridie hugged her to her, all her confusion at seeing little Julia so grown up and smart looking a regular lady, disappearing under the warmth of Julia's embrace.

'Bridie it's so good to see you, so good.'

'You too darlin' girl, and its fit and well you look.'

Now the rest of the maids gathered round Julia, shaking her hand and calling her ma'am. It was clear that Julia had not changed, under all the style she was still the quiet good natured girl she had always been. When the family moved towards the drawing room John took Julia's arm and propelled her forward. She cast a look of longing over her shoulder to where Mrs. Walshe and the others were returning to the kitchen.

The ground rules were soon laid down. Julia had no intention of keeping her distance from her friends in the kitchen. At first she tried to work with Bridie Walshe, turning up in the kitchen in the mornings when John rode out with his sister and the Major, and before Lady Grace had risen from her bed. But there was a new woman in her place. They had managed to secure the services of Mary Deegan, a local woman who had worked under Mrs. Hayes, the cook at the Manor House.

Julia soon realised her presence in the kitchens was not appreciated so she had taken to visiting Bridie in her own quarters when she could.

'You have to get to know your place now alannah. As Mr. John's wife you must stay at his side. I am always glad to see you, but I think it would be better if you did not come to the kitchen so often.'

When she knocked on Lady Grace's door the morning after their arrival and heard the gentle voice bidding her enter, it was to find Miss Armstrong, the old governess, obsolete now, all her pupils departed, folding Lady Grace's clothes.

'Sit down Julia, how nice of you to visit. Miss Armstrong has been helping me to manage since you went away. and we are getting on famously,' she motioned for Julia to take a seat near her, and, trying to hide her confusion, Julia did so, but the conversation was stilted and neither woman was at ease.

'It will take time for us all to get used to our new positions. But we will soon find our feet.' Lady Grace patted Julia's clenched hands and her eyes were kind. Poor girl, she thought, this is more difficult for her than for any of us.

I do not belong anywhere now, Julia thought later on that evening as she returned from visiting Jem and Nellie and the children. She had set out from Leigh Court to walk to her old home, laden down with presents for all the family but Sadie was the only one whose greeting was natural and joyous when her sister arrived at the door. Jem and Nellie were sitting at the table taking tea and they started up, confused, not able to look at Julia as she stood before them.

'Are you not going to offer me a cup of tea after my walk?' Julia laughed, trying to put them at ease.

'We are, oh we are' Nellie was wiping her hands on her apron, clearing the delph and the crumbs off the table.

'You will have to excuse the state of the place' she said, nearly falling over herself in an effort to tidy up.

'Sit down woman for God's sake; its only our Julia.' Jem spoke sharply, his face red.

'Of course it Is.' Julia's laugh was nervous, she felt as ill at ease as Nellie so obviously did. 'Look what I brought for you and for the boys.' Julia started to unpack the basket, handing each of them a gift. Sadie squealed with delight when she tore the paper off her parcel and jewel bright hanks of fine embroidery threads fell out onto her lap, together with packets of needles and crochet hooks.

'Oh Julia, how lovely, I never saw such colours' and she stood up and hugged Julia.

Nellie held up the lace blouse and Jem laid the white cotton shirt over the chair reverently.

'The boys are out in Kerrigan's wood, they won't be long. I told them to be back before sundown'.

Nellie was pouring tea for Julia, taking her coat and touching the fine material wonderingly as she went to lay it on the bed in the back room. When she came back there was a sudden silence and all eyes were on Julia.

Nellie was carrying a baby, a little round faced infant with a downy growth of red hair covering her head.

Julia felt faint, the room was spinning around her. She sat down quickly, her hand to her throat and Sadie walked over and put her thin arms around her.

'This is Estelle'. Nellie came forward and offered her the child. Making a supreme effort, Julia held out her arms and took her. The little body squirmed in her arms and the tiny face puckered.

'She wants her bottle' Sadie said. 'Would you like to feed her Julia? She's no trouble, honest to God, she's as good as gold.'

Julia nodded, lifting the child up to her face, she kissed her gently and the eyes opened in surprise. She found herself staring into a pair of startlingly blue eyes and her heart leapt; My God, the child has Kitty's eyes. Julia felt the tears welling up in her throat, but she forced them back and smiled instead. 'Estelle' she said softly and she saw an answering smile dawn in the baby's eyes. Estelle Anne Whelan, you are a little beauty.' The baby was gurgling up at her, her hunger forgotten for the moment and Julia sat gazing in wonder at Kitty's baby, knowing she loved her already.

As she lay in the big bed beside John later on that night, Julia was reflecting on the strangeness of her new life.

'I don't belong anywhere now, not at Leigh Court with your family, I am not one of them, not a high born lady and I don't belong with my own kind, they think I have left them behind and maybe I have. A little knowledge is a dangerous thing' she sighed.

'You belong right here, at my side Julia.' John was leaning on his elbow, gazing down at her. 'The thing to do about a little knowledge is to add to it. After Christmas we will take time each day to study, you and I. We will discuss what is happening in the world and here in our

own country. It is time I took your education in hand my dear. You have
a fine mind and it's hungry for knowledge. But not now, my darling,
this is no time to discuss mundane matters.' And he turned out the lamp
and took her in his arms.

After Christmas Julia applied herself to her books again with a will.
Now she had time on her hands and she could spend long hours
studying. She spent most mornings in the room John had had fitted out
for her on the first floor beside his study. While he tended to his ever
growing number of patients, most of them from labouring families and
tenant farmers, who had never had a doctor in their house before, Julia
cleaned their apartments, she insisted on this in spite of opposition from
both upstairs and downstairs. Then she took tea with Bridie Walshe in
the cook's little parlour.

She spent three hours at her studies, reading the books John marked
out for her and the papers, so that they could talk about the happenings
at home and abroad. John insisted that she take a keen interest in
politics, teaching her facts about Ireland's history that she had never
known. Talking about the struggle for Home Rule that was going on in
England's Parliament. After luncheon, which they took with the Major,
Lady Grace, and Lou-Lou when she was at home, they would ride off
together in the pony and trap or walk arm in arm around the demesne.
They were a familiar sight, clipping along the roads or strolling, heads
close together, along the pathways. Dinner was always a quiet, leisurely
meal and then John and Julia would retire to their own apartments to
read, or Julia might sew or embroider, while John read to her, or talked
late into the night, about his hopes for the future. He confided all his
dreams of a better world, where every man would have a decent way of
life and the means to marry and raise a family with dignity.

'I think you were born into the wrong family, are you sure you are
the Major's son?' Julia asked him jokingly one night as he told her they
would live to see the working man a power to be reckoned with.

'I have seen such misery Julia, both in England and here. Such
appalling inhumanity perpetrated on innocents whose only crime is that

140

they were born poor. I don't consider myself a religious man, but there is a God who created all of us for His own good reasons. I am damned sure He did not create some to be the slaves of others. No. Liberty, Fraternity, Equality started many years ago and the French gave voice to what is in the heart of most men of goodwill. It will have to come Julia, here in Ireland and all over the world. It is coming even as we speak.'

Julia would listen enthralled, when John talked like this. She could not understand everything he said, but she knew he was saying things her heart and mind agreed with. She would sit at his feet before the fire, gazing into the flickering flame- light and listen, dreamlike, to his soft voice, while he stroked her long hair, lifting it every so often and letting it fall around her like a cloud of dark silk.

Those were the times she loved best, she wished they could stay like that forever, together in their own peaceful world.

Chapter 23

Helen Leigh Kerrigan had not put in an appearance since John and Julia arrived home. The last time she had forced an entry and tried to harangue her father, he was ready for her. Drawing himself up to his full height and bringing the weight of his military experience to his aid he managed to subdue Helen's angry voice. Forcing her to sit down, he told her in no uncertain terms that Leigh Court belonged to her brother John. 'That's how it is Helen, and that is how it has always been. The eldest son inherits. Of course you and your sister are well provided for, things have improved over the last few years and you are a rich woman in your own right, apart from your husband's wealth. You can draw on your inheritance any time you want to, but the house and land belong to John and his heirs.'

When she started to protest wildly, he held up his hand for silence and continued: 'Should anything happen to your brother, should he die without issue, I have seen to it that the estate passes to the next of kin; in this case yourself. So you see, my dear, the house and property will always be owned by a Leigh. You are welcome here, Helen, and should you ever want to return to live at Leigh Court, you may do so, your room is still as you left it. This is my last word on the matter. Your mother and I want you to make peace with John and his wife. This is our dearest wish'. But as he looked at Helen's face, black with rage, he knew he was whistling down the wind. Sighing resignedly, he made it clear that he had no wish to discuss the matter further.

'You will live to regret this decision father.' Helen's voice was low and harsh. 'I won't set foot in this house again until I come to claim what is mine.' She strode from the room without a backward glance and the Major watched through the window as she climbed into the trap and drove off, taking stones from the drive as the wheels skittered along at too fast a speed.

'Poor Helen' he muttered. 'Poor girl.'

There was little or no entertaining done any more. In a way Mrs. Walshe was glad, she was getting too old to cope with anything other than the simple meals for the family but now and then she looked back longingly to the old days when the Major and Lady Grace had entertained on a grand scale. She heard from Mrs. Hayes that things were as bad at the Manor, worse, because the mistress usually dined alone.

'Himself is never at home now, out gallivantin' all over the countryside and he drunk out of his mind most of the time. Lord, I'm waiting for them to carry him home and his neck broken one of these days and he riding that horse like auld Nick himself was after him.'

The two cooks were having their weekly visit, this time Mrs. Hayes had called to Leigh Court. Hynes the butler, too old now to take a very active part in the household, sat with them, enjoying his afternoon tipple. He had no complaints, Miss Julia saw to his every comfort, looking after him better than any daughter would. 'A grand little girl, never forgot her place. She takes good care of the servants, remembers what it was like to live below stairs,' he told Mrs. Hayes.

'Well I can't say the same for Helen Leigh, she treats us like muck, never even allows that we are alive at all unless she has something to complain about. I never knew such a disagreeable woman, she gets crabbier with every day that passes. Wouldn't you think she would be delighted to see her brother so happy?'

'Delighted is it?' Bridie Walshe spluttered into her tea cup. 'That wan would kill Julia Whelan with her bare hands and then turn and strangle her brother if she thought she could get away with it. It's going between her and her rest that she can't have the whole place here to rattle around in, though God only knows what she would do with it if she had.'

'God forbid that she ever will, Mrs. Walshe, God forbid,' Hynes murmured piously, casting his rheumy eyes up at the ceiling, as if the deity he was calling on lived in the first floor of Leigh Court.

'Wait till she hears that Julia is going to have a baby. That will really set her off.' Bridie Walshe chuckled delightedly, glad to be the one to pass on the news and sure it would reach Helen Leigh's ears before nightfall now that Hayes had it; sure that one couldn't hold her water, everyone knew that.

Julia's baby was born in October, nearly a year to the day after Kitty's death and Estelle's birth. They named him John, after his father and his grandfather and the Major was as proud of his grandson as any man could be. At the baby's christening, his relatives on both sides brushed shoulders. John's aunts and cousins travelled from Ireland and England. The birth and christening of a son and heir was a solemn occasion in the family.

Jem and Nellie put in a brief appearance, uncomfortable in their Sunday best. But of Helen Leigh-Kerrigan, there was not a sign.

Lady Grace held the baby for the official photograph and then Julia sat with him on her lap, John standing behind them, hand on her shoulder, looking every inch the proud Papa, for their first family portrait. The birth was not too difficult, Dr. Cosgrove looked after her well. John had insisted that she be given the chloroform, much appreciated by Queen Victoria at her many confinements. If the Queen of England could have it, then so could his wife, he told Julia, allaying any fears she might have before the child was born. He was afraid she might be remembering the night Kitty's child came into the word, but Julia had no worries. Healthier and happier than she had ever been, she sailed through her pregnancy and John James Leigh arrived safe and well on a mild October evening.

'See how accommodating he is?' John said, 'He made sure to arrive before nightfall so no one would have to travel after dark.' And it seemed that baby John was indeed a thoughtful child. He slept peacefully and ate when he should.

'A thorough little gentleman' the Major was fond of proclaiming much to Lady Grace's amusement.

'His father all over again, the little lamb' was Bridie Walshe's pronouncement on first viewing the new arrival.

'I have to fight to hold my own son even for a few minutes of the day' Julia laughingly complained to her husband.

'Well we must have another, so that you can have him to yourself' was John's quick rejoinder. But it was three years before their second child, a daughter, Catherine, was born.

Life at Leigh Court was idyllic. So much so that Julia Leigh often felt afraid that so much happiness was being given her. The children were strong and healthy, the Major and Lady Grace were happy, even though Grace was growing frailer with each winter. They enjoyed their grandchildren and if Helen's absence from their lives pained them, they never spoke of it. Louise had bought a pony for John and was already teaching the little lad to ride, boasting that he had a marvellous seat. 'The child is a natural, an absolute natural' she told the Major delightedly.

Julia had only one complaint and that was that John worked too hard. He wore himself out, caring for the sick of the parish and his fame had spread so that he was called out to visit people in Wexford and even further afield. John drove out in all weathers and no distance was too far for him to travel. The plight of the poor people tormented him and he complained bitterly to Julia, often sitting late into the night, his head in his hands telling her of the dreadful conditions the people were enduring.

'There's no decent sanitation in the town Julia, it's a wonder there's not more typhoid about, especially in the hot weather, and tuberculosis is rampant. At least country folk are not living in such crowded conditions, they have a slightly better chance.' He did what he could for their own tenants, seeing to it that their housing conditions were improved and giving them attention and medicines without charge when they were sick. The Major complained now and then that John was bankrupting the family and squandering his inheritance. But he approved of what his son was doing and so did Lady Grace.

On New Year's Eve 1899, a party was held at Leigh Court.

'We have to mark the beginning of the new century' the Major said, and John agreed that indeed they must throw a lavish party and invite everyone on the estate. 'Everyone must come Julia, we must signal the beginning of a whole new era. A time of great change and we will be in at the birth. We will let it be seen that Leigh Court is in the forefront of the new age.'

His enthusiasm was infectious and everyone including the servants set to with a will. It was years since they had entertained on such a lavish scale and the old house seemed to preen itself on the night as the people arrived. The lights could be seen for miles around and the sound of music welcomed the guests as the string quartet John had hired for the night started up in the front hallway.

Bridie Walshe and Mary Deegan had excelled themselves and some of the local women had been cc-opted in to lend a hand. Hynes the butler, his eyes sparkling, rejuvenated, like the old house, for the night announced each guest as they arrived. And Julia standing bcside John and the Major, with Lady Grace seated in front, welcomed each one, people she knew and those she didn't know, delighted to see such diverse company mingling under one roof. Whatever about tomorrow, tonight they were all one at Leigh Court. When the chimes rang out and the cheering started, John Leigh kissed Julia, she could hardly make out what he was saying over the din; but she knew he was making a toast to the New Year and the New Century.

Chapter 24

'The old queen is in failing health, we may soon have a new king to rule England. Wouldn't it be prophetic if this should happen in the early years of the new century?'

John was talking about his favourite subject and Julia, sitting at his feet mesmerised by the flickering fire-light was trying to stay awake to listen to his words.

'Ireland will get Home Rule now and we will be able to build up a new economy if England's stranglehold on our foreign trade eases. The workers in England have banded together in a strong union movement and the Irish worker will do likewise.

'Why, in Dublin the Union is growing by leaps and bounds and it won't be long until it moves out to the smaller towns. When people realise that unity is their strongest weapon against the injustices meted out to them by the ruling class they will flock to join the unions and the employers will have to accept it.'

Even still it surprised Julia to hear her husband talk like this. She wondered where he got his understanding and love for the poor working people. But then she remembered the quiet thoughtful boy he had been. Walking around beside the Major, John Leigh had said little, but he had seen much that gave him food for thought and helped to ally his sensitive soul with the people who suffered so much from poverty and ignorance, even here on his father's estate. His time in England practising medicine in a hospital that serviced one of the most depressed areas in the world, the East end of London, had further opened his eyes and his heart to the plight of his fellow men.

'I want to do what Count Tolstoy has already done in Russia. After my father's time, when the estate is in my name; I intend to give each man the right to purchase his own bit of land. I want to help the people to become self sufficient, if they work together and cooperate they can make at least this little part of the country a beacon light for the rest. We don't need all this land Julia, our children can be educated and learn to earn their own living. I plan to set up a proper practice, maybe even build a small hospital in the area, entice a few more doctors to join me. We could research, given the proper conditions and funds, maybe even eradicate some of the worst diseases. I know myself, if the people had proper housing and sanitation we would not have such a dreadful mortality rate, especially amongst the children and young people.'

Julia turned her head so that she could watch John's face. His beloved features looked flushed in the glow from the fire and his eyes were shining and animated.

'You should enter parliament yourself John' she said.

John shook his head: 'No, no Julia, I would be useless. My struggle is here with the people, doing what little I can'.

'You are doing more than a little John, already you have transformed the lives of most of the people on the estate, except for those who are too stubborn or ignorant to listen to you. The women are looking after themselves much more now and they are starting to call you out to the difficult births. See how they bring the infants to your rooms in Ballyleigh, more and more every week?'

John had taken a house in the village and opened a clinic for mothers and babies on certain afternoons each week. He sighed heavily. 'It's just a drop in the ocean Julia, painfully slow. Sometimes I feel I am taking one step forward and two steps back. But all I can do is my best, what was that Chinese proverb you read out the other day for me: 'Better to light a candle than sit and curse the dark'.'

'Yes John, that was in the book of verse you gave me for Christmas; I am so enjoying it. Listen; here's another couplet; Chinese too:

'*I saw you coming down the western road,*
and my heart laid down its load'.'

'Beautiful my darling.' John repeated the words softly: 'Beautiful, and how apt; my heart laid down its load the instant I saw you. We will live to see a new Ireland my dear, a whole new world.'

Julia shivered suddenly and John was immediately filled with concern. 'Look at me keeping you sitting here when you should be getting your rest. Are you cold darling?'

'No.' Julia was getting to her feet reluctantly. 'No John; someone has walked over my grave.'

John Leigh roared with laughter until Julia shushed him in case he would wake the sleeping baby.

'Oh, Julia. You're such a strange mixture; ancient Chinese couplets one minute and the next you are talking nonsense and old wives' tales. Better get to bed my dear, our little girl will be awake at dawn, demanding to be fed,' and he hugged Julia to him, still grinning as she opened her mouth to defend herself.

On her birthday at the end of January, John Leigh gave Julia a small gold locket, beautifully engraved with their initials intertwined. As she exclaimed over it, complaining as usual that it was far too expensive a gift, he stroked the side of her face with his finger and then lifting her chin, bent and kissed her gently.

'Julia, my Julia; nothing in the world is too good for you. I could never begin to tell you what you mean to me, how you transformed my life'.

'Why John, those are the words I should be saying to you, without you I would have no life, you gave me life when I was dead, how could I ever thank you?'

'By living, my love, just living your life, that's all the thanks I would ever want.'

Julia was remembering his conversation that night as she carefully cut both their faces from a photograph, the first one they had ever had taken on an afternoon in London, on one of those Halcyon days that were fast taking on a dream-like quality as time went by. She pressed the two tiny scraps of paper into the locket and closed it, then kissing it she fastened it round her neck. Dear John, he was growing even more thoughtful; if that was possible.

Early in February the annual shoot began on Kerrigan's land. The Major never took part, even before the trouble with Helen; his health had become too precarious for such pastimes and he spent more and more time in his study, poring over old papers and books. John often remarked that he believed the Major was refusing to enter the twentieth century, preferring to stay with his memories.

From early morning the guns could be heard and late into the evening.

Towards the end of the week the baby, who was teething, had kept Julia awake most of the night before, so when John asked if she felt like taking a walk in Kerrigan's wood before evening closed in, she declined, saying that she was too tired to try to move outdoors, so he set off alone for his evening stroll. The light was already fading and a faint outline of the moon was appearing as John strode through the woods. The crisp crackle of frozen twigs and leaves under his feet and the cawing of the rooks at the White Cross, the only sounds, with now and then the report of a lingering, persistent hunter, still determined to add to his bag.

John paused to enjoy the view from the rise, it was a calm evening but a wind was rising, its edge razor sharp with the threat of frost yet to come. John pulled up his coat collar and turned to head back. Then on an impulse, he left the path and made for Kerrigan's pond, where he had first seen Julia. Reaching the little clearing, he stood still and looked out over the dark silent waters. Cold and forbidding, with the hoar frost already starching the surrounding grass and the lowering sky touching the tops of the silent trees, ghost-like in the gathering gloom. Yet John could close his eyes and see her again, his silver maiden, glowing and shining with moon dust dripping from her slender frame.

Suddenly a single shot ripped the silence asunder and John Leigh fell forward onto the frost hard ground and lay without movement. A stain spread out across his coat under his left shoulder, black on black and the rooks rose from the white oak in a mad frenzy of sound.

Julia was putting baby Catherine in her crib, little John watching from the doorway, when the shaking began. Laying the infant down carefully, she wrapped her arms around herself and moaned softly, she was suddenly freezing, and then the tears started; 'Oh no! Oh God no, John, John!' Julia's cries brought the little boy to her side, his eyes wide and anxious, thinking it was his name she was calling. Julia knelt and grabbed him to her and his little arms went round her neck.

Later that night as the men carried her husband's body up the driveway of Leigh Court, Julia stood dry-eyed, watching their approach.

'I see you coming, my darling, but my heart will never again be able to lay down it's load. I will be strong John, I promise you. I will never give in to the darkness, not as long as I have breath left to breath'.

She went through the wake and the funeral, white faced but composed, taking the hands that were offered; consoling the Major and Lady Grace, who was too over-come with grief to leave her bed.

The whole neighbourhood was shocked and numbed by John's death. It was rumoured that Luke Kerrigan had been found wandering in Kerrigan's wood, blind drunk and that his gun was found near John Leigh's dead body, but the official verdict was that by a cruel and unfair twist of fate a freak bullet from the shoot fired by a person unknown had taken the life of Dr. John Leigh.

Helen Leigh arrived at the big house the day after the funeral and demanded to see the Major. Ignoring his haggard appearance she started in immediately he entered the room. 'You must sign everything over to me at once Father and I will take control. It is unthinkable that that woman and her brats could lay claim to the Leigh estates; don't forget she is catholic and so are her children. I know my brother gave in to her in this as in everything else. I have been well informed over the years.'

The Major sat at his desk, his head in his hands, hardly aware of what she was saying. Helen stopped suddenly, a cunning look on her sharp features: 'Father, you look worn out, let me get you a drink.' She turned to the sideboard and poured some whiskey from a cut glass decanter. Handing her father the glass, she paused, her hand on his shoulder. 'You need someone to see to things, you will have to take care of Mother, and Lou-Lou is useless. Julia has the children to care for. Let us bury the past and only think of one another.'

'Yes, yes,' the Major agreed, thankful that Helen was doing the decent thing at last. Thank God she was rowing in. Well she was a Leigh after all.

'I will pack some things and move here for a while, just until you are all stronger again.'

'Yes do Helen. So glad to have you,' the Major caught her hand, tears standing in his eyes and Helen made herself smile at him consolingly.

One week later Helen Leigh faced Julia across the same desk, her face hard and bitter in the early morning light.

'You will be provided for of course, but you can see that it is impossible for you and your children to stay under this roof. Without my brother's protection, you would not be accepted. I have seen to it that you will be paid a monthly allowance and I have made over three properties in Wexford to you. The rent to be paid to you to support your children. I would like you to sign this paper, giving up all claim to Leigh Court and the estate in return for these settlements. Otherwise I will have no choice but to throw you out with nothing. Think of your children my dear, and do the decent thing.'

Julia looked back at her, the depth of the hatred in the other woman's eyes almost physically wounding her. 'What does the Major say about this?' she asked, keeping her voice level.

'This is all in accordance with my father's and mother's wishes' Helen answered. 'Now sign'

Julia took the pen and signed her name, knowing that she would never be allowed to stay at Leigh Court, Helen would fight her in every court in the land and with all the weight of the family behind her. She knew also that the Major and Lady Grace were too devastated by John's death to try to stand up to Helen, even if they wanted to.

'I want no money,' she said, her voice coldly determined. 'The house for the children and myself to live in and the rent for John's and Catherine's upbringing, yes, but I will work to support myself as I have always done. I will take from this house only what I own and I will be gone before nightfall.'

Without looking at Helen she turned quietly and left the room.

The coach carrying Julia and the children, a bag with her few possessions and another with the children's clothes, pulled away from the front door and headed off down the driveway as the night closed in around the big house. Julia sat with the baby on her knee and little John opposite, wrapped in a rug. She had not been allowed to even say goodbye to Major Leigh and Lady Grace. The staff had stood, tearful and frightened when she went to say her farewells. Bridge Walshe whispered that she would see her soon as Julia kissed her old friend. Now, her face pale but resolute and her eyes on the road ahead, she left Leigh Court forever.

Julia was twenty-five years old and already she felt she had lived two lifetimes.

Chapter 25

A thousand times during the dark night that followed, Julia regretted her hasty flight and upbraided herself for not thinking of what faced her. And a thousand times she thanked God for Bridie Walshe's foresight in pressing her to take with her a basket of food and provisions.

Even Lonegan felt sorry for her as he helped to carry her scant luggage into the dark hallway of the little house in Crown Street.

It was obvious that the place had been uninhabited for quite some time and the dank smell of must and mould that greeted them when the door was opened almost made Julia's stomach turn. The second doorway led into a small kitchen with a black, open hearth and a table and two rotten looking chairs. A rough dresser against the wall with a few pieces of filthy delph hanging crookedly and some mouldy logs beside the hearth completed the furnishing.

'Begod Missus, you'll have to light up a fire or them two children will be perished before morning.' Tom Lonegan tipped his cap back on the back of his head and with uncharacteristic generosity offered to help.

'A fire. Yes.' Julia had been wondering where in God's name to begin. If she thought for one minute that she would be let back into Leigh Court, even for a few days while she tried to make this place habitable, she would have climbed back into the coach and begged Helen Leigh for some sort of mercy, but she knew she would be wasting her time and her energy. Helen had at last rid Leigh Court of the woman she considered the usurper; and her children.

There was no going back, and Jem and Nellie had no room. Maybe she should send the children back with Lonegan and ask him to bring them to her brother's home.

The little boy was crying now, his arms around her legs. He stood, afraid to move, calling for his Papa. No! She would keep them with her.

Rummaging in the basket Bridie had pressed on her, she found what she had prayed would be there, three candles tied together with string.

Lonegan produced a box of matches from his pocket and handed it to her without a word.

Julia lit one of the candles and stood it carefully on the table, she took John into her arms. Thankfully the baby was sleeping peacefully in the little crib she had brought with her.

Lonegan disappeared and when he returned he had the rugs from the coach with him. 'Here'. He thrust them at her roughly 'Them children need these. I don't care what the other wan says.'

Julia shushed the little boy and sat him on one of the chairs. 'You have to be a big boy now, and brave. We are going to have an adventure like the one in your book. This is the prince's castle . . . '.

'All black now, because of the wicked witch's spell.' John interrupted her, his eyes wide with excitement.

'Out of the mouth of children' Lonegan muttered. 'The wicked witch is right' and he disappeared into the dark hallway again.

'Yes, black now, but tomorrow you and I will make it beautiful again . .' Julia said.

'And live here happily ever after,' the little fellow interrupted again, clapping his hands delightedly.

'Yes,' Julia turned away so he would not see the tears in her eyes.

Lonegan came in again, with an armful of dry kindling and sticks. Julia could not even guess where he had found them . . . he knelt down at the hearth and started to light the fire.

'There's a water faucet out the back Missus, and there's a kettle. Give it a good rinse out and fill it, I won't be long getting this going'.

Julia did as he told her, finding a tap in a little lean-to off the kitchen. When she returned the fire was already blazing and Lonegan was breaking up an old stool. 'I found this in the other room, it's dry anyhow and it will keep the fire going for you; you'll be alright in the morning, at least you'll be able to see what's what. I'll have to be getting back before I'm missed.'

'Thank you Tom, I won't forget your kindness to me this night.'

Lonegan nodded gruffly: 'You wouldn't leave a dog in this place without doing something for it.' He left this time, slamming the door after him and Julia took off her coat and rolled up her sleeves, not giving herself time to think of her position. She had two children to look after; they had to be protected and made as comfortable as possible. She took the cloth covering the basket and laid in on the table without even trying to clean the dirt off it; everything would need scrubbing tomorrow. For now she would do what she could.

Later, when the children were fed and asleep, John in a makeshift bed on the floor, Julia sat at the fire which was still glowing with the last of the wood. The room was warm, at least the windows were intact. The little house, what she could see of it, seemed sound enough, if filthy, damp and neglected. Now that the children were looked after and she had time to think, the darkness began to try to take over her mind and she found herself beginning to shake uncontrollably.

Standing up she started to pace the floor, talking to herself in undertones, so as not to disturb the sleeping children.

'Now Julia girl, you cannot afford the luxury of giving in to this nonsense. You have two children depending on you, and you owe it to your husband's memory to stand up and live . . . Oh John, John,' she stuffed her knuckles into her mouth, trying to stifle the sobs. 'No, none of this.'

It was as if there were two people under her skin and in her head and not one. Most of the night the argument went on, until sometime in the small hours Julia lay down, totally exhausted, pulling her coat over her, she slept the sleep of the dead.

The baby's cries woke her next morning and as she fed the infant she took stock of her surroundings.

The house was sound alright but she would need money to make it habitable. Why had she refused the allowance Helen Leigh had offered? Her anger and stupid pride would cost her and the children dear. What would she do when the last of the food in Bridie's basket was gone? She would have to turn to Jem for assistance until she sorted herself out.

The sun was shining through the dirty window pane and Julia chose to look at it's rays dancing and to ignore the dismal dirt of her surroundings. The baby settled and John munching on some bread and honey, she raked out the fire, delighted to find a little glow at its heart.

Following Lonegan's example of the night before, she went foraging and to her delight found quite a decent mound of turf outside the back door. Thank God, I was never afraid of hard work, Julia thought, as she set to with a will. Little John helping to make the castle shiny, followed her around, busily getting in her way but she was glad to see him so engrossed.

As she lost herself in scrubbing and cleaning, working in the old familiar way, doing things she had not engaged in for years, Julia's spirit started to lift until she realised with a start, sometime around mid afternoon, that she was beginning to feel a sort of happiness she had not experienced since John's death. Feeling almost guilty, she paused where she knelt, on the floor of the tiny kitchen. Suddenly it was as if she heard John's voice: 'Live my dear. Live, that's all I want you to do.'

'I will John,' she answered, her voice loud in the little room. 'Oh I will, I promise you.'

That evening, as little John and herself finished off the last of the provisions, Julia knew there was a God and one who had her welfare well and truly in hand.

She jumped with fright as a loud knocking echoed through the house. It must be Tom Lonegan back to see if we survived the night she thought as she went hesitantly to the front door.

It was not Tom Lonegan, but Bridie Walshe who stood in the doorway and she caught Julia in a bear-hug when she opened the door. The coach from Leigh Court stood on the roadway with Lonegan sitting on the driving seat, staring straight ahead. When Julia managed to disentangle herself, she drew Bridie into the hall, asking in amazement how she managed to get time off to come and visit so soon.

'Well, that's it Julia my love. I have all the time in the world off. I left! Walked out. I don't care' she said defiantly, as Julia's face registered shock. 'I won't stay under the same roof with that vixen'.

'What about the Major and Lady Grace?,' Julia asked.

'The Major deserves what he gets for letting her do what she did to you and the children and Armstrong will look after her ladyship. Of course Louise won't miss any of us; won't even notice that we are gone.'

'What are you going to do Bridie? Where will you go?'.

'Well that's up to you, my dear'. Bridie Walshe's voice wavered and she looked at Julia hopefully. 'I have my money, I saved plenty over the years. Thank God I still have my health and I can do my bit. If you'll have me I'll stay here with you and the children and we can work something out between us; that's if you'll have me'.

'Oh, Bridie.' Julia threw her arms around the little fat figure, crying and laughing at the same time. 'If I'll have you; the good God sent you in answer to my prayers.'

Bridie allowed herself to be hugged and kissed, her face wreathed in smiles. 'Well, my girl' she said at last, pushing Julia away, 'I have been called many things in my day, but never an answer to prayer. Stop your nonsense now.' She surveyed the hallway with a jaundiced eye, her hands on her ample hips. 'I can see we have plenty of hard work ahead of us; tell that good for nothing Lonegan to carry in my things, so that I can get my apron. Is the kettle boiling? There's a box of provisions on the floor of the coach; get the tea like a good girl, I can do nothing without a good strong cup of tea.' She bustled down the hall, crowing with delight when John, coming to see what the commotion was, threw himself into her arms.

'Well my own lamb, my little soldier. And did you think I would leave you here without me to look after you?'

'It's a castle Bridie, a prince's castle, we have to make it shine.'

'And so we will my own little mannie, so we will'.

Julia watched as they went into the kitchen hand in hand and then she blessed herself. 'Thank you God, you are there after all'.

She smiled up at Tom Lonegan, who coughed and shot a stream of tobacco juice out the corner of his mouth. 'Begod, it never took Julia Whelan long to fall on her feet; a cute hoor that wan.' Lonegan would not have admitted, even under torture, that he had ever lifted a hand to help Mick Whelan's brat. 'Deserves all she gets, looking to rise to places she had no right to be, and the auld Walshe wan runnin' to join her.'

But even as he growled, Lonegan knew she was luckier than those who remained at Leigh Court under the rule of iron Helen Leigh was already imposing.

Part 3

Chapter 26
WEXFORD 1905

There were quite a few people taking the air on Wexford's Quays. People liked to promenade along the wooden-works on Sunday mornings after Mass. It was particularly pleasant on late spring and early summer days when the docks were quiet and peaceful and the fresh breeze off the sea brought a bloom to the cheeks and blew away the tiredness of the week's work.

Mothers were careful to keep their children from the edge, it was too easy to fall into the water and Julia Leigh kept a weather eye on John and Catherine.

John was tall with his father's dark hair and pale skin, a serious eight year old boy; too serious by far. Julia often longed to see him running free like the other lads on the street, but John preferred to stick his head in a book or spend his time indoors industriously writing or sticking cut-outs into his scrap book.

Catherine on the other hand, a pudgy little girl who followed her brother everywhere, like a lap dog, was never serious, her good humoured face smiling or on the brink of a smile at all times.

Julia worried about her son, wondering if the sudden move from his former life of luxury at Leigh Court had damaged him in some way. But Bridie Walshe wouldn't hear of this idea, saying he was his father's son and highly intelligent with too much sense to go gadding about the streets with the rough neighbourhood boys.

This morning it was Catherine who insisted on straying out to the very edge to look at the waves. Julia was taking them to the Crescent Quay to join the crowds of young people fishing for crabs. Bridie had shooed them out when they came back from Bride Street Church: 'I'll take care of the dinner; you go and get some fresh air into your lungs. Off with you now and don't come back here before one o'clock or I won't let you in.'

John and Catherine joined the children already lying flat at the quayside, pieces of string baited with bits of bread or whatever scraps they could find, dangling into the murky waters, waiting hopefully for the quarry to clasp the bait, when, with much squealing and shrieking, the crab would be hoisted ashore and dropped into a waiting jar or can. John carefully tied the bait to Catherine's string and saw to it that his little sister was safely back far enough from the edge before getting himself settled. The children had no jar, John would not allow Catherine to actually keep a crab. If they were fortunate enough to make a catch, it had to be returned safely to the water after being examined minutely and scrutinised carefully. Catherine was never too happy to see her crab dropped back over the edge and allowed to scuttle off into hiding on the mucky sea floor, but John insisted it would be cruel and pointless to keep the crab; nobody at home would eat it and unless she was prepared to do so it must be set free.

The little girl reluctantly agreed to her brother's line of reasoning; as she usually did.

Julia joined the other adults on the low wall skirting the semi-circular inlet. She closed her eyes, breathing in the tangy air. The children were safe now, she could relax and enjoy the beautiful June morning. Dressed in the usual sombre black which she had adopted after John's death, her dark hair peppered with grey, Julia looked older than her thirty years. Bridie Walshe was forever taking her to task about her 'widow's weeds,' as she disparagingly called the black clothes Julia favoured.

When are you going to get out of that mourning garb?' she scolded, urging her to go out a little more and make some friends. But Julia was quite happy as she was. She had the children and Bridie and her good job in Behan's Drapery Shop in North Main Street where she did the books and looked after the accounts, working the full week from eight a.m. to six p.m., with half day Saturday and Sundays off. She had her beloved books and now and then she bought a ticket for a variety show or a touring opera when one came to the Theatre Royal. She had even seen two moving pictures over the last year or so, but the latter were not really to her liking. She knew very well the other women and girls at work considered her stand-offish, but this did not bother her in the least. Julia liked her solitude. She never visited Ballyleigh. Not since that night, five years ago now, when she fled from Leigh Court and all it contained. Her life in the big house was like a dream, hazy and unclear. She often wondered about this; if it was a deliberate trick of the mind to avoid painful memories or if that was how it was for everyone as they grew older? Her youth in the little cottage at the edge of Kerrigan's wood grew fresher as time went by, indeed her memory painted it in vivid colours, leaving out the harsher realities and only highlighting the good times.

'Time tinges everything with a rosy hue, especially when we want it to' Bridie remarked when Julia discussed it with her. John Leigh she carried in her heart so he was never far from her thoughts. She never asked about Leigh Court and when Jem or Nellie visited she discouraged any talk of the big house, preferring to bury that part of her life and leave it. Now and then she caught a glimpse of Helen Leigh or Luke Kerrigan on Wexford's streets or in a shop, but she hastily averted her face, unsure if they would even remember her and not wanting to risk finding out.

The moneys from the rent of the two other houses she allowed to accumulate for John's and Catherine's education when they needed it. Her own wages and Bridie's contribution were adequate for their simple life style.

Most of all Julia liked her new independence, which had been hard won.

During the first few years in Crown Street, she fought her depression and misery and learned, inch by painful inch, to stand on her own feet and plan her own destiny. She realised now, with hindsight, that she had been totally dependant on John. She had often told him he was her life and this was so to such a degree that his death had left her like a plant deprived of food and water; incapable of sensible thought or action. But for the presence of Bridie Walshe and the motherly love and care she bestowed on all three of them, Julia doubted if she would have made it through that terrible time. Bridie encouraged her to go out, to look for employment after their first year in the town. She insisted that Julia look further than housekeeping or cooking and menial jobs and made her apply for the position in Behan's, it was advertised in the weekly paper.

'You can read and write with the best of them and you have a great head for the figures.'

To her surprise, after being interviewed by the owner and in spite of the fact that she had no papers to show, Julia was offered the job at twelve shillings a week and a special discount to purchase goods in the store.

'I like the cut of your jib ma'am.' Barnabas Behan, the slightly unorthodox and highly eccentric proprietor of Behan's High Class Drapery and Ladies' Outfitters told her after listening to her answers to his questions, his head on one side and his pocket watch, to which he referred now and then, in his hand.

Barnabas was a fair and kind employer and his staff were happier than most workers in the town. Although he had never been further than the Quays, or for a brief Sunday sail up the river with a friend, he adopted a nautical air and turn of phrase. That and his preoccupation with the time of day and the state of the weather gave rise to much merriment on the part of the townspeople. But Julia liked him and her four years in his employ had helped her to grow in self confidence. So on this sunny June morning, as she sat on Wexford's quayside, she presented a slightly prim picture of a young widow, a little withdrawn perhaps, still mourning the loss of her husband, but tranquil and serene for all that.

The children's interest in crabs exhausted, they wondered home, watching the ships riding on the tide at their moorings and the gulls wheeling and soaring in off the water and up over the slate grey buildings of the three-tiered town.

Julia had grown to love Wexford. It held all the delights and comforts of town life, while at it's edges it meandered off into countryside. One could walk quite easily out along leafy lanes or take a boat across to Ferry-bank or an excursion train to Rosslare on Sunday afternoons.

St. Brigid's band often marched out on Sundays too or gave a brief recital in one of the church yards and there were G.A.A. matches and touring shows and now there was talk of a new picture house to show moving pictures all week long.

When the children turned the corner they started to run and Julia saw her brother Jem's trap outside the house in Crown Street.

Strange for Jem to visit on Sunday, and unannounced. Usually Nellie and himself called when they were in town for the monthly groceries. On Fair Day when Jem had business buying or selling, he sometimes called. He had his own small holding, bought with money scrimped and saved during his years at Leigh Court. He was glad to be out of there, he told Julia and she suspected that Helen Leigh Kerrigan had made it impossible for him to stay the stables after her own departure.

She entered the kitchen to find Jem with Catherine already seated on his knee. He looked up and smiled and Julia's heart settled back to it's normal pace. Even after all this time she suspected the worst, a habit that would probably stay with her for the rest of her life, she thought ruefully.

'What brings you to town on such a fine morning?' she asked after greeting her brother.

'I'm off to the match in the park; have you forgotten; Wexford are playing today?' Julia had forgotten, if she had ever known in the first place. She had little or no interest in athletics, she supposed that was why young John hadn't either.

'He has sandwiches. Did you ever hear the like? As if we couldn't give him a bite to eat. Keep the sandwiches and sit in with us to the dinner.' Bridie Walshe bustled around. Busy as ever though she must be galloping up to the seventy, Jem Whelan thought, watching her dishing up the Sunday meal.

As he finished eating, Jem turned to Julia, a serious look on his face. 'I know you don't like me to mention Leigh Court, but you will hear it soon enough. The Major is poorly. They don't expect him to last the week.'

Julia shook her head and then motioned him into the front room. She never talked about the Leighs nor allowed anyone else to do so in front of the children. As she closed the parlour door she said in a low voice: 'It was good of you to tell me, you meant well I know, but it is nothing to me. When Lady Grace died they never told me and my letter to the Major went unanswered. Since they professed no interest in me or the children since I left, I have taken it that they don't wish to know us. We have a new life now, Catherine does not remember anything other than the home here and I don't think John does either. I tell them about their father, that he was a doctor and a good man and that's enough. I will pray for the Major, I bear him no ill will. He did what he had to do, but I will never set foot in Leigh Court again and neither will my children. I hope you understand.'

'I do Julia, I don't blame you. You're better out of it and from all I hear so will the Major be when God calls him. The Helen wan gets madder every day'.

Julia held up her hand. 'Please Jem.'

'I'm sorry, I know how you feel. I'll say no more.

'I'll be off now. I don't want to miss the start of the match. Thanks for the dinner, Mrs. Walshe is still the best cook in the country'.

'Give my love to Nellie and Sadie. Tell Estelle we are all looking forward to having her for the holidays and bring the boys to visit; if they'll come, that is.'

'I will if I can catch them' Jem laughed, then shouting his goodbyes, he joined the men on the street, all hurrying in the same direction, bound for the big match.

Chapter 27

Late in the afternoon, Julia put on her light coat and a straw hat and headed out again. Bridie Walshe was snoozing in the front room, her glasses on the end of her nose and her book of recipes, the only book she ever bothered to read, open on her lap. The children were in the back yard, Catherine busy with her dolls and John poring over a book.

Julia called a cheery goodbye, saying she would be back in an hour or two and telling them not to disturb Bridie's rest. Then she made her way out onto the sunlit street, closing the front door behind her.

Heading up Distillery Road and past Pierces foundry, Julia drank in the air eagerly.

'You can take the girl out of the country, but you'll never take the country out of the girl.' She smiled, remembering the words Bridie often quoted at her in winter when she paced up and down the front room like a caged lion. She usually ended up braving the elements and walking in the rain and wind; sometimes even sleet and snow. Julia found it impossible to stay indoors, but walking on pavements in town was a very poor substitute for rambling through Kerrigan's wood listening to the wind rushing through the tree-tops or lashing the storm clouds before it and throwing thunder at the distant hills. During the late winter and early spring, she spent her weekends in the fields at the top of the Rocks Road, the children in tow. When they reached the meadows at the summit of the road, with its breathtaking view back down over the town and out over the harbour as far as the eye could see, Julia forgot she was the mother and soon there were three children racing free through the tall grass and climbing the rocks and ditches.

This afternoon the air was still; the sky blue and cloudless. Julia strode out until she came to the end of the town and then she slowed down to a gentle stroll, removing her hat and opening her coat. She had left the last of the walkers well behind her and she had the countryside to herself. The ditches glowed with wildflowers. The white stitchwort and the golden celandine, blue veronica and purple foxglove making a rich tapestry, with dog roses and wild violets running rampant. The scent of the wild woodbine and brilliant yellow furze vied with one another for supremacy on the shimmering air. Julia stood enraptured, her eyes closed she turned around and around on the country road, intoxicated with the look and the feel of it all.

Such largesse, she thought, nature parades herself without shame, like a strumpet in love with life.

How good it would be to be able to dive headlong into Kerrigan's pond, or better still into the wide ocean and swim and swim forever.

Julia threw her arms into the air and laughed with the sheer joy of it all. Then running across the road she climbed the far ditch as quickly as she could, hampered by her long skids. The green and gold fields stretched back down, like a chequer board, and the town, shimmering and swaying in the haze of heat rising, its twin spires pointing heavenward. The waters of the estuary and the harbour beyond merged with the sky, palest aquamarine, and the clouds were hills and mountains on the blue bruised horizon.

> *'I will arise and go now and go to Innisfree,*
> *and a small cabin build there*
> *of clay and wattles made.*
> *Nine bean rows will I have there,*
> *a hive for the honey-bee,*
> *and live alone in the bee-loud glade.'*

She spoke the lines of her favourite poem. Somehow she had to release the pent up feelings that threatened to blow her head right off her shoulders, surrounded as she was by so much beauty.

She paused now, drinking in the scene before her.

Suddenly a voice behind her continued:

> *'And I shall have some peace there,*
> *for peace comes dropping slow,*
> *dropping from the veils of morning*
> *to where the cricket sings.'*

Julia turned slowly, wishing the ground would open and swallow her. Her face flaming, she looked down at the man standing on the road. She was struck dumb.

Aware of the spectacle she must present, perched on top of the ditch, her coat hanging off, her hair falling around her flushed face, quoting poetry. All the wonderful joy and exuberance drained away like water through a colander and she was a mad woman, wild and witless.

He was leaning on a walking cane, a tall figure, bare headed and dressed in black. His head on one side he gazed up at her, a smile beginning around his mouth.

'Yeats; what a poet, and that's my favourite poem, would I be right in thinking it's yours too?'

Julia tried to clamber down without falling on her behind and compounding her total embarrassment. She clutched her coat around her and clamped the hat firmly onto her head. Pulling herself up to her full height and still wishing she could disappear, she cleared her throat and opened her mouth. When no sound emerged, she closed it again, firmly. Her tormentor continued to gaze at her. Now that she was standing on the roadway, he was looking down. He was quite a tall man, well over six feet. Julia had the feeling she had seen him somewhere before and her fervent hope was that she would never see him again.

'I beg your pardon, ma'am. I had no wish to startle you. But seeing your obvious enjoyment of the view and hearing you quote from my favourite poet; I couldn't resist the urge to join in.'

His voice sounded serious enough, but Julia couldn't help feeling she was being laughed at. She looked up at him sharply and tried out her voice again.

'You gave me quite a turn, I climbed up to pick some woodbine and I thought I was quite alone. I don't usually go around the countryside speaking poetry out loud you know?'

'More's the pity ma'am, more's the pity.' He was laughing at her, she was sure of it.

'I must be getting home now, please excuse me.'

Gathering what she could of her shredded dignity, she turned and set off determinedly down the road.

'Excuse me ma'am; Mrs. Leigh isn't it? I should have introduced myself. I am Pat Vernon, one of your tenants I think. I live in number fifty six Crown Street.'

Julia paused. She never touched the monies from the two houses. She knew nothing of the arrangements.

He had taken over on her and was walking at her side, his long stride clipped to match her slower gait.

'Oh yes, I knew I had seen you before; you often pass up and down, I think you must work in the foundry.'

'Indeed I do, I'm a fitter in Pierces, for my sins. I have seen you many times. You enjoy the opera, as indeed I do myself.'

Julia was slowly beginning to recover her composure, but only slowly. He was going to accompany her the whole way home, this was becoming obvious. There was no way she could get rid of him, no turn off on the straight road back into town. He strolled along at her side without a care in the world.

Imbecile, Julia thought, can't he see how embarrassed I am?

'I know you are widowed, as I myself am. I was not blessed with children as you are. I have had many conversations with your son John, a fine boy, and an intelligent lad. We share an interest in stamps.'

Julia looked at him in surprise. The cheek of the man, speaking to her in such a personal way and getting to know John without her permission.

'Indeed; John speaks to everyone on the street. He is a friendly boy' she said primly.

There was a short silence. Then he began again: 'I am a blunt man, Mrs. Leigh, I speak my mind. Life is too short for pretence. I have admired you for some years now and I am delighted to at last find myself in conversation with you. I have often wondered if I dare call on you but fate has been kind today and thrown us together.'

Julia stopped and turned to face him. 'How dare you speak to me like this, you are no gentleman. You crept up on me when I was, well, at a weak moment and now you are taking advantage of me. Please allow me to continue my walk unhindered. I have no wish to be accompanied.'

Her face was red with anger and if she was bigger she would have actually punched the despicable man.

'I most humbly apologise Mrs, Leigh for my forwardness. But you see I feel as though I know you'.

'Well you don't. Julia was nearly in tears, the traumatic events of the last while threatening to overcome her completely.

'I apologise yet again ma'am. He bowed slightly. 'Maybe at some future date you will allow me to call on you?'

'Never!' Julia flounced off ahead, leaving him standing, looking after her. Surely now he would have the manners to let her alone.

All the way into Crown Street she was conscious of his step on the road behind her and it seemed hours before she got into the shelter of her own hallway where she stood in the dimness trying to cool her flaming cheeks and calm her racing thoughts.

Call on her indeed! What a nerve the man had, and no manners whatsoever. Julia had certainly never met anyone like him before in her life.

Chapter 28

Pat Vernon was not a man to let the grass grow under his feet. On Monday evening after supper Julia heard a knock on the front door. She was sitting reading in the front parlour and before she made up her mind to answer it herself she heard Bridie making her way along the hall. It was unusual for them to have callers, especially on Monday at such a time and her curiosity was aroused as she heard the murmur of voices. Then Bridie appeared in the doorway, an impish grin on her face: 'You have a gentleman caller ma'am she announced in respectfully servile tones, winking broadly at the mystified Julia who rose as if to go into the hallway.

Before she had taken more than a few steps, a tall figure appeared behind Bridie Walshe.

'Mr. Patrick Vernon to see Mrs. Leigh' Bridie intoned, ushering him into the room and stepping out into the hall, she closed the door with a flourish.

Julia was nearly as flustered by his sudden appearance now as she had been on the previous day, but remembering her manners she held out her hand and bade him good evening.

'What can I do for you Mr. Vernon?' she asked, barely resisting the impulse to lift her hand to smooth her hair and straighten her collar.

'I came to see if I could make up for my gauche behaviour at our first meeting. I'm really not such a bad fellow, but I'm afraid I forgot my manners in my anxiety to speak to you. Won't you forgive me and give me another chance to get acquainted? I brought a book of poems you might like to see. It has Mr. Yeats' latest collection.' He held out a slim volume, looking, Julia noted, quite penitent and remorseful. So much so that she could not suppress a smile. Seeing her face, Pat Vernon sighed with such exaggerated relief that Julia could control herself no longer and she burst out laughing. At this he too began to laugh and soon the two of them were helplessly shaking, tears of merriment running down Julia's cheeks and his loud guffaws making Bridie, who had paused outside the door, shake her head in amazement.

Wiping her eyes, Julia nodded, barely able to talk with the effort to keep from laughing again.

'I forgive you. We have only met twice and on both occasions you have managed to take my breath away. Sit down and I will ask Bridie to get us some tea and we can talk to one another in a civilised manner. It seems I am going to have to get to know you, you are obviously not going to go away.'

Pat Vernon sat down, sticking his long legs out before him and managing to look totally out of place in the overstuffed armchair with the starched antimacassars on the back and arms. Julia left him there while she went to fetch some tea.

'Tea is it?' the grinning woman said in a wicked voice, 'Is that all you are going to offer the poor man and he having the courage to beard the lion in her den?'

'Bridie Walshe, behave yourself and put on the kettle, tea is good enough. You know I don't encourage anyone to drink anything stronger, certainly not under this roof.'

'Oh, all right, all right, don't go all high and mighty on me. Give the poor man a bit of encouragement won't you? It's about time you had a friend; a man friend, if you follow me'

'Not alone do I follow you Bridie, I'm ahead of you. Mr. Vernon is not a man friend, he is simply someone I met while out walking and he has kindly brought me a book to read. Now don't make any more out of it than that. And certainly not in front of the children.'

Bridie went to make the tea, still grinning and John, who was listening to the women's conversation, asked if he could go in and talk to his friend, Mr. Vernon.

'Certainly'. Julia was glad to see him show some interest, he had been listless all evening, complaining of a headache. Now Catherine wanted to meet the visitor too, so she trotted after her brother.

When Julia carried in the tray, John was showing Pat Vernon his stamp collection and Catherine was already sitting on his knee, her arm twined around his neck. This did not surprise her, apart from being a friendly child, any man who came into the house was immediately taken over by Catherine. She loved male company. He seemed quite at home with the children, answering John's many questions patiently and letting the little girl fix his collar and play with the large fob watch he took from his pocket.

Julia sat back and observed him silently. He was not a handsome man. His long pale face and receding hairline gave him an appearance which was not helped by the large walrus moustache adorning his upper lip. His hair was fair, turning to grey. It would be hard to know what age he was; early forties she guessed. He was quite well spoken, with a trace of a country accent noticeable at times. A well read man, probably self-educated, she thought, quite an interesting man.

As if sensing her scrutiny, he looked up and caught her eye.

'You have two lovely children Mrs. Leigh.'

'They are not too bad' Julia laughed, 'but I think it's time they went to bed now or they will not be able to get up for school tomorrow.'

'I don't think I am going to go to school Mama' John said. 'If my head is not better' This was so unlike John that Julia was worried. Usually he could not be kept from school for any reason. Julia put a hand to his head and was startled to feel how hot it was. He looked paler than usual too and Bridie said he had eaten nothing all day.

'Go to bed dear and I'll bring you some hot milk. If you are no better tomorrow we will have to see about getting you to the doctor.'

The children were never sick, apart from a chill now and then she had never had to worry about them. There was always a lot of illness about the town, especially during the summer months when fevers could spring up and turn into an epidemic. Julia made up her mind to have Bridie bring John to the doctor in the morning. Now the children made their goodnights and Julia promised to come and tuck them into their beds as she always did.

'You must come and see me again soon,' Catherine announced firmly as she reluctantly took leave of her new friend. 'Promise?'

'Oh I most certainly will' he said, looking over her head at Julia.

Much later in the night when she left him to the door, Julia realised she had not enjoyed anyone's company so much for longer than she could remember. She had talked to this man, who was a virtual stranger, telling him about herself and her life in Ballyleigh, even mentioning John; letting herself remember and speak of things buried deep in her memory for years. He in his turn spoke of his young wife who had died in childbirth after only two years of marriage, and how he had mourned the loss of both her and his little stillborn son for many years.

'I am not a religious man. I prefer to call myself a humanist' he told Julia. 'So I decided to dedicate myself to the betterment of society; especially Irish society, the working man in particular. We are trying to unionise the workers here in Wexford. Have you heard of the Union? You have; well some of us are organising. We want to see the Union established in the town and we have a tough fight on our hands.'

Julia listened, enthralled, to his quiet voice as he spoke of the plight of the poor people, the ordinary working men and their families, and how they were being exploited, to make the rich men richer. It was as if she could hear the echo of another voice which spoke of such matters with different words, but shared sentiments. When at last he rose to go, she felt she was waking from a long reverie, and when he asked if she would care to accompany him to a concert in the Theatre Royal the following evening, for which he just happened to have acquired two tickets, she agreed without hesitation.

'Thank you for a lovely evening, I don't know when I enjoyed myself so much Julia. I may call you Julia?'

She nodded.

'And you must call me Patrick, or Pat if you like.'

'I shall call you Patrick' Julia said shyly, 'I prefer Patrick.'

'Very well then, Patrick it is and I will call for you tomorrow night at seven thirty. Until then goodnight dear lady. I hope your son will be well, but I would advise you to have a doctor look him over. I have no wish to alarm you but there are cases of scarlet fever and meningitis in the town. Better to be sure than sorry.'

The following morning John seemed a little brighter, but Julia decided he must stay in bed. 'We will leave him another day and see how he gets on' Bridie Walshe said when Julia suggested they might call the doctor. As she cycled to work she hoped she had made the right decision. One did not like calling out a doctor if it was not really necessary. But when she arrived back at dinner time, John was again complaining of a bad headache and was flushed and feverish. Julia made up her mind. She would drop in to Dr. Roche's rooms on her way back to work and ask him to call later in the afternoon.

It was with some relief she heard Bridie's account of the doctor's visit when she got back to the house after work.

'He says the child is spending too much time at his books. He needs fresh air and outside activities. He gave me a bottle and John is sleeping soundly since shortly after I gave him the first spoonful.' Bridie was happy enough and when Julia looked in on her sleeping son he seemed peaceful.

'Still I won't go to the concert with Patrick Vernon. I would not like to go out again in case he needs me when he wakes up.'

'You will indeed Miss. This is the first time you have gone out with a friend, let alone a man-friend, since we came to live in this blessed town. Get yourself ready now and be off with you when the man calls. I am well able to look after Master John. I won't hear another word about it' and Bridie folded her arms across her chest and glared at Julia, defying her to speak again.

So Julia was ready and waiting when Patrick Vernon arrived at the door. They walked to the theatre through the balmy evening and enjoyed the concert of local talent which was, as Patrick said: 'Like the Parson's egg; good in spots.'

Later, walking home along the quiet streets, Julia felt totally at ease in his company. He is a kind man, she thought, and we seem to have a similar sense of humour, we laugh at the same things. I could grow to like this man, maybe we can be friends.' It would be good to have someone to talk to again.

Coming around the corner into Crown Street, her musings came to an abrupt end when she saw the coach outside her own house. Her heart racing, she started to run, Patrick loping along beside her. A distraught Bridie Walshe opened the door: 'Julia. Oh Julia, I thought you'd never come, I had to get Mr. Black next door to run for the doctor. The poor lamb is worse, he kept getting sick and he didn't know me. The doctor is with him now,' she sobbed.

Julia ran past her and up the stairs. Dr. Roche was in his shirt sleeves bending over the bed. She could hear John's voice, but she could not make out the words. The child was raving, his body tossing and thrashing, his eyes open and staring straight ahead with a glazed unseeing look.

'Oh My God. What is it, what's the matter with him?'

The doctor was holding a cold compress, trying to apply it to John's steaming forehead. 'It's a fever Mrs. Leigh, a bad fever. The temperature is dangerously high, I am afraid to move him until it breaks. Then I must get him to the infirmary. I think the child may have meningitis.'

'Oh no'. Julia dropped to her knees beside the bed, calling John's name and trying to hold him still, 'What can I do Doctor? Tell me what to do.'

'Keep applying cold water, sponge him over until the fever breaks. I will stay with you, we can do no more except pray'.

All through the night Julia knelt at John's side while he tossed and turned, muttering and moaning feverishly. People came and went in the little room and she was vaguely conscious of their presence. Towards dawn he seemed quieter and Dr. Roche urged her to take a rest: 'Go and take some tea, you are exhausted and the night is not over yet.'

Julia made her way downstairs, surprised to see Patrick sitting in the kitchen beside the settle, where Bridie Walshe slept worn out with grief and anxiety. He poured a cup of tea, putting it into her hands.

'Drink it Julia, you have to keep your strength up.'

Julia forced down the hot tea, shaking her head when he offered her some bread. She was freezing, shaking with the cold. 'Oh God no.'

Julia dropped the cup onto the floor where it smashed into pieces as the tears started. She turned and ran back up the stairs, Patrick Vernon close on her heels. As she entered the room the doctor was rising from his knees, shaking his head.

'I'm so sorry, Mrs. Leigh'

Julia stood looking down at the little body, lying still, his eyes closed.

The trembling was so violent she thought she would fall until someone took hold of her and held her in a strong grasp. She turned, tears blinding her and buried her face in Patrick Vernon's black jacket, her body racked with shuddering sobs.

Major John Leigh's obituary took up a full page in the local paper that week. He was laid to rest in the family grave at Ballyleigh with due pomp and ceremony. His grandson, John Leigh was buried quietly in a new grave in Crosstown Cemetery just a day later.

On an evening in late October, Julia Leigh and Patrick Vernon were married quietly in Bride Street Church. Julia's brother Jem and his wife and family, her sister Sadie and Estelle Whelan, Kitty's daughter, and Patrick's two bachelor brothers from Ballyerin came to share a meal with the bride and groom in the house in Crown Street.

Bridie Walshe, thinner now and quite feeble, insisted on cooking the meal. The couple did not go away together. Patrick had to work the following day, and there was an important meeting taking place that night which he was obliged to attend. The workers were determined to bring the Union to the town and Patrick and men like him were needed if they were to succeed.

Julia knew from the outset the pattern of her life with Patrick. She was his wife but his first love was the welfare and freedom of the working class.

Chapter 29

Two years after their marriage, Julia gave birth to twins, a boy and a girl. The boy was named John, the girl Elizabeth.

The following year she had another girl, Bridie, named for Bridie Walshe.

Her daughter, Catherine, loved the babies, which was just as well, because the little girl was happy to put away her dolls and help her mother to look after the growing family.

Bridie Walshe never really recovered from young John Leigh's death and she too had to be cared for. She spent her days sitting beside the kitchen fire, her once heavy frame shrunken and twisted with arthritis, but her quick wit and her sharp tongue had survived unscathed and she was still a force to be reckoned with.

Julia had changed too. If John Leigh had cosseted her and treated her like a piece of Dresden china, more like a beloved child to be sheltered and guarded from harsh reality, her second husband did none of this. Patrick Vernon was the third son of a poor tenant farmer, a man who could identify with Julia's former life in the cottage on the Leigh estate. An intelligent man, he had started work in Pierce's foundry at the tender age of thirteen years. He educated himself, learning to read and write in what little spare time he had and making use of the Reading Rooms set up in the town to help such men as himself. His disdain for the landed gentry was matched only by his hatred of England. His dream was freedom for the workers and freedom for Ireland. He had no time for the Redmondites and Home rule. In Patrick's mind there was only one way for men like himself to claim their birthright and that was to free Ireland of the yoke of tyranny and free the workers from the equally heavy yoke they laboured under, and revolution would achieve both these objectives, but not bloody revolution, there was a better way; the men must unite; stand together as a nation against the tyranny of English rule. He spent himself for both causes, working tirelessly to bring the Union to Wexford.

He was not a demonstrative man, nor was he given to polite conversation. Julia had no doubt that he loved her in his own way. He spoke so much at meetings that he liked to sit quietly during the brief spells he spent in his home. He treated her like an equal, something Julia grew to appreciate over the years. But he criticised her lack of interest in, or knowledge of, the affairs of her country. He talked to her of politics and the situation at home and abroad. He brought her papers and pamphlets and urged her to read them. She soon became familiar with the works of James Connolly and Jim Larkin and knew what was happening in the halls of Parliament in England and the cities and small towns of Ireland. The front parlour was stacked with books and papers. The house was constantly filled with men who had important matters to discuss with her husband. Julia accepted all this as part of her life with Patrick, but her own time was given to the rearing of her young family and the managing of the house. Money was scarce; she never touched the funds from her properties; never thought about it even. She had discussed it with Patrick shortly after the marriage but it was anathema for him to even think of using Leigh money or to have his wife and children do so.

Julia was happy enough, her days were full. Never one to shy away from hard work, she enjoyed the challenge presented to her to run the house and keep everyone fed and comfortable. More and more she returned to her country roots. First it was a few hens in the back yard, then she bought two young pigs from her brother and fed and fattened them in the garden. Proud of her achievements she drove them herself to Hill Street on Fair Day in July and sold them for a fine profit, buying two more banbhs and new outfits for the children with money to spare.

Her neighbours in Crown Street did not know what to make of the little woman who kept so much to herself. Before her marriage to Patrick Vernon they had referred to her amongst themselves as 'Lady Muck,' allowing that her standoffish manner was due to a feeling of superiority. It was rumoured around the place that she had been married to one of the Leighs of Leigh Court, but there was never any trafficking between the house in Crown Street and that quarter. In latter years she was turning the back garden into a small farm, and this was not appreciated. But Patrick Vernon was one of their own; they could relate to him. He had a word for everyone and open house for the men to air their grievances. His father before him had stood with the workers in Pierces in the 1890's when they tried to bring the Union to the foundry. Now Pat was one of the leading lights in the movement himself, working to get better conditions for the families of Wexford.

The Irish Transport and General Workers Union had been founded in Dublin the year before, in 1909. At first it was based among dockers and carters but it was committed to organise the broad mass of unskilled labour. Pat Vernon was eager to see it established in Wexford. The Act of Union which imposed the burden of Free Trade with the wider English markets helped to destroy native Irish manufacture. Also the Irish middle and lower classes who had wealth were reluctant to invest that wealth in industry, preferring the security of Bank Investments and Treasury Bonds. But Wexford was an exception to this rule. Maybe because it was a seafaring and trading town, with an important trade with the Port of Bristol. The town was more like Britain or North east Ireland, with a thriving foundry industry. The main product was agricultural machinery. The skilled workers had organised in the late eighteen hundreds but now a great wave of unrest was sweeping Britain and Ireland, resulting in the hunger for trade unionism amongst the unskilled. The people were bitterly discontented with working and living conditions and a man named James Connolly, who had just returned from America, saw the Irish Transport and General Workers' Union as a force to join socialism and nationalism and he became an organiser for the I.T.G.W.U. The Union used the tactics of the sympathetic strike and the blacking of tainted goods to fight the employers policy of using blackleg labour, rather than talk to the workers. The Employers feared the Union and tried to suppress it. They could not or did not read the signs of the times. The attitude among the workers had changed. They were no longer docile and obedient, the old complacency had been replaced by a stubborn need to change an intolerable tyranny. Patrick talked to Julia late into the nights. It was hard not to be caught up in his excitement and enthusiasm and in spite of her tiredness, Julia listened, eager to understand.

'We will live to see a new Ireland, Julia girl.' Patrick's dark eyes were on fire, sometimes this smouldering fervour frightened Julia and she remembered a quieter voice, speaking in gentler tones, but then she invariably felt a sense of guilt, as if she were betraying both men by this unfair comparison.

But Julia could not help worrying. The very idea of violence of any sort was abhorrent to her gentle nature. She believed that no cause was worth the shedding of blood, no matter whose blood it was. Sometimes when she stood in the crowd listening to the speakers at the open meetings, she shuddered when the oratory became to inflamed. Please God grant that they would accomplish all they wanted to do without any real trouble. But even as she made the prayer and remembered some of the scenes from her own life in Leigh Court, she knew that likelihood was slim.

It's really a fight to the death, the death of one way of life, the birth of another and birth never takes place without blood. She returned home on such occasions and buried herself in her work and her children, pushing everything else resolutely from her mind.

Chapter 30

The streets of Wexford were packed! It was the eve of the New Year 1911 and the people were parading as was the custom. There was an air of celebration about the town and the music of mouth organs and melodeon could be heard over the excited voices of the populace.

Julia and Patrick, with twelve year old Catherine, who had begged to be allowed to join in the fun this year, made their way to Cornmarket just as the church bells solemnly tolled the midnight hour.

After a few minutes the joy bells started to peal and people called greetings to one another.

The excitement was infectious and Julia felt curiously light headed. She always loved a parade of any sort, especially if there was music involved. No one could resist the joyous noise the bells made, ringing out over the dark streets, lighting up the frosty night with a sort of heady pagan lustiness. She glanced sideways at her husband's profile, impassive as usual, and seemingly immune to the revelry in the air about him.

She sighed and held Catherine's hand tightly. Their marriage had been a mistake. She knew that with a quiet certainty that brooked no argument. In the beginning she had pushed away such treacherous thoughts, making herself avoid guilty comparisons, but as time passed she stopped blaming herself and realised the gap between Patrick and herself could never be bridged. His frenetic obsession with freedom was just that, an obsession. He had no sense of balance, no patience with her own or anyone else's humanity. Like a man driven, he was single minded in his belief in freedom as the answer to all ills. When the workers were their own men, when Ireland was free of the oppressive occupation by England, then the world would be perfect and Utopia would be upon them.

Julia listened and tried to learn. She was unsure of her own thoughts and feelings, too new to argument to make any case of her own. But somewhere in her soul was a nagging doubt that would not be silenced. Patrick was a good man and a brave man, this she did not doubt, but there was another side to her husband; a darker side that troubled and disturbed her. His moods of exhilaration and hope too often gave way to long periods of melancholia and gloom, when he seemed to go to pieces before her eyes. At such times he kept to himself, barely speaking and even the children's company failed to lift his depression. He loved the children. Julia never doubted his kindness and concern for his family but she could not follow where he went and she was unable to help him when the black humour was upon him. When she tentatively voiced an opinion now and then, he scornfully silenced her and brought her yet another book or pamphlet to read. In her heart of hearts she believed, in spite of what he said, that if a man is not free in his own heart, free and at peace, no amount of outward freedom will lighten his load or improve his lot. The struggle begins in one's own heart and mind, this was her stepping off point, but Patrick believed that once relieved of the outward burdens the hearts and minds would follow. Little by little their conversation dried up and they became awkward with one another. She knew Patrick blamed her for this estrangement, feeling that she compared him unfavourably with her first husband who had, as he pointed out, been one of the gentry, a member of the privileged classes. Once and once only had they had a ferocious row. It began, Julia knew with the wisdom of hindsight, in the pain and inadequacy they both felt, and it blazed into flames before either of them realised what was happening. Her feelings of anger had amazed her, she hurling abuse at him and provoked a responding burst of anger, preferring it to his silent absent presence.

When he slammed out of the house, leaving her bruised and shaken in spirit, she had run to Bridie Walshe for consolation. Bridie, who had heard the angry voices through the thin walls was troubled and slow to speak. When at last she answered Julia's entreaties for understanding, she was cautious and tried hard not to take sides. She had watched Julia and Patrick trying to come to know one another, she herself had had serious misgivings at the suddenness of their decision to marry but her own struggle to come to terms with young John's death had occupied her completely. Julia was still young and impetuous; one of those women who would never really leave girlhood behind and would suffer the consequences. Her love affair with John Leigh had been just that, a love affair, which never had time to grow old or sour, or even develop into a mature relationship. Who knows what would have happened if they had been given time to grow old together. John Leigh was an unusual man, sensitive and shy, apart from her own love and adoration for him, Bridie knew enough about humanity to realise he was that rare and precious thing, a really good man. His love for Julia was the stuff of dreams. He had made her the centre of his world, endowing her with all the qualities he believed a woman should possess and she, so young and impressionable, had only to step into this dream landscape and move through it, with him to guide her every step.

Yes, who knows if she would have always been content to live out John Leigh's dream and if as she grew and developed, she wanted to be her own person, would John have ever been able to let go of the dream and settle for the reality?

Julia had had to grow after his death and her hasty withdrawal from Leigh Court and its cushioned environment. When young John died she started to fall to pieces and looked for another saviour. Patrick Vernon was there for her, but she had to pick up the pieces herself and go on with her life. This time she had found the strength within herself and had emerged a strong woman, stronger than her new husband. This was the problem now, Julia wanted to follow Patrick Vernon's lead, to find no fault with him, she wanted him to lead and shape her as John Leigh had done. This was the one role she knew as wife.

He on his part could not and would not treat her in this manner and even if he had, she would not have been able to accept it.

Bridie could not have put words on this but she could see, in her own way, what was happening between the two.

'Musha alannah,' she said now trying to calm Julia. 'You will have to control your temper and let the man be. He is what he is and you won't change him. Think your own thoughts and give him the freedom to think his. You are married now, with a family to rear, and you will learn to live together if you give it a chance. The past is gone Julia and we can glorify it or let it rest in peace. Who knows the future? We have only the day that's in it to do the best we can with. Pat Vernon is a good man; not a saint, not a devil, just a man doing his best to live his life. You can help him or hinder him; only you can choose. We always have a choice you know, between heaven and hell. Some people refuse to join us in heaven, but if we choose hell we can pull everyone in with us.'

Julia remembered Bridie Walshe's words often over the years and she tried to act accordingly. Bridie was a wise old woman, this she knew and even though the going was not easy she valued the older woman's advice. There was no point trying to make Patrick into something he was not. Maybe that was what love was, living life as it is; not what we would like it to be. Julia made a New Year resolution once again and faced into 1911 with renewed hope.

There were nearly twelve thousand people living in Wexford in 1911 and a large number were dependant on the foundries for work.

Pierce's foundry, where Patrick Vernon was employed was the largest, with over four hundred men manufacturing agricultural machinery and bicycles. There were two smaller foundries in the town. The workers were trying to unionise. In July of that year a dock strike spread from the British Isles to the docks at Wexford and their demands were eventually met. The workers began to realise the strength and power of organised labour. The Irish Transport and General Workers' Union spread from the docks to the foundries. But the management in Pierces who had successfully quelled a similar effort in 1890, tried to do the same now and warned that the company would close if the men persisted in joining the Union. The organisers were determined to succeed this time and the town was buzzing with rumour and counter rumour.

Patrick Vernon was seldom at home and when he was he spent his time closeted in the front parlour with men of like mind. The low drone of their voices went on into the small hours. Julia kept her own council.

She was well briefed on all matters pertaining to the workers and her own background gave her a unique insight into the mind-set of the employers. There would have to be compromise on both sides if a peaceful settlement was to be reached. Julia had strong doubts and misgivings and no one to voice them to.

Towards the end of August, on a sultry day when the heat in the house was oppressive she decided to bring the children for a picnic to her favourite spot at the top of the Rocks Road. Packing a bag with bread and jam and taking a bottle to fill with fresh water at the Folly Spring, she set off with her little brood of excited children running along before her. The twins were not over robust. The boy, John, quiet and shy, but without his namesake's sharp intelligence, Lizzie was the leader, a skinny little tom-boy with her mother's wide green eyes. The baby, Bridie, a fat little girl with solemn round face and good humour, reminiscent of Catherine at that age. Catherine was in Ballyleigh for the month, staying with Estelle at their uncle Jem's cottage. The two girls were inseparable and often watching them, heads together, one red, one dark, Julia remembered Kitty with a dart of pain, so sharp it took her breath away even after all the years. Estelle never asked about her parents. Jem and Nellie were the only mother and father she knew, even though she was told about Kitty and Julia often spoke to her about her real mother.

Of Luke Kerrigan, nothing was ever said. Julia wondered if Estelle knew the truth. The people of Ballyleigh had long memories and she was sure they had let the little girl know her history, one way or another. But Estelle never asked and Julia never told her the story, maybe when she was older the opportunity would arise.

Kerrigan never made any move to see his daughter. He lived a bachelor existence in the Manor House, surrounded by his dogs and horses. Stories of his drinking and carousing were legend in the area, but he managed to farm the land his wife allowed him to hold on to.

Helen Leigh was living at Leigh Court with Louise. She ruled the estate with an iron fist driving anyone who could, possibly, get work elsewhere, away.

Lonegan still held on, he had his ever increasing brood to feed and it was rumoured that he was the only man who was not afraid to face Helen Leigh. People said the only reason she kept him on was that she enjoyed fighting with him.

Today Leigh Court and its inhabitants were far from Julia's mind. She sat on the sun-warmed rock, looking back down over the glorious panoramic view of town and harbour, shimmering through a haze of heat, like the ancient towers of some exotic Mediterranean port. She thought what it must be like to travel to foreign lands, to set off unhindered and follow where the spirit leads. In her mind's eye Julia had visions of all the places she read about, places so colourful and exciting, the very names made the head whirl. Constantinople, Bombay, Athens, Florence; Julia spoke the names out loud, savouring the sounds, and her children rolling and laughing on the green grassy slopes, barely noticed. Their mother often talked to herself, they were used to it.

When the little band wended their way home in the first coolness of evening, Julia was surprised that the streets were so empty. When they came to Distillery Road corner and saw groups of men standing around outside Pierce's foundry, she knew something had happened. The men should be inside at this time in the evening, still working away.

Hurrying the tired children along, she walked quickly down Crown Street. As she approached the house the door opened and Patrick emerged, a stack of papers under his arms, his face animated: 'Julia, its happened. We are locked out, the struggle has begun in earnest.'

As Julia started to ask questions, he shook his head impatiently, 'I can't stay, I am expected down town. We were given our choice; leave the Union or else . . . The men stood together, it was magnificent. So Pierce locked us out. Now I must go.'

He hurried off after hurriedly greeting the children. Julia stood looking after him down the street where here and there little knots of men stood together In some of the doorways, women in aprons stood quietly, hesitant to ask questions, their closed faces betraying the anxiety they were feeling.

Julia gathered the children and went inside. The house was quiet. Bridie was asleep in her chair beside the empty range. There was a feeling of foreboding. Julia wondered if it was inside herself or if the children too could sense it as they stood, tired and subdued in the shadowy hallway.

Chapter 31

Very soon Julia realised that life in the house in Crown Street would never be the same. The lockout in Pierces, and the other foundries in the town who soon followed Pierces lead, affected most households. As the weeks and months dragged on it became clear that this would be a long and bitter struggle. The employers feared the militant Irish Transport Union, founded by Jim Larkin, for the unskilled or semi-skilled workers. The southern organiser of that Union was in Wexford. A Dublin man named Peter T. Daly; he addressed a large crowd in the Bull Ring and Julia stood beside Patrick listening as he urged the men to stand firm for their right to join the Union and gain recognition for their skills. For wanting this right the men had been denied the right to work. She began to understand at last how Patrick felt and his burning passion for the Union movement. This was more than just a skirmish between workers and employers, it was a struggle for the very soul of a nation, beginning here in their own town. Julia came away convinced and Patrick, sensing her mood, hugged her close.

'Stand with me Julia girl, I need to know you are there. We must hold out whatever the cost to all of us, we must win, this our chance, our time in history.'

But the mood in the town grew ugly as time passed. Eight foremen who tried to keep the business going at Pierces had to be escorted to and from work by policemen.

Talks were arranged but no agreement was reached. Patrick went out every day as usual. When he was not on picket duty, he was busy elsewhere, but Julia had never seen him so ebullient, so animated. He barely came home to eat and his talk was all of what was happening on the street or in the lives of the locked out men.

On the evening of September 9th he came home to fetch Julia to a meeting in the Faythe. She was resting, tired after a long day and was reluctant to stir, but Patrick was adamant 'You must come my dear, Jim Larkin himself has arrived to address the people.'

Later as she stood in the open square listening to the impassioned words of Larkin she was glad she had not missed this night. She could see why the men called him 'Big Jim' as she watched the tall imposing figure, long arms raised over his head, his defiant words ringing out towards the people thronged into the wide street. Larkin contemptuously dismissed the proposals that the men should either join separate craft unions or a local union. This would mean no I.T.G.W.U recognition and a local union would be ineffective, just a sop to get the men back to work under the same conditions. The roar of the crowds and the caps flung high into the night sky signalled the men's approval as he finished his speech. Patrick and Julia walked home through the deepening darkness in companionable silence. Julia had never felt so close to her husband, they were united now as never before. How odd, she thought, that something like this could draw us together. It's surely true what they say about the ill wind bringing good somewhere.

It was an ill wind that blew through the streets of Wexford town all through the winter of 1911 . There was hardship in the homes where people struggled to feed their children with no money coming in. There was suffering too on the streets when the employers brought in blackleg labour, adding to the unrest. R.I.C. reinforcements arrived in the town and marched along the quays towards Barrack Street. The people threw stones and they retaliated by baton charging the large crowd. There were many nasty injuries and Patrick came home that night, his head streaming blood from a deep gash which he received while trying to control the crowd.

As she bathed his wound, Julia tried to urge him to stay at home for the rest of the week.

'This is an ugly wound Patrick, you could have concussion. Please rest for a while until it heals.'

But she might, as Bridie Walshe said, have been talking to the wall. On the following night, Thursday, he headed out as soon as he had eaten and shortly before midnight as she had given up waiting his return Julia heard the key in the lock and a white faced Patrick arrived in the kitchen. She was shocked at his appearance, thinking he had been hurt again, but he shook his head in answer to her question. 'No, but there was terrible brutality tonight, an innocent man was batoned as he passed by on an errand of his own. They have taken him to the Infirmary, but it looks bad. I thought myself he was dead'.

Patrick was visibly shaken, the ugliness of the scenes he was having to witness on the streets day after day was wearing him down and his former hope and excitement was fast deserting him. Julia was becoming more and more anxious about him and a few days later she accompanied him to the man's funeral, for indeed he did die; a quiet unassuming man who was unfortunate enough to be in the wrong place at the wrong time. The funeral was the largest seen in the town for many years. The shops and business premises were closed as the cortège passed, led off by St. Brigid's Fife and Drum Band. The bitterness of the people against the police was palpable on the near silent streets.

There was opposition to the strikers too as Julia found to her cost when she tried to shop for her groceries in some of the local shops. She was ostracised too by some of her neighbours whose hardship increased the longer the men were out. They had always suspected that she had money and private means, especially since she owned her own house and it was rumoured that she also owned property all over the town. In actual fact, Julia was finding it harder and harder to manage. Bridie Walshe's money had dried up long since and if it wasn't for Julia's shrewdness and culinary skills they would be hungry.

Some families in Crown Street were destitute and it broke Julia's heart to see the state the women and children were in. She knew Patrick would never agree to her using the money accrued to her from the Leigh Estate and she herself had no idea how much there was or what she was entitled to.

As January 1912 came and with it no sign of a cessation, James Connolly arrived in the town and his very presence gave a new lift to the hearts of those suffering appalling levels of poverty. The Union was doing what it could in helping with strike payments and there were various aid committees organising concerts in aid of the workers. Help came from Dublin, Belfast and Cork and even from Britain. The Orangemen in the Queen's Island Shipyard in Belfast organised a collection after Connolly addressed a rally in Belfast seeking support.

But Julia was resolved secretly to do something herself; she could not bear to see her children in need. Pride is one thing, but this is rank stupidity, she said as she made her way to the solicitor's office. She would find out what was available and Patrick need never know. She took Bridie into her confidence and she agreed wholeheartedly saying of Patrick with a sniff: 'What he don't know won't hurt him.'

James Hennigan treated Julia with the utmost courtesy and respect. He had often wondered why she never made use of any of the moneys, indeed never showed head at all in his office. She could hardly disguise her amazement when she heard the amount in her name, deciding to tell the sympathetic man in front of her what she wanted to do with the money and enlist his aid in figuring out how best to use it to help the people in need in the town.

Hennigan listened carefully without comment and when Julia finished he sat quietly for a few moments.

'I think, Mrs. Vernon, that you must first look after your own future and that of your remaining child, Catherine isn't it? You can certainly afford, if you are inclined, to donate quite a large sum of money to the strike victims. I take it you want to remain anonymous. We can arrange this for you. So I will draw up the necessary papers and you can call back and sign them this afternoon'.

Julia decided she would draw a modest sum monthly and made sure there was an ample amount set aside for Catherine's education, after all this was what the money was meant for in the first place; John's and Catherine's education. The rest she would donate to the working people; the irony of the situation was not lost on her; Leigh money to alleviate the sufferings of the locked out workers of Wexford. She could see from the sardonic smile on the solicitor's face that he too enjoyed the strange joke fate was playing on the remaining members of the Leigh family.

In mid January, Patrick and Julia were amongst the crowds who welcomed P.T. Daly back to the town and escorted him from the North Station to his hotel. Shortly afterwards on Saturday 27th January, Daly was arrested at the Union office in Charlotte Street. He was charged with 'incitement' and brought before the magistrate at the barrack at George's Street and sentenced to three months detention in Waterford prison, pending trial.

The news spread through the town like wildfire and crowds gathered on the streets. Julia stood at the North Station for the second time that month, but this time the people were angry, not jubilant and though Daly was conveyed there in a closed carriage, he could hear the spontaneous outbursts of cheering along the route. As the carriage arrived in Redmond Place, opposite the railway station, Julia was almost swept off her feet as the crowd surged forward. She caught sight of Patrick on the far side of the street but he did not see her, he was pressing close to the carriage as were so many others, men and women, trying to shake Daly's hand. As the train eventually steamed out, the people cheered and waved handkerchiefs and hats. Later, as she walked home, Julia came on a noisy scene where people were groaning and hooting and throwing stones after a walking figure. She did not wait to find out who they were attacking but hurried past, eyes averted. Scenes like this were common place and it was not wise to linger on the streets of Wexford, especially after dark.

After Daly's arrest the situation looked even grimmer. With the cold miserable winter lingering on and some of the people in a state of near destitution, James Connolly arrived back in Wexford. He called for more common sense and less abuse and Julia felt hopeful after listening to his words at a meeting on February 2nd. The hope she felt was rewarded when on the evening of Thursday, February 8th, terms of settlement were unanimously agreed. The Irish Foundry Workers Union was formally established. Two Wexford men, Nicholas Lacey and Richard Corish, who emerged as a natural leader of the people all through the harrowing times the town had endured, were elected President and Secretary.

The Lockout was over and the people were jubilant. Bonfires and tar barrels were lit, men and women and children thronged the streets. Julia and Patrick, with the children, joined in the torch-lit procession led by the Foresters Brass and Reed Band and the St. Brigid's Fife and Drum Band. They marched to the Town Hall and from there to the Faythe.

Julia could hardly recognise Patrick; he was a man transformed and his happiness was infectious. The children skipped along, not really understanding but delighted with their parent's obvious good humour and the joy all around them. The music of the bands and the general air of *joie de vivre* was fed by the peoples' relief and gratitude that their long ordeal was over.

As the crowds dispersed and the Faythe quietened down to darkness and the night, Julia stood remembering the glorious speech she had heard. James Connolly's ringing tones still echoed in her ears: 'You of the working class of Wexford have reason to be proud of yourselves, and I believe that Ireland is proud of you today . What we have won is one small moiety of what we will win for you in the near future. We have only begun that long, mighty upward march for the uplifting of the working classes. You will continue to march until you have acquired not only the right to be protected by Unions but until you of the working class have acquired the right to own the country you are living in'. She felt some of this pride herself, for her long dead love and for her husband, Patrick. Both men's dreams were beginning to come true and their children would reap where they had sown.

Chapter 32

The first euphoric days gave way to a harsher reality as the town counted the cost after a lockout that lasted nearly six months.

The men reported for work on February 12th many of them wearing I.T.G.W.U. badges. So that the whole thing would not break up again the men agreed to remove the badges if all the blackleg labour was dismissed. There was widespread poverty and illness in the town, tuberculosis was rampant. For some the hardship was too much and nearly one hundred of the workers had left Wexford to seek work elsewhere, mostly in England. It soon became evident that in spite of their promises to the contrary, some of the workers would not be given back their jobs. On one pretext or another some of the ringleaders were let go.

Patrick Vernon was one of these casualties. Julia's heart bled for him as she watched him listlessly move through the days. He wanted to believe that no sacrifice was too great and to endure the loss of his job gladly for the greater good. But with it had gone not only his livelihood, but also his self respect and his main reason for living. She urged him to seek work elsewhere and this he did, half heatedly. When he came home at night, tired and depressed, she mourned for him, but silently, for now that the strike was over their new found closeness seemed to have ended too.

P.T. Daly was brought before the Wexford Assizes on March 5th and was sentenced to one month's imprisonment in Waterford. The town planned to celebrate his release and on Sunday April 14th he arrived back to Wexford with Mrs. Daly and Jim Larkin.

Julia and Pat were present at the station to meet him along with a large crowd. The bands were out again and again the parade headed for the Faythe where Richard Corish read an address to Daly from the workers.

Later that night a massive torchlight procession took place. The town turned into a veritable fairy land with bunting and Chinese Lanterns and the people put candles in their windows. Julia watched the march past from an upstairs window, too tired to venture out again, the children by her side, waving excitedly to Patrick as he passed by. But Julia saw that his head did not turn as he passed the house, he was unaware of their presence, his gaunt figure stiff and upright and his face resolutely set, his eyes staring straight ahead. She sighed and Bridie Walshe patted her arm.

'He's gone from us Bridie' she said sadly, 'in all but body.'

'There's nothing you can do girl, you've done your best. Some men never settle, their spirit is too restless to be content with domestic arrangements. Pat Vernon is one such, leave him free to do his own thing, that's the kindest thing you can do for him now.'

That night Patrick told Julia he was going to Dublin. 'Larkin has offered me a job organising' he said with a flash of his old excitement. 'I must go Julia, there is nothing for me here.'

'No nothing,' Julia answered, biting back the angry words that sprang to her lips.

'It's for the best' he said, avoiding her eyes, 'I will earn good money and of course I can come home often. Better than taking the boat to England.'

Julia nodded, turning away and busying herself folding the children's clothes.

Maybe it was for the best, the children would miss him and maybe she would too, but the struggle would be over. Bridie was right, she had done her best; she felt no guilt, maybe even the beginning of some relief. She was losing a husband she had never really had and he was going to his first love, leaving her to her memories.

The days and weeks after Patrick's departure were busy ones for Julia. Estelle came to stay so that she could attend the convent school with Catherine. Neither of the girls were scholars but Julia wanted them to have a good education. They would both probably end up working in some shop in the town, certainly Estelle would as this was the height of her ambition. Julia hoped Catherine might train to be a nurse, she showed interest in medicine and her good humour and compassionate nature would stand her in good stead if she did choose that profession.

Patrick wrote regularly, his letters full of Union news and praise for Connolly and Larkin. He sent money every week and remembered to enquire after the children but his promised visits failed to materialise. Julia was happy, she worked hard looking after Bridie and the children and at night she had her beloved books.

Jem and Nellie visited regularly and even persuaded her to come to Ballyleigh with the children for a visit during the summer months.

So it was that on a bright July afternoon Julia stood once more looking out over the dark waters of Kerrigan's pond. She was alone, Jem had taken the children out across the land for a walk and Nellie and Sadie stayed behind to get everything ready for a celebration tea.

How small the clearing seemed to her now, had it always been so overgrown? The mossy bank was still green, the sound of birdsong filled the air, but Julia would never again find joy in Kerrigan's Wood, only in her memory could it be as it was, only in her thoughts and dreams could she dance through the green gold air and let her spirit soar as it had when she was young. The reality now was the image of a still form, with blood darkened coat and arms outflung, dying alone on the bank they had loved so much.

Stifling a sob Julia turned and walked resolutely back along the narrow pathway. She would never come here again, better to let memory lead us gently down roads we should not walk alone.

Chapter 33

Julia stood, her hand to her throat. The face looking back at her from the mirror seemed unfamiliar. It caused her to pause in her work and stare. Unfamiliar and yet familiar but not her own face. Now she realised what had startled her about the reflection, it was for a fleeting minute her mother's face she saw. She rarely looked at herself in mirrors, she was not vain about her appearance, never had been, but now she wondered when the change had come about. She was forty, about the age her mother had been when she died. How odd, she thought, sitting down on the sprigged eiderdown, I thought my mother old; an old woman and yet I don't feel old. How odd suddenly to be faced with undeniable evidence of the passing of time, the greying hair, the lined brow, the fading eyes. Is this how it comes upon us, like a thief in the night? Julia had often wondered about old age, in fact she secretly feared it. She did not think death held any real terror, but to be old and helpless, unable to work. These were the thoughts that came to freeze her heart on sleepless nights. And today was the first time her nightmare had come upon her in daylight hours, a fleeting glance, a brief encounter and a shiver through the heart. What had she achieved? she who still waited for it all to begin. Those few brief years with John, that dream time which she knew and admitted in moments of rare honesty, she endowed more and more as life went on. Bridie warned her now and then saying how empty we become if we insist on living in dream world.

'But you are so brave Bridie' she cried the last time they sat together, she holding the older woman's pain gnarled hands in her own, holding more than Bridie's hands, willing her to stay and not to think of leaving them.

'Old women are always braver than young ones, they have no option Julia love'

'What would I do without you Bridie?' she asked.

'You would do quite well,' Bridie answered adding with a trace of her old fierceness. 'No one is so important they can't be done without. Only the good God Himself; and He's not going anywhere.'

Today it was not easy to shrug off the melancholy thoughts and Julia lingered, letting her mind ask the questions. It was four years since she had seen Patrick. He still wrote now and then and the money came regularly, but it was clear their marriage was over and Julia held no ill feelings towards him. When she thought of him at all it was of an absent friend. Maybe they should have stayed just that, friends, but then she would not have the twins or young Bridie. No, there is a reason for everything, or so it said in John's bible which she kept in the parlour and took down now and again, much to Bridie's horror. She was convinced no good could come of reading the 'Protestant Book' as she called it.

'Too many questions girl, you ask too many questions for which there are no answers. You shouldn't fight with life, you'll only lose. Things are as they are and they always will be'; that was Bridie's credo.

'You think too much.' This made Julia laugh when she was in good humour and cry when she was in bad form. 'How can you not think Bridie, for God's sake tell me how to turn off thought if you can.'

'There, more questions' Bridie always ended their conversations shaking her head hopelessly and advising Julia to go and do something. 'Keep yourself busy alannah, that's the cure for all complaints, keep yourself busy and the world goes on anyhow, without your worrying about it'.

Julia's world had gone on after Patrick's departure. He had fought another lock out in Dublin in 1913 and now he was a member of the Volunteers. That force was growing rapidly rallying to the cause of Irish Independence. They were drilling here in Wexford, exchanging military salutes in the streets. Last year the third reading of the Home Rule Bill had passed in Westminster and there was a massive parade in the town. The bunting was out again and the nationalist flags flew from the buildings and the ships in the harbour. Julia took the children out to see the rockets and fireworks filling the air.

But then the dreadful headlines in ' The Free Press' on the first of August had announced the beginning of the 'Great War.'

Julia gave up reading the reports of the war and atrocities, especially after word came towards the end of that first year of the death of her own brother, Jem's twin, Jack, at a place called Gallipoli. Poor Jack, he must never have married, because the telegram for next of kin came addressed to the Whelan family of Ballyleigh.

There were many such notices coming to homes in Wexford and all over the country; and Wexford sailors were the heroes of many maritime encounters. There were efforts going on locally to recruit more men. Julia herself had seen a major rally in the Bull Ring in June with the Band of the Royal Dublin Fusiliers playing and a Magic Lantern slide show of pictures of atrocities in Belgium projected onto the sides of a van.

But life went on much as usual. The new cinema opened at last and she had managed to attend the first film show. But moving pictures were not really to her liking, she preferred the live concerts.

Julia shook herself out of her reverie. The children would be home from school, ravenous as usual and she still had plenty to do. Next week was Holy Week and Easter would be upon her before she had the spring cleaning tackled. She wanted to have everything ready for when Catherine arrived from Dublin. Julia was proud of her daughter and secretly amazed at Catherine's courage in going to Dublin to work as a student nurse in the Mater Hospital. The girl got few holidays and the work was hard, but she took to it like a duck to water and her letters home were full of happiness. Julia missed her but rejoiced in her success.

Estelle was happy too, working for Julia's old employer, Barnabas Behan and coming home each night to the house in Crown Street. So the house was scrubbed and scoured from top to bottom and in between attending the ceremonies in Bride Street Church, Julia baked and cooked 'Enough to feed a regiment' Bridie told her.

Catherine would come by train on Easter Monday as she had to be on duty until then, so Julia set out to meet her with the twins and little Bridie in tow. The train was late very late, and Julia's anxiety was growing with the children's restlessness. There were others gathered at the station, quite a crowd waiting for relatives and friends. People started to move towards the office determined to find out what the delay was all about. Reluctant to join them, Julia stood back waiting. There was a stirring of activity around the door as the station master emerged and held up his hand. A clamour of noise broke out and Julia who was too far away to hear what was being said strained to hear the man in front who was craning over the heads of the crowd and turning to address his companion. 'Please, what is it?' she asked tentatively.

'Some sort of Rising in Dublin; Freedom Fighters have taken over the G.P.O. The city is in turmoil. No train tonight I'm afraid.'

Catherine managed to get word to them during the week that she was safe and well but working beside every available nurse and doctor in the city. By this time Enniscorthy had fallen to Rebel Nationalists and steps were taken for the defense of Wexford. Of Patrick there was no news. The Volunteers stood with the R.I.C. and five hundred Wexford citizens including the Mayor were enlisted as special constables. The town held it's breath.

There were random shots fired and arrests made. Extra troops came from Cork and there was a military camp at Drinagh, south of the town.

In May the homes of Sinn Fein supporters were raided and there were many more arrests. Amongst those taken was Richard Corish, but most of those arrested were released within a month.

Julia stayed at home, fearful to venture out onto the streets. She found it hard to contain the children, especially Lizzie, who wanted to be in the thick of things. She worried about Catherine and Patrick. She knew in her heart that Catherine would be well, but she also knew without being told that Patrick was involved, beside his hero James Connolly.

Within two weeks most of the extra troops were gone and the Mayor congratulated the people of Wexford for their calm and orderly conduct. The Easter Rising was over but at a terrible cost. The majority of people all over the country had little sympathy for the rebels but as news of their barbarous treatment filtered through, the tide turned. Julia cried, something she had not done for many years, when she read of James Connolly's death.

The following month she received a card from a Welsh prison. Patrick was thankfully alive but wounded and in jail.

The war in Europe went on and Julia knew she had never in her wildest dreams realised just how much blood it would take to see out the old order and usher in the new. She was not alone in this, the world asked itself the same question.

In the spring of 1917, Patrick Vernon came back to Wexford, an old and broken man.

'Tread softly' Yeats had written, because you tread on my dreams.' But Patrick's dreams had died in Kilmainham along with his comrades in arms.

Julia sat night after night wiping the sweat from his white face and holding his trembling hands as he relived the horrors of those awful days.

'Why was I left?' he groaned over and over 'There is nothing for me now, nothing left.'

As she hushed his cries for fear of waking the children Julia spoke to him as she had to Kitty years before, comforting him and telling him she was there in the darkness beside him. Slowly his body recovered but his mind was slow to follow and she resigned herself to the fact that Patrick would be an invalid for the rest of his life, an old man sitting in the sun, a rug covering his knees and his head bent as if in prayer.

In 1918 the United States Air Force had a Sea Plane Base at Ferrybank and it was in use for the last few months of the war. That year too Julia walked after John Redmond's funeral; to the family vault at St. John's Cemetery. He had come very close to achieving independence by democratic means but now he too was gone.

The bands and tar barrels were out again on Wexford's streets with the ending of the war. This time Julia stayed at home with Patrick and the children went alone to the parade.

An influenza epidemic swept across the world now, and Wexford did not escape, over one thousand people were afflicted.

Bridie Walshe and Patrick both succumbed to the terrible disease.

What she had dreaded had come to pass and Julia was alone again.

Chapter 34

It had rained all morning and now the air was vibrant with smells and colour.

Her hands plunged deep into the rich moist soil, Julia knelt and let life flow into her from the earth until she felt it coursing through her veins, heating the blood and bringing her to new awareness She blessed the ground and the never failing miracle it worked for her. This little plot, bounded by a box hedge and a rough stone wall was her world garden where she could rest from mind toil. The mid morning silence, broken only by bird call with the rain of slanted shower light falling on her head was where the windless communication that sustained her existence took place. There were no words for what happened here, but deep in the core of her being understanding came silently and she knew and was at peace. All in a moment she could see why people were prepared to die for their country, whatever its name. Patriotism has nothing to do with language, with flags or creed, it is the pull of the earth under one's feet, the invisible umbilical cord that never breaks and bonds what is original in man's soul to his parent clay. Remember man thou art but dust . . .' Dust is all there is; but what an all.

Throughout her life she had a heightened awareness of this truth which grew stronger as she aged. It called her into deeper and deeper union until all her needs seemed to fuse and be fed by this communion. Was the God she found it hard to speak to in prayer the instigator, the silent conspirator in this time out of time. She hardly knew or cared. It sufficed, and was good.

The evening noises of the town began to intrude at last and reluctantly she returned to present duties and needs.

The children would be home shortly demanding to be fed. They brought her the outside world, young and innocent as she liked it and in their company she was young and happy. The pigs, long gone, had blessed the garden with their presence and her flowers were magnificent. She grew mostly flowers now. Jem brought her fresh vegetables and all the good things she needed from his ever increasing plenty. His careful husbandry of the land gave back a thousand fold and Nellie and himself prospered. They had fine sons to help with the work and Sadie carefully preserved in the hot house of their love and concern enjoyed her life still. They were blessed to live in the country, the town was not a good place to be, there was so much unrest. The Barrack was filled with troops all of the last year since they had arrived from Devonshire. There were constant riots on the streets. The soldiers were looking for Sinn Fein supporters. They questioned people and when they did not like the answers they got, they assaulted them. Despite the intervention of the R.I.C. the people fought back with stones and bottles. It was not safe to linger on the streets of Wexford and homes and businesses were raided; people were searched at gunpoint.

Since January martial law was enforced and all dances, fairs and marts were suspended and anyone caught bearing arms could be executed. The names and ages of everyone had to be displayed inside the main door of each house and all meetings were banned.

Then in February, an irregular military force called the Black and Tans because of the colour of their uniforms, were recruited to supplement the R.I.C.. They were rough, cruel men and Julia found it easy to believe there were many criminals amongst their ranks as was strongly rumoured.

It was hard not to worry about the children. The twins were fourteen now. John still a quiet youth but Lizzie was ripe for any devilment. Only last week she had had a lucky escape and Julia's heart still froze over as she remembered the incident: both the twins collected slop from the Barracks for an old man at the end of the street who kept pigs. He was kind to all the local children and paid them a few pence for their help. Julia was returning from evening devotions when she met up with John and Lizzie, both laden down with heavy buckets of slop. John walking slowly, painstakingly taking care of his bucket. Lizzie, skittish as usual, prancing along beside him. Neither of them heard her approaching and just as she was about to call out Lizzie tripped. The pig slop poured out over the pathway and as she bent to help Lizzie to her feet Julia saw what looked like a bundle of paper or rags lying burst on the ground. Before her horrified eyes could register the contents, Lizzie was frantically gathering together and throwing it back into the nearby empty bucket, regardless of the stinking liquid she knelt in. But she was not quick enough to keep Julia from seeing the bullets gleaming wetly. Julia gasped and Lizzie looked up, her eyes dilated with fear and in that instant Julia knew she was aware of her deadly cargo. The twins were transporting stolen ammunition from under the noses of the auxiliaries at the barracks and carrying it to a Sinn Fein house. Julia grew faint with terror; my God they would all be shot. Lizzie flashed her a warning look. Quick as lightning she poured some of the contents of John's bucket over the parcel in her own bucket and picking it up, shoved John before her and proceeded on down the street as if nothing had happened.

That night Julia quizzed a frightened John and a defiant Lizzie. How many of the children were involved in this dangerous game? she asked. John swore he knew nothing and she believed him but Lizzie was another matter.

'You are better off minding your own business mother.' Her face set, her eyes stony, she stood her ground and Julia knew she was looking at Patrick Vernon's daughter.

'I want you to promise me you will give up this madness she pleaded, but Lizzie would not budge. John can do as he pleases, but I will help work for the cause until this country is free.'

Julia turned away, her legs trembling. 'Does the nightmare never end? Dear Jesus, did I think I would hear those words in this house again and so soon.'

She knew she could do nothing. Lizzie was adamant, she had picked up the gauntlet and the battle continued.

Chapter 35

The night was heavy with the musky smell of autumn. A white mist rising from the fields disguised and changed the familiar countryside into an eerie haunted landscape.

A captive moon, struggling to escape from angry ragged clouds, shone fitful bursts of light earthwards and tried half-heartedly to pierce the grey white curtains covering the land.

The six men moving silently along the road cursed the sometime beams. The smoky half dark suited them well. Their business was secret and they wanted no witnesses. They had no eyes or ears for autumn splendour as they covered the ground quickly, staying close to the ditch. The leader stopped suddenly and pointed, his followers looked across the fields and grunted in assent.

On the horizon, rising from the mist, the outline of a great house loomed huge and majestic. Even at a distance Leigh Court was an imposing sight, its graceful black lines drawn cleanly against the pearl grey backdrop of the autumn night. The beauty of the line, the stately silhouette meant nothing to the watching eyes, they saw the enemy. Heads down they moved on again, crossing the style opposite Kerrigan's wood, they made their way sure-footedly through the fields to the little copse beside the driveway leading to the mansion. Dressed in raincoats; their hats and caps drawn down, keeping their faces shadowed, their familiarity with their surroundings betrayed the fact that they were local men. Their movements swift and sure, they flitted through the trees like night hawks, noiselessly passing over the ground without seeming to bruise the grass under their feet. Emerging at the rear of the stables, they broke into two groups. Three men proceeded on towards the main house and three entered the first stable building. The three who moved towards the house paused and one whistled softly through the darkness. An answering whistle signalled the approach of another figure, crouched low and running towards them across the lawn. Not wasting time on greetings this new arrival urged them towards the east side of the house where a low door opened to his touch and he led them into the cellars.

Once inside, Tom Lonegan turned a grinning face to his companions.

'Well boys, I told you I'd get you in. Have you the stuff?' The men made no answer but fell to work, their movements quick and sure. Lonegan watched them, rubbing his hands together nervously. As time ticked slowly by and they went about their task with silent and deadly earnestness he began to grow anxious: 'Hurry on boys, for God's sake hurry on, that wan sleeps with one eye open. Sometimes I think she's a bit of a witch. If she happens to wake up we're done for'.

'Shut up Lonegan,' the leader spoke for the first time through tight lips, his voice low and business like. 'We've no mind to botch the job for fear of a woman.

What can she do if she does see us. She knows none of us and it won't take three of us to subdue her.'

'She knows me begot and she would be well able for ten men. I'm gettin' jittery at the thought of it'.

'Sit down and keep quiet' the speaker hissed, losing patience with the nervous Lonegan.

Before Lonegan could answer a loud explosion rent the air and the house seemed to rock.

'Jaysus' he screeched, running for the door. The other man was on his feet and pulling the door open before Tom Lonegan got to it. Already scarlet tongues of fire were issuing from the blackened mass of the ruined stables.

'Christ Almighty' Lonegan babbled, sweat streaming down his terrified face. 'What happened; we'll all be destroyed'.

'Shut up you fool, the explosion went off too quickly, Sean was to wait for my signal. Can't be helped now, we continue as ordered. If you don't shut up I'll shoot you down.' He drew a black pistol from his pocket, pointing it at the cowering man in front of him. Turning back into the room where the other two still knelt, heads bent over their task he spoke briskly: 'How much longer lads?'

'A few seconds more and we should be right' one of the men answered unrolling a ball of wire and moving back towards the door.

Catching Lonegan by the scruff of the neck the first man dragged him after him and all four backed out through the doorway. Two of them pulling Lonegan along with them made for the shrubbery leaving their companion to deal with the fuse.

The night was lit up now with scarlet billows whooshing up into the sky and great streamers of smoke jostling with the clouds. The remaining figure bent over the fuse line was too intent on his work to hear the frantic voice behind him.

'What are you doing. Stop. Stop or I'll shoot.'

Helen Leigh Kerrigan, shotgun in hand screamed again and this time he heard.

Before she could raise the gun he pushed the plunger and a second explosion boomed out, blowing the door, through which they had entered not twenty minutes earlier, before it.

With a shrill screech, Helen raised the gun and fired but even as she did a single shot rang out and she dropped to the ground, her own shot passing harmlessly over the crouching man's head. He rose and took to his heels, not pausing to check the fallen woman.

The sound of running feet hammering off the driveway and the crackle of flames igniting, mingled with the high pitched screams of the horses stopped Louise in her tracks as she came around the side of the house. She had awakened from a nightmare in which she had fallen at the ditch in Kerrigan's wood, her beloved stallion on the ground injured. She knew by his screams that he was badly hurt and then she woke to realise the screams were real. The horses; she had to get to the horses.

Turning from the sight of her sister's prostrate form she saw the blazing inferno that had been the stables. The horses were being burnt alive. She could hear their agonised screams. She must get them out. Rushing across the yard she plunged without pausing into the furnace with no thought but to reach her beloved children.

Helen Leigh Kerrigan moaned softly and Lonegan, on his knees at the edge of the driveway heard the low sound.

'Oh Jaysus Christ it wasn't supposed to be like this' He had wanted to see them burn the bloody place to the ground all right, but he never meant anyone to be hurt.

She was alive, what could he do? If she lived he'd swing. No doubt about it, or she would shoot him herself.

Whimpering with terror, he knelt on the wet ground too paralysed with fright to move.

With a mighty crack the first floor of the house went up, shooting glass and smoke out over the yard. Lonegan roared with terror and watched mesmerised as Leigh Court burned before his eyes.

The horses were silent now as the roof of the stables caved in and their pyre burned on. Of Lou-Lou there was no sign.

Helen moaned again and Lonegan's horrified gaze turned from the blazing building to where she lay.

Begod he couldn't let her die like a dog. His mind made up now he sprang into action.

Blanching as the heat from the wall of the house hit him, he ran forward and lifting her into his arms, moved back in a half crouch, half carrying, half dragging her lifeless form into the safety of the lawn.

She looked dead. Her face white, the front of her nightgown scarlet with seeping blood. What to do? Lonegan was half mad with terror, his wits deserting him completely under the weight of the horrifying events of the night.

'Kerrigan, begod, I'll go for Kerrigan.' Leaving the hapless Helen lying on the mist covered lawn, while above her Leigh Court blazed and crackled, a mighty bonfire in the night, he turned and ran towards the fields that divided the Leigh land from Kerrigan's Manor House.

Luke Kerrigan and his men met him halfway. The raging inferno, lighting up the countryside and dispersing the mist was drawing men from all quarters. Lonegan, rasping for breath, gabbled out his news as he approached.

'The boys have blown up Leigh Court. Miss Helen is shot, Miss Louise is burned . . . The boys did it, the boys!'

Luke Kerrigan shook him off and ran ahead. Helen. My God, Helen.

He found her where Lonegan had left her, laid out on the grass, the white heat of the fire surrounding her and the terrible cracking and grinding of the house in its last agony giving the surrealistic landscape nightmare qualities he would never forget. He found a thread of a pulse; she was still alive, and he shouted to the approaching men to go quickly for his motor car.

The drive to Wexford seemed to take forever but at last she was being looked after. As he strode up and down the dim corridor Luke tried to marshal his thoughts. He could see her as she was when he had first loved her, haughty and proud, riding out to hounds. Young Helen Leigh, a fairy tale princess, or that's how he had seen her. How far from him she had appeared then and he had loved her and wanted her so much. He had never cared about Leigh Court or the blasted name, that was his father's doing, tying them to that bloody building. Well now it was gone and it had been the death of her as he had always said it would be.

The grim faced doctor moved towards him down the long hallway.

'Mr. Kerrigan, your wife is alive but only just . . . the bullet is lodged too close to her heart for us to remove it. I'm afraid it's only a matter of time. I'm so sorry'.

'Can I see her?' Luke asked and the doctor nodded. 'Why not? She is barely conscious, she won't be able to talk to you I warn you, she is very weak.'

Luke entered the room and walked across to the bed. Helen lay, her hair spread out around her, her face white as the sheets covering her body. He stood looking down at her, his own face drawn and strained. What to say to her if she did know him? What was there to say now? After all the years it had come to this.

Helen opened her eyes and looked straight at him. She was trying to say something. He knelt and bent his head low, straining to make out the hoarse whisper.

'Julia Whelan, must see Julia . . .' Her voice trailed off.

Had he heard right? Julia Whelan, what in the name of God could she want with Julia Whelan? Why he didn't even know where the girl had got to. He had not had any dealings with the Whelans since Kitty died. Again the hoarse insistent whisper: 'Julia Whelan, get me Julia Whelan.'

She caught his arm and tried to squeeze it with her lifeless hand. Her eyes were pleading silently, he nodded and she seemed to relax. 'All right Helen, I'll get her, hold on.'

The lids dropped over the distracted eyes. Luke turned and walked away, moving as gently as he could. Where was he to find Julia Whelan? If he was to bring her to Helen he would have to be quick about it. He had seen enough of death to know he had very little time to accomplish his task.

Chapter 36

Loud and persistent knocking woke Julia from a troubled sleep. Her first thought was of Lizzie: Oh God, was the child after drawing the Tans to their door?

Hastily pulling her robe around her, she went out onto the landing, relieved to see Lizzie and John standing close together, pale faced and afraid. Estelle was emerging from the back bedroom, rubbing the sleep from her eyes.

'Stay here all of you and don't make a sound.' Julia's voice was low and harsh, covering her own fear and demanding obedience.

She calmed herself as she went slowly down the narrow stairway, willing herself to face whatever was at the other side of the door with a courage she did not feel. The rapping was insistent and louder now, echoing along the still dark hallway. She pulled back the heavy bolt and opened the door. Her first feeling was one of relief to find not a bunch of brown clad soldiers but one lone man standing outside on the chilly early morning street.

It took her some moments to recognise the tall grey haired figure and even then she could not quite believe that Luke Kerrigan was frantically tearing on her door in the early hours of an October morning.

For his part, Luke showed no sign of recognition, his face distraught he spoke roughly without preamble: 'Julia Whelan, I'm looking for Julia Whelan. I was told she lives here.'

Something about her stance. The stillness, the hand to the throat made him pause; 'You are Julia Whelan?' It was half statement, half question.

Julia nodded. 'I am, though it's a long time since anyone called me by that name. And you are Luke Kerrigan.'

'Yes, yes, for God's sake can you come with me, my wife is calling for you, she hasn't long. Please, please come.'

Julia stepped back; what in the name of God was he talking about? He was clearly in a state of near frenzy, 'Please come in.,' she stood aside so that he could enter the hallway, she could sense the presence of the youngsters on the stairs behind them, wide-eyed with curiosity now that their fears of an early morning raid were gone.

He walked rapidly past her into the hall, the quiet inside the house and her own calm demeanour seemed to help him.

'I'm sorry to disturb you this way ma'am; but it is a case of extreme emergency. Leigh Court was burned last night and my wife Helen Leigh was shot. She is in the County Infirmary even as we speak and she is near death. She wants to see you; I promised I would bring you'.

Julia was weak with shock, her legs were trembling uncontrollably and she had to lean back against the wall to try to steady herself and keep from falling. Estelle ran forward and caught her. 'Julia. Julia are you all right' she put her arms around Julia and held her up.

'Yes, I will be grand.' Making a superhuman effort Julia straightened herself and patted the young girl's arm. 'Take Mr. Kerrigan into the kitchen and make him some tea while I get dressed. Please,' she said to the still distraught man, 'Go with Estelle, she will look after you. I have to dress. I will be as quick as I can.'

She walked on her still shaking legs, back down the hallway and up the stairs, past the curious twins, who knew that this was no time for questions.

Hurriedly dressing, her fingers numb, her brain in a whirl, Julia wondered why Helen Leigh should want to see her of all people. She would have to go with Luke Kerrigan, she knew instinctively that if she refused he would pick her up and carry her, or drag her all the way there.

The man was nearly out of his mind and there would be no point in trying to reason with him. When she returned to the hall he was still standing, having refused to go into the kitchen and Estelle, brewing the tea, looked as if she would not be able to keep from asking the questions that were jumping out of her curious eyes.

'Will you take tea Aunt Julia?' Julia shook her head and reached for her coat and hat.

Hardly giving her time to put them on, Luke Kerrigan grabbed her arm and propelled her towards the door. As she jammed the hat down on her head he opened the back door of the automobile standing at the kerb and ushered her into the seat, he himself sat beside the driver, a young man Julia did not recognise and barked an order: 'Quick, to the Infirmary, as fast as you can.'

Julia had never been in a motor vehicle and she held on for dear life as the machine spluttered to life and took off down Crown Street at a frightening speed.

The morning was cold and a sharp wind tore at her, nearly ripping the hat from her head, and whipping her hair around her face. She felt sick to the stomach before they were well on their way and despite clutching at the shiny leather upholstery she slid from side to side like a rag doll. She was sure they would be killed before the nightmare journey came to an end. Kerrigan never uttered a word, he stared straight ahead, his body tense, his back straight as if willing the vehicle to move even faster.

When they shuddered to a stop beside the hospital steps he was out of the car before it was properly halted and Julia protested as he grabbed hold of her and nearly dragged her out onto the road. For the first time he looked at her and paused as if realising how roughly he was treating her. 'I beg your pardon ma'am I am afraid she will be gone before I get back. Please excuse my behaviour; I cannot think . . .' he added pathetically, and Julia nodded.

'Yes we will be as quick as we can; don't worry, she will wait for you'.

Together they climbed the stone steps; Luke Kerrigan trying to harness his impatient long-legged stride to wait for the tiny figure at his side.

When they reached the silent white room the doctor was leaning over the bed.

He looked up as Luke hurried to the bedside and drew him back slightly.

'She is still holding on; only just. Is this the woman she wants to see?'

Luke nodded, 'Yes, this is Julia Whelan.'

As he spoke, Helen Leigh's eyes flickered and then opened. She made as if to raise her head and the doctor motioned Julia forward.

Staring down, Julia could hardly see any sign of Helen in the bloodless face.

The thin hair was grey-white against the snowy pillows and the countenance, that of a very old woman. Then as she bent down the eyes snapped open and she was looking into the sharp ice-cold depths she remembered so well.

The eyes focused and she saw a flicker of recognition dawning, then the claw-like hand came up and caught her arm, drawing her down closer.

Helen was trying to speak. Julia could see the effort in her eyes and a thin rasping sigh escaped the white lips. She bent down until her face was close enough to feel the clammy coldness of Helen's skin and whispered, 'Please Miss Helen, don't try to speak.'

But the awful rasping came again and then the words 'John. John. Shot.'

'She thinks she is back at John's death; she wants to be forgiven for not coming.' The thought flashed through Julia's mind.

'It's all right, it's all over a long time ago' she whispered. But there was no dawning look of peace or ease in the eyes looking back at her.

With what must have been a tremendous effort Helen Leigh drew herself up until her head was raised from the pillow, her eyes burning into Julia's, she spoke clearly, in a strong voice: 'I shot John, I shot him!'

Julia tried to draw back, but the hand holding her arm was like a vice. The eyes held a different look now and with a sigh Helen Leigh fell back on the pillow. The doctor leaned over her and shook his head.

Julia stood rooted to the spot; as Luke Kerrigan fell to his knees at the far side of the bed.

'She's gone' the doctor said and Luke began to sob: 'Poor Helen, poor girl, she wanted to get rid of the terrible secret she carried all these years.'

Julia heard his voice as if from a distance and decided she must keep her own secret now. What she had seen in Helen Leigh's dying eyes as they looked into her own had not been sorrow or remorse, but triumph! As she waited outside the door for Luke to emerge, Julia's overriding feeling was one of deep abiding sorrow and heaviness. To her own surprise she could find no anger in her heart for the dead woman, only pity and a deep, deep sadness, so that when he did come towards her she could look at him with sincere sorrow.

'What can I say, Mrs. Leigh, it is Mrs. Leigh, isn't it?'. He was seeing her as if for the first time that morning and she was seeing a much different man before her. His face certainly bore the ravages of a misspent life, but his eyes were kind and gentle.

'Mrs. Vernon' she said 'I remarried, but Patrick Vernon is dead.'

'Oh, I did not know. I'm afraid I lost touch with your family'. Was there a touch of shame in the voice?

'Yes, we all had much to forgive and forget.'

Startled, he looked into her eyes and what he saw there made him speak impulsively:

'Could you come and take breakfast with me in an hotel or somewhere? I would like to talk to you.'

'No; but you must come to my home. There is someone I want you to meet. I think it is time.

The wide green eyes, he remembered her now, the eyes had not changed, looked steadily into his and he inclined his head and followed without another word.

Chapter 37

A vivid yellow burst of daffodils danced defiantly in the long grass of what had once been the carefully manicured lawns of Leigh Court. Their tossing golden heads made valiant efforts to draw the eye from the blackened ruins behind them. Nature was doing all she could to cover the shame of the great house, throwing out banners of ivy and creepers to bandage the naked remains. Already the lichen and green moss padding was softening the harsh outlines, and the wild flowers and brambles reasserting their hold on the land.

Three years had passed since the burning, but still the daffodils came to herald the spring.

'Let mankind do its worst, nature will ignore as much as she can and all his puny efforts will come to naught in the long run. The land will do what it must, and it can wait as long as it needs.' Julia spoke aloud, standing at the end of the driveway, a wilderness already, her thoughts and memories came tumbling down the years. She had not wanted to come but Estelle had insisted. The car from the Manor House had collected her this morning and here she was, drawn as if by a magnet. Like someone before whom a terrible gaping wound has been revealed, she could not tear her eyes from the horrible sight even though the looking was a knife pain opening wounds she had thought long healed.

Estelle wanted to come here with her but she had refused, saying she would rather go alone. The pilgrimage, for that's what it felt like, had to be made; old ghosts must be laid to rest. She knew she must stand alone before the past and engage in hand to hand combat if she was to have peace. Julia had always faced the darkness, she could not live with shadows, not then, not now.

The answers she found might only be to her own questions but that was all she needed. When she was able to sort out the little questions it was enough, she had learned long ago to leave the unanswerable alone.

For years she had blocked this place from her mind, obliterated it completely. Now she deliberately opened the floodgates herself, it was time, she was ready. She was fifteen again, trudging the mucky back road to work here in the kitchens, but even as a great sob threatened to crush her chest another image pushed to the forefront of her mind; a dancing barefoot free spirit, spinning like a top under the trees in Kerrigan's wood. She remembered staring out at these trees the day her mother died, and waiting as John's body was carried towards her, up the driveway, but again the pain was pushed aside and she could see John as he stood under the roses on the back walk, taking her hand and kissing it shyly, and she laughed as she remembered how she felt. They had known such joy. Her first son was born here and Catherine, dear Catherine. What plans John had for this place. How strange she thought, the world turns and rearranges everything and Mick Whelan's grand-daughter would be mistress of Kerrigan's Manor and the lands which once belonged to the Leighs of Leigh Court. Indeed, even now, she could lay claim to that title since Luke Kerrigan had acknowledged his daughter and brought her home to the Manor House within a year of Helen Leigh-Kerrigan's death.

And the country itself? A treaty had been signed and Ireland was now a Free State. Michael Collins had fallen, but the war was over and it was up to the people to make Ireland their own. Much would have to be forgotten and forgiven and peace might prove more difficult than war for many. I have lived to see your dream come true John, and you too Patrick for just last month Richard Corish was elected to the Dail.

Yes, I have lived to see it turn full circle.

Julia shivered, the pale April sun was hidden behind a dark rain cloud and the air was suddenly chill, her feet were freezing and if she did not move she would catch cold. Turning away she walked briskly towards the gate, trying to bring some feeling back to her numbed limbs.

Over by the ruins of the stables she caught sight of a woman with a black shawl wrapped around her shoulders. She was bending, probably gathering sticks for her fire. A little girl, barely visible in the long grass, moved ahead of her. As she drew closer, Julia saw that the child was clutching a bunch of primroses. She held out the flowers. 'Don't you want them yourself?' Julia asked. She shook her head; 'I can pick some more, there's plenty for everyone; nobody lives here any more'.

'What's your name?'

'Mary Ann' she smiled shyly up at Julia. 'What's your name?'

'I am Julia Whelan, thank you for the lovely flowers.'

The woman straightened up and shading her eyes she called to the child who turned and ran back through the long grass, waving goodbye as she went.

Julia buried her face in the flowers and drew in the sweet fragrance. The sun had burst out again and she could feel the heat on her shoulders. The air was alive with promise and outside the gates the road was bright,

Epilogue
NOVEMBER 1946

My Granny died yesterday. I didn't really know her but I think I liked her. She was a funny lady though, she always had a long black dress on and she never turned on the light in the front room or pulled back the curtains. It was always very dark when my Daddy brought me to see her.

She had a piece of paper in her hand when they found her. It was writing from the Bible. I thought only the Protestants read the Bible but my Daddy said she had another husband, before Granda, and he thinks that man was a Protestant. I asked my Daddy to tell me about it but he didn't know very much. He said Granny never talked about it.

My aunts said she was very sad. Lizzie said she was a bit mad. I think they were wrong. She had lovely eyes. Her eyes looked sort of far away, as if she was looking at something no one else could see. I wish she had waited until I was grown up. I wanted to ask her what she could see. I would love to know all about her but nobody seems to know very much, if they do they wont tell me. Someday I'll find out though, when I'm big.

Granny left me her lovely brooch. She always wore it at her neck, Daddy says it's called a cameo. She left me her gold locket too, but I won't get it until I am seven.

I think my Granny liked me. She really liked my Daddy. I think she liked everyone but they just didn't know.

The house in the Faythe

by Vonnie Banville Evans

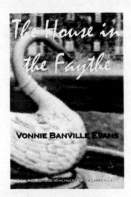

"This is an attractive little memoir somewhat in the spirit of Alice Taylor or Maura Laverty: a childhood remembered with affection by sounds and smells and feelings; by the happiness of the great outings to Rosslare; the excitement of the mighty games of taws, when every child in the area walked around with a little cloth purse full of marbles...you want to know more about these people who lived in a world where children feared the bogeyman, drank water from the pump, listened to Dick Barton on the wireless and saw every film that came to town."

Maeve Binchy - The Irish Times

Anna's Dream

by *Vonnie Banville Evans*

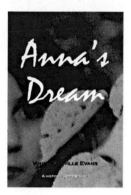

"The rocks which rise behind Anna Dunville's house in Wexford are the gathering place for her gang of friends, where they build huts and plan adventures. But no adventure could match the one that awaits Anna in Vonnie Banville Evans' Anna's Dream...a gripping story that leads Anna and her friends to delve into the terrible events of three hundred years before, when Cromwell and his troops laid waste to the town."

Gordon Snell - The Irish Times

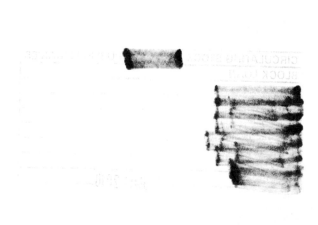

Lightning Source UK Ltd.
Milton Keynes UK
23 April 2010

153209UK00001B/11/P

9 781907 215124